HOW TO BE A BADASS DETECTIVE

HOW TO BE A BADASS DETECTIVE™ BOOK ONE

MICHAEL ANDERLE

DISRUPTIVE IMAGINATION

Copyright © 2021 Michael Anderle
Cover copyright © LMBPN Publishing
A Michael Anderle Production

LMBPN Publishing supports the right to free expression and the value of copyright. The purpose of copyright is to encourage writers and artists to produce the creative works that enrich our culture.

The distribution of this book without permission is a theft of the author's intellectual property. If you would like permission to use material from the book (other than for review purposes), please contact support@lmbpn.com. Thank you for your support of the author's rights.

LMBPN Publishing
PMB 196, 2540 South Maryland Pkwy
Las Vegas, NV 89109

First US edition, May 2021
ebook ISBN: 978-1-64971-733-7
Print ISBN: 978-1-64971-734-4

THE HOW TO BE A BADASS DETECTIVE
BOOK ONE TEAM

Thanks to our Beta Team

Rachel Beckford, Kelly O'Donnell, Mary Morris

Thanks to our JIT Readers

Daryl McDaniel
Wendy L Bonell
Zacc Pelter
James Caplan
Veronica Stephan-Miller
Deb Mader
Debi Sateren
Dave Hicks
Dorothy Lloyd

If We've missed anyone, please let us know!

Editor
The Skyhunter Editing Team

To Family, Friends and
Those Who Love
To Read.
May We All Enjoy Grace
To Live The Life We Are
Called.

CHAPTER ONE

The Alchemist stood in front of the mirror, admiring what she saw with a calm sense of satisfaction. Important work would need to be done momentarily, but not at once. She would do things at her own pace.

She had not turned on the light in the bathroom. Sufficient illumination was provided by the wall-mounted lamp in the hallway behind her.

The woman in the glass before her was of considerable age, but she could pass for thirty, thirty-five at most. She was on the taller side, trim but not skinny, and it was difficult to discern her ethnic background by looking at her.

Adding to the impression of relative youth was her hair, which covered her right eye and was dyed bright turquoise. Such styles were more common among the young, after all.

What really fueled her enigmatic attractiveness, however, was something that most people could not name or identify or even understand. It was not merely physical. Rather, it was the faint perception of a mystical life force, a creative vitality, that shone from beneath her skin and hovered around her at all times.

1

Like an aura.

"Oh." She sighed and ran her fingers over the smooth, bright surface of the mirror. "I'm doing well lately, but there's no reason not to do even better. One can always use a recharge. And it's not as though *they* are going to make good use of all that beauty, is it?"

Fluttering her eyelids one last time, she turned away and marched out of the bathroom to her studio, where her newest acquisition waited.

There was only one window in the studio, and it was permanently covered by a heavy dark blue curtain. The walls were painted a similar color, giving the room the appearance of being underwater. The floorboards were dark and glossy. Off to the sides, piled against the walls, were the Alchemist's various tools and pieces of gear that she put on her person whenever she needed to go out into the night and acquire a new piece of art.

In the center of the studio was a table, and on it rested the painting she had stolen.

The Alchemist approached it slowly, drinking in the sight—the living presence—of such a fine creation, endowed as it was with so much talent and potential. Alas, it had all been squandered by both the artist and the buyer. Neither of them had the slightest idea of what they were doing.

Thus, the Alchemist had been forced to rescue the piece. She alone could give it the appreciation it deserved. She brushed her turquoise forelock away from her face and angled her head to the side, staring at the painting with both eyes.

It was an Expressionist work depicting a distorted, androgynous human figure, grotesque and beautiful at the same time, surrounded by a swirling vortex of a landscape, as though the protagonist's whole environment was a product of his or her turbulent emotional state. Something about it was unsettling, yet it had an air of breathless hope and optimism lurking behind the shadows and chaos.

The artist was a young man named Luis Domingo, who, while not yet widely known, was beginning to be the subject of a certain amount of buzz within the art world. Discerning critics had praised his early works, proclaiming him an up-and-comer worth paying attention to.

And so the Alchemist had come to Southern California once she'd heard the announcement that Domingo was offering one of his paintings at an auction in Los Angeles. She spent much of her time in the vicinity of New York and Paris, more traditional hubs for the fine arts, but was more than willing to travel around the world as needed.

"It's a travesty," she declared in a whispery voice as she gazed at the painting. "Art of this exceptional caliber should not be *for sale*, particularly not for such a pathetically low sum. Domingo must have allowed desperation to get the better of him. And his buyer is even worse. She knew better. She was being cheap and deliberately mendacious in her quest for a good deal. Wretched people. Idiots." She shook her head, then crouched to retrieve the tool she needed from a black bag of supplies.

She knew in the back of her mind that Domingo could not entirely be blamed for letting his masterpiece go for far less than it was worth. He was young and not yet well established, and the amount that the buyer, Mrs. Corvina, had offered probably seemed like a large figure to him. In fact, it was nothing.

He should have picked up a second day job and held out for a respectable sum. Other artists had done similar things in the past.

But even then, the thought of selling an excellent piece was an affront to good taste.

The Alchemist stood back up and returned her eyes to the painting. In her right hand was an ornate knife, its hilt well-worn ivory trimmed with silver, with a curved blade about seven inches long of dark, rippling Damascus steel.

It was an object designed to take life...and transfer it elsewhere.

The woman breathed in deeply and slowly let it out, waving her left hand, fingers splayed out, over the surface of Domingo's modern Expressionist masterwork. She could feel the force of its vitality; her skin tingled.

When a person stooped to the abysmal level of exchanging money for true art, they *killed* that art. They revealed their own crassness, ignorance, and crudity and their lack of ability to appreciate the life essence and creative spark contained within the work.

Since such philistines could not appreciate the vitality anyway, they were not using it, so the Alchemist did not feel she was stealing anything. A few people had told her otherwise, that theft was theft, but she had ignored them.

"Now," she said, "to make manifest to the eye what is already obvious to the spirit."

Her knife hand plunged downward, forward, and then up. The blade punctured the canvas and sliced it apart, ripped it to shreds. In the space of a hundred seconds, Luis Domingo's painting lay in jagged and tattered pieces upon the table. In particular, the Alchemist had obliterated the humanoid figure at the center of the composition.

As the knife destroyed the painting's physical form, she imagined its ethereal eternal form flowing into her and rejuvenating her with its mixture of vivacious warmth and powerful coldness. Each cut of the knife gave her a visceral, nearly childish satisfaction—a sense of getting away with something naughty. But the part of her that was older—far older—knew that it was the right thing to do.

Finally, it was done. The painting was destroyed, and the Alchemist felt good, as though she had spent all day getting exercise and fresh air, followed by a healthy meal and a nice soak in a jacuzzi.

Furthermore, she felt...inspired.

The Alchemist left the knife sitting atop the ravaged canvas and turned to another canvas, blank, upon an easel near the northwest corner of the studio. Brushes and oil paints had been set up beside it since she had expected the current rush of motivation to begin a new work of her own.

As her hands moved over the empty surface, filling it with colors and patterns, her mind went wild with fantasies of Domingo's genius flowing through her, guiding her brush strokes. The painting that began to materialize bore more than a passing resemblance to the one that had laid on her table moments before.

But it would not be identical. Insofar as the creative spark was being channeled through *her*, it would be her own work.

She painted for three hours without stopping or resting and barely paused to appraise what she had done. During the final half-hour, though, her mind started to wander to the next important task she had to undertake—returning the painting to its "owner."

The Alchemist smirked. Each time she helped herself to a piece of artwork some fool had destroyed through their greed, she made a point of delivering its remains to those same fools. The painting was worthless to them after having been bartered for like a mule or cart full of groceries, so the Alchemist's knife simply emphasized the obvious.

And Mrs. Corvina deserved to have that emphasized as much as possible.

The Alchemist sighed as she finished painting for the evening. "Too bad about Domingo, though. Perhaps one day he will learn not to sell himself short."

Kera MacDonagh had finally ended her employment at the Mermaid last week. However, she had known as well as everyone else had that it would not be a clean break. Her presence there would be...phased out. Gradually.

"Kera!" announced Jennifer, her former fellow bartender, as she strode through the front door. "Welcome back...again. Like you actually planned on leaving us behind for more than a week at a time, haha."

Kera smiled and advanced past the array of dining tables toward the bar. She was wearing her riding leathers, which clung to her slim frame atop her regular clothes, but had removed her shiny black motorcycle helmet before she came in. Her hair, naturally blonde but dyed black, spilled across her face, and she brushed it aside.

"Hi, again," she said. "I had some time and I was in the neighborhood, so I figured I would stop by and say hello, maybe have a quick drink and a bite to eat."

What she had said was *mostly* true. However, she also needed to talk to Stephanie and would prefer to do so in person rather than over the phone or via text.

Jenn gave her a squint of fake disapproval. "Well, if you plan to order food, why'd you come up to the bar? Have some manners, woman, and get yourself a table."

"Yeah, sure, whatever." Kera chuckled. "Actually, do you have any extra appetizers back there? Or a bowl of nuts or pretzels is fine. I'm not eating as much lately as I used to. Oh, and I'll have a beer. Whatever you have on hand."

Jenn fetched her some pretzels and a bottle of nice seasonal ale. Kera then listened as Jenn related what-all had been happening at the place since her departure.

Kera noticed a slim, thirtyish man with dark hair and eyes rushing between the tables out front and the kitchen area in the back. "Who's he?"

"Oh," said Jenn, "that's Arash. Cevin hired him a few days ago. He bounces back and forth between washing dishes, bussing tables, and bringing out food and drinks when the waitresses are busy since he's got experience with all of the above."

Jennifer flagged the man down and told him to come out and talk when he got a minute or two. He was in a hurry but nodded his agreement.

"He's pretty cool so far," Jenn added. "One thing I'll say for Cevin is that he knows how to hire people who aren't incompetent or complete assholes, unlike some other bosses I've had in the past."

Kera agreed, though her thoughts turned inward. Soon she would be running a business of her own, and the question of who to hire—who to *trust*—weighed heavily on her. She already had a core crew, but there might come a time when outsiders had to be brought in to help with the mundane legwork and paperwork.

Stephanie and Arash appeared more or less simultaneously. Kera and Steph hugged, then the new guy introduced himself.

"Hi, I'm Kera." She shook his hand. "I used to bartend here. I quit right before you started."

"Oh?" He seemed genuinely curious. "What made you leave? This seems like a pretty good place."

To Kera's annoyance, Jennifer answered on her behalf. "Entrepreneurship, isn't it? Our girl's going to be a businesswoman! How will you get the startup capital, though?"

Dammit, Jenn, Kera lamented in her mind. *That's exactly what I do not want to talk about right now, not to mention you're putting me on the spot.*

Kera had never divulged to any of these people how rich her parents were. Her former coworkers all struggled to make ends meet, let alone get beyond living paycheck to paycheck, so the last thing they'd want to hear about was Kera's inheritance.

Of all of them, only Stephanie knew the truth, and Kera had to hope she wouldn't blab if Kera told a little white lie.

Kera cleared her throat. "Well, I was having trouble with that part also, so I accepted an internship with a detective agency.

They're a small company, just getting started themselves, really, so in a way, I'll be one of the people who helps the place get off the ground. That's the plan, anyway."

Stephanie gave her a weird look but kept her mouth shut.

To seal the deal, Kera sent her expanded consciousness toward her friend, conjuring up a wave of emotional signals meant to convey anticipation. She did not yet know how to beam thoughts into other people's heads, but she could influence their feelings in ways that usually got the point across.

"Huh," Jenn replied. "Yeah, that's one way to do it. What kind of agency are they, exactly?"

Kera spread her hands. "I'm not sure; we're still working on that part. Ideally, I want to take on cases that are, you know, big and significant. The kind of stuff I can tell my grandkids about, if I have any, and that would get mentioned in documentaries. Especially if I'm doing good in the world. It would be a lot more fulfilling than devoting my time to petty stuff like spying on someone's cheating significant other or figuring out if an employee is going truant and misusing company funds or whatnot."

Jenn nodded as she worked on a drink for one of her customers. "Sounds about right. You're the type who seems to want to do important things. What's the word I'm looking for? 'Grandiose,' that's it. Something grandiose."

Arash snapped his fingers, his eyebrows rising and his face lighting up. "That is a great idea. Like the UFO landing at Roswell. You could investigate that, figure out what really happened. Say your client is the American people and ask everyone in the country to mail you one cent for it. You would be rich!"

Kera laughed. "That would be interesting and maybe worth a shot. I don't think our government would like it very much, though. You know how the feds get with people who disagree with them, hold them to standards, or expect them to divulge information. Last thing I need is the Men in Black coming to my door."

And she thought but did not say aloud, *Especially since I'm already guilty of multiple felonies as part of my career as a vigilante. I'm sure the warrant for "Motorcycle Man's" arrest is still one hundred percent active.*

Arash's smile dimmed, but he was clearly still enjoying the idea. "Well, it is something to think about, no?"

Jenn had a suggestion of her own to offer. "Or you could finally solve the John F. Kennedy assassination. I always wondered about that, like, with all the weird facts that don't add up and all the conspiracy theories. Although," she frowned, and her eyes went distant, "the feds might be even *more* pissed off about that than they would be about Roswell. Damn."

Before Kera could reply, Jenn saw one of her customers trying to wave her over and hurried to help him, leaving the conversation behind for the time being.

Still, the others seemed to expect Kera to address what Jenn had said. "Well," she began, "I don't think I'm qualified to investigate the JFK incident. At least, not yet. But maybe later when I hit the big leagues. Plus, aren't they supposed to declassify some of the information on that soon?"

Stephanie nodded. "Mmmhmm. My grandmother was hoping she'd live long enough to find out the truth about all that, but I don't know if she'll make it. Damn shame."

Cevin, the owner, had wandered toward them midway into the discussion. Kera suspected he had other things to do, but he obviously wanted to hear what they were talking about and make a contribution or two of his own. He was a tall man, though he tended to slouch when standing, in his early thirties, and less self-assertive than he ought to be. His confidence had improved, though, since he'd begun dating an extremely attractive woman (with Kera's, Jenn's, and Stephanie's help) a month or so ago.

"Hey, now," he said. "Leave Kera alone. No need to prod her into doing stuff she's going to get in trouble for."

Jenn, returning to their vicinity as she grabbed a fresh glass, remarked, "Well, *that's* no fun."

Waving the comment off, Cevin continued, "It's best to start small with things you know you can handle but will still make you look good. When you're a new business owner, that's how you build a foundation for expanding your business later. Take on jobs you're proud of, and treat your clients and customers the best you can. Word will get around, and you'll have stuff you can brag about later when more people start getting interested. Speaking of which..." He turned around and shuffled back to his office.

Kera rubbed her chin. "He's right. Granted, um," she coughed, remembering her cover story of getting an internship, "it's not really my business, not yet, but still, I might be able to make suggestions to the owners or pick and choose which cases I work on. I'll keep that in mind. Focus on what I'm good at and use that as a stepping stone to bigger and better things."

The conversation trailed on as Kera finished her beer and pretzels, then everyone else went back to work. Stephanie seemed too busy for Kera to be able to pull her aside, unfortunately, so she resigned herself to having to speak in code over a text message and wait till later to talk to her in person about what was going on.

As she got ready to leave, dropping her tab plus a generous tip on the counter for Jenn, Cevin appeared again and motioned her to come to his office.

"What's up?" she asked. "I don't have another partial paycheck coming, do I?"

He scratched his nose. "Nice try, but no. I was just wondering —for my own conscience, I guess—did you decide to leave us because of the lower hours you were getting? I hope I didn't do the wrong thing by letting the other girls kind of pressure you into being the one who always went home early."

Kera hadn't expected the question, but Cevin was the type of man she could see worrying about something like that. Before she could answer him, however, he spoke again.

"Wait, or is it because of what happened when that asshole shot your bike because I wouldn't cooperate with him? God, I still feel bad about that. This place's reputation is improving again, but I don't think I'll ever live down that period when we were the local bucket-o'-blood tavern or whatever. Ugh."

Kera held up her hands, palms toward him. "No, no, nothing like that. Really, Cevin. But I appreciate you asking. Besides, you paid to have my bike fixed. You didn't have to do that. Thanks again. It's only because, well, I want to move on and do other things. You didn't do anything wrong. This is probably the best place I've worked so far."

He sighed in blatant relief, wiped his brow, and hazarded a smile. "Oh, good. That takes a load off my shoulders, seriously. Well, I'm not going to lie, I'm sad to lose you, but I understand. Slinging drinks isn't everyone's permanent calling in life. And you stuck with me through the roughest period we ever had. Now, things are turning back around. We're a respectable establishment again, and business is picking up."

"Good." She laid a hand on his shoulder. "I wish you the best, and I promise I'll continue to stop in at least, uh, once in a while. I won't make promises as to *exactly* how often, ha, but I'll make an effort since I don't live too far away. We'll keep in touch."

It went without saying that Stephanie would act as the messenger, given that she would continue working there.

Cevin agreed. "Okay, great. Well, I have to get back to the boring number-crunching stuff. You're going to have all kinds of fun once you start doing that at your new place, I'm sure. At a startup, you're going to wear many hats, but I know you're up to it. Best of luck."

She gave him a hug, which seemed to embarrass him, then turned and left. On her way out, she caught Stephanie between tables and told her, "I'll talk to you more later this evening."

Steph nodded and hurried off.

Frowning, Kera contemplated helping her friend with her tables but felt as though it would be somehow inappropriate since she was no longer on the payroll and the customers might be perturbed to have some strange biker chick suddenly grab their empty dishes. Pushing it out of her mind, she left the bar behind and found her ride in the back lot.

Zee stood on his kickstand in the same parking space Kera had always used as an employee next to Cevin's truck. He was a Kawasaki Z-900 and as spotless and smoothly maintained as when he was new. The two of them had been through a lot together, and she rewarded him with proper maintenance whenever she had the time.

And now that she was technically unemployed, she had more time than ever.

"Okay, Zee," she said, putting her helmet back on. "Time to go home and get started on the next phase of our lives."

Kera revved the engine and sped into the street, merging with the usual heavy LA traffic and weaving around it when she could.

Driving relaxed her, even when the streets were congested. Her mind wandered.

She had expected to come away from the Mermaid in a bittersweet, sentimental frame of mind—good months had been spent in that place, with good people, and she was leaving them behind. It was her one remaining link to a "normal" life. And it was gone, barring sporadic visits. She was on her own.

But it meant that she was *free*. Her inheritance was in the process of clearing—a large amount like that had understandably flagged eyes at the banks—but it would be hers soon, and she would have as long as she needed to get her agency up and running.

As she drew closer to the warehouse she had converted into her home, she recalled that there was still one lingering problem: her alter ego.

"First order of business," she promised herself, "is getting rid of the 'Motorcycle Man' phenomenon once and for all. Fame has its perks, but it will be nice to be free of *that*, too."

CHAPTER TWO

James Lovecraft and Mother LeBlanc sat on one side of the dining table, and their student Ezeudo sat opposite them. The sun was streaming through the eastern window, so they hadn't bothered to turn on any electric lights as they ate their omelets and toast, washed down with coffee and orange juice.

James swallowed a mouthful of his food. "All right," he began, pointing his fork at Ezeudo, "you're doing well, and I mean that. I know it's rough. Normally we don't push our recruits this hard, but, well…you've already heard all this anyway."

"Yes," Ezeudo confirmed, trying not to sigh too obviously, "I have." He assumed James was summing things up in this fashion as a prelude to some momentous announcement.

Nodding, James went on to say, "So, currently, the plan is to, well, continue the plan. Since you made up your mind that you were totally on board with us and our organization's mission, I would say that your progress and performance have improved. You're on the verge of pulling ahead. If you do outpace the schedule, we may be able to afford to give you a short break from time to time. But the one thing we cannot and will not do is to fall behind schedule, no matter what."

He glanced at Mother LeBlanc, giving her the opportunity to add any comments of her own. She was far older than James, though she looked younger than he did, if anything. She could have overridden his decisions if she wanted to, but she tended to allow him to take the lead where the subject of Ezeudo was concerned.

"I agree," she stated. "If things continue as they are, all should be well."

She reached into the folds of her diaphanous multicolored dress and pulled out a pepper shaker, upended it over her omelet until it was coated with black sprinkles, then put it back where she had found it. Ezeudo wondered if she would ever divulge the secret of how she always managed to produce exactly what she needed or wanted from the strange garment.

He didn't have high hopes on that front, however. Even James was confused by the dress, and if *he* didn't understand it, what chance did Ezeudo have?

Ezeudo gave a vague nod and returned to his breakfast. He was somehow disappointed, having expected a new development or a strange reversal.

No, he told himself, *I have agreed to remain here of my own free will and have told them I believe in the role they have set for me. Magic is much too powerful to be allowed into the hands of fools and renegades. My yearnings for freedom and action are as nothing compared to the greater needs of the world. Was it not the betterment of our society that led me to wander the world to begin with?*

Ever since he had fled the Nigerian village of his boyhood, he had drifted around, sometimes on jobs for the United Nations or various nonprofit charitable organizations, other times for himself. He rarely stayed in one place for more than two or three months at a time.

But after these two had come to him in Geneva, he had somewhat grudgingly agreed to be trained by them in the arts of thaumaturgy over the course of an entire year. And though it had not been stated outright, he had serious doubts that he would be allowed to leave James's estate during the whole of that period.

They were a strange pair, his teachers. James Lovecraft was an average-looking white man in his middle thirties with glasses and short side-parted hair. He resembled an accountant or a computer programmer rather than the incredibly powerful magician he was.

In contrast, Mother LeBlanc looked the part. Though Ezeudo suspected she was at least a century old, she had the appearance of a beautiful black woman of perhaps twenty-five. She had a mysterious air of dignity and formality in her mannerisms, a Creole accent, made references to the traditions of New Orleans, and of course, there was her outlandish dress.

Ezeudo was about to ask what today's lessons would be when a faint electronic bell sound came from James's laptop, which he had left open on the edge of the table.

"Ah," James acknowledged the alert, "someone sent us a message, probably a magical one, though it might simply be a mundane piece of spam or a promotional offer or some crap like that. A couple of years ago," he explained to Ezeudo, "I figured out how to route psionic messages to my email. Makes life far simpler to be able to read those things at my own leisure rather than have them pop directly into my head when, for example, I'm trying to enjoy my breakfast."

Ezeudo chuckled as James turned his fork back to his eggs, though his curiosity had been piqued. "I take it the message is from the council?" he offered. "Psionic messages, from what I have read, are not a beginner's spell."

"Perhaps." James shrugged, apparently indifferent.

Mother LeBlanc pursed her lips and turned a critical eye on her partner. "Really, James, you have become far too reliant upon technology. The reason these gadgets exist is to act as a crutch for people who do *not* possess the gift of magical aptitude. By letting your inbox field your messages for you, you are acting like a man with functional legs who uses crutches because he is too lazy to walk."

There was something playful in her tone, and James, who had worked with her for years, snorted. "Hilarious. What are we to make, then, of you being too lazy to walk over to the counter and get the pepper shaker from there? Oh, no, you had to conjure one out of your dress."

LeBlanc waved a hand. "That is the complete opposite of the point I was trying to make. However, it was a nice effort on your part to turn my criticism back on me, albeit one that failed miserably. Now, are you going to end the suspense of this mysterious message, or will I have to stoop to reading your email for you?"

Grumbling, James set down his fork and turned the laptop toward him, examining the message with eyes that suddenly went from dull and complacent to wide with alarm.

Ezeudo tensed, sensing something was wrong. LeBlanc did likewise. The vibe of shock and danger all but electrified the air.

"What is it?" Ezeudo asked. He wondered if it was something to do with him. Perhaps the council was objecting to his independent experiments with scrying on Motorcycle Woman or wishing to change his training schedule.

But obscurely, he knew it was worse than that.

James's mouth fell open, but it took another couple of seconds before he could speak. His skin had grown pale and clammy.

"We, ah…" he began in a hollow voice as LeBlanc moved in beside him and put a hand on his arm. "We are being challenged for control of the North American continent. And by 'we,' I mean, the council."

"*What?*" LeBlanc snapped at a startling volume. "Who *dares?*"

Ezeudo felt his stomach sink as he watched and listened.

James swallowed. "Oh, I think I can guess who. Let's see if they had the decency to sign their little message." He scrolled down through the email. "No. They did not."

Biting her lip with impatience, Mother LeBlanc insisted, "Play the message as it was *intended* to be received. That might give us a hint."

The two thaumaturgists locked eyes and Ezeudo watched them closely, trying to figure out what was passing between them.

"Fine," James said after a moment. "But since it sounds like a threat, don't blame me if hearing it in its original form ruins the rest of your day."

LeBlanc inhaled and folded her arms. "Agreed."

James turned to the screen, touched it with his right hand, and performed a gesture with his left while intoning something under his breath. The missive played in the minds of all three of them, vanishing from his inbox at the same instant.

You, a terrible voice began, *have failed to govern your own territory.* It was a woman's voice, full and throaty and with a noticeable Eastern European accent, though augmented with various distorting effects that made it echo through their minds like the condemnation of an angry goddess.

You have transgressed in ways that cannot be forgiven, and you have revealed your weakness. You shall therefore be shown the strength that must govern North America in your stead.

Then an image burst before their minds' eyes of dark figures, nine of them, standing in silhouette before a sheet of eerie green fire. The flames roared, shrieked, and hissed, then both sound and image vanished, leaving their minds reeling in darkness and cold.

Ezeudo gasped, and his hands clawed the table. He looked to his teachers for reassurance, hoping they were not as terrified as he so they could offer him some condolence that such an evil and threatening vision was merely a bluff, a cheap trick.

But James and LeBlanc appeared shaken. Less so than he, which gave him hope, but they clearly were not about to make light of what they had all experienced.

"Well," James muttered, sticking a finger under the collar of his shirt, "that made the point rather clearly, didn't it? They're not interested in negotiating, only in getting us to back down or risk destruction. Or something along those lines."

"That," remarked LeBlanc in a low voice, her eyes narrowed, "was my impression as well. And I believe I know who sent it."

She and James nodded in unison.

Breathing heavily, Ezeudo leaned across the table. His eyes felt like they were nearly as wide as the breakfast plates before them. "Who?"

He did not like the way the others' faces changed when he asked. In fact, when he saw the looks on their faces, he was very sure he did not want to know.

"The Orthodoxy," Madame LeBlanc said quietly.

There had been a certain amount of debate over where the next meeting would take place. Kera knew that her warehouse, located in downtown LA, was inconveniently far from Lia's house in Long Beach, and Lia was the second most crucial member of their burgeoning organization.

But Long Beach was inconveniently far from everyone *else*, so they had decided to congregate at Kera's place, with the promise that the next meeting would be at Lia's to keep things fair.

Distance notwithstanding, Lia was the first to arrive. Unlike Stephanie and Chris, she did not have a day job. Yet.

Someone knocked on the side door of the warehouse right on schedule. Kera peeked out the window to confirm it was Lia. Nodding in satisfaction, she opened the door for her friend and business partner.

"Hi," Kera greeted her. "I made coffee. It only got done about five minutes ago tops, so it's still fresh."

Lia inclined her head and gave a faint smile. "Thank you." She was a petite woman, probably in her late twenties, of Korean descent, with long black hair and a somewhat aloof and professional demeanor. She always wore business clothes, suits, or suit-dresses regardless of the occasion. A briefcase, presumably containing her laptop and any papers or other gadgets she might need, dangled from her slim, pale hand.

Kera took the case and set it on the kitchen table while Lia helped herself to some coffee. "The good news," Kera reported, "is that Stephanie's working a split shift today, so she'll be out in an hour or so, though she has to go back to the Mermaid at ten. The bad news is that Chris has to stay late, so he won't be around 'til about the same time as Steph."

Lia returned, seating herself on the couch as she sipped from a steaming mug. "I see. Well, that will give the two of us time to go over the organizational specifics before we begin delegating things to them. As you can see, Johnny didn't come. I'm starting to believe he's *serious* about not wanting to be fully involved in our operation. Still, he tentatively agreed to help us once in a while when necessary."

Kera shrugged and sat down in the chair opposite her. "Okay, that's fine. He's definitely been an asset so far, but I can understand wanting to divorce himself from the underworld and 'the life' or whatever as much as possible, even if it means he has to stick with retail for the time being."

They talked a bit about their daily lives for the sake of relaxing and reestablishing rapport before turning to business. By then, the caffeine was kicking in.

"So," Kera began, "are you sure you're okay with the place being called 'MacDonagh Investigations?' I mean, yeah, I'm the one providing the startup capital, and I'll be the CEO, but you've been as instrumental as I have, so we can add your name to it if you want."

Lia shook her head. "No, that's fine for several reasons. Three, specifically. First, as you said, you are the one who is incorporating the firm. Second, there are certain individuals who might recognize my name and grow curious as to what I was up to, and, given my past, we don't want that."

Lia, along with Johnny and their mutual friend Sven, had worked for an up-and-coming drug syndicate and various other petty criminal endeavors before Kera had overthrown their leader Pauline and set them on the path to becoming law-abiding citizens.

"And third," Lia concluded with a slight sigh, "many people cannot pronounce my surname anyway. I am not among those Koreans fortunate enough to be named something easy like 'Kim' or 'Park.'"

Kera laughed, thinking about the Kim family that owned the grocery a mile or so down the road, who were good friends of hers. "Well, technically 'MacDonagh' should be pronounced with more of a gargling sound than a hard 'G' at the end, but that's how Americanization works on people's names, I guess. Anyway, yes, we'll keep things simple by just naming the whole outfit after me. A bit self-aggrandizing, but it works."

"Self-aggrandizement," Lia pointed out, "or more properly, self-promotion, is one of the cornerstones of success. Case in point, here is my, um, rough draft for our company website. I'm open to constructive criticism, and there will likely be bugs to work out, layout to be improved, and so forth, but I believe I'm on the right track."

She turned the laptop around and showed the screen. Kera leaned forward, examining it and running her finger over the scroll pad as needed.

"Huh. It looks like...a lawyer's website? Somehow I would have thought it would be more, I don't know, like, police-esque, or maybe resembling one of those tactical gear stores or something."

Lia's mouth realigned itself into a sly smirk. "Exactly. We're not private defense contractors. Detective agencies primarily deal in information. In that regard, they are quite similar to attorneys. Most lawyers' websites are boring and staid, yes, but they are people whom their clients trust to handle their dirty laundry, so to speak, and protect them from legal repercussions. We want to convey an image of being trustworthy and legitimate, and one of the hallmarks of that is looking boring."

Kera took a swig of coffee, thinking it over. "Yeah, I'd say you're right. Besides, while we need to start building a reputation soon, we also don't want to attract too much outside attention, so it's best to avoid anything overly sensational in our advertising."

She looked around the warehouse and sensed that Lia was also contemplating what sort of office they should maintain if any. Kera's place was probably not the best location.

"Well," Lia added, "you're right that we will need to establish ourselves with a kickass case, one at which we can succeed with flying colors so that our customers are all too willing to leave us a nice review, spread positive word of mouth, and so forth. But like you said, due to both of us having things in our pasts we don't want to be scrutinized too hard, we want to avoid becoming downright famous."

Kera chortled at that. "I'm already famous, albeit not under my own name or identity. So yeah, I agree. We want to stay off of the front-page news. It's better to be one of those 'well-kept secrets' people whisper about at the water cooler. But how do we get a case that guides us toward that? And can we somehow link it to my plan to get rid of 'Motorcycle Man,' so to speak? I think a sudden disappearance would stir up as many rumors as anything, and I want to make sure it goes the opposite way."

The latter issue was one of the things she had wanted to discuss with Steph, and she hoped her friend would get out of work and show up soon.

Lia shrugged. "That is indeed the hard part, but difficult is not the same as impossible. I have several ideas for ways we might approach the problem, which I put into a flowchart here..."

Kera marveled at the level of work her partner had devoted to the task. After all, they had not even officially begun.

"I'm surprised you've done all this," she admitted to Lia. "It's a different line of work from anything you're familiar with, and part of me assumed you would want to coast for a while, get your bearings, before plunging right in."

Lia shook her head. "No, if we are going to do this, I insist on *doing* it, full stop."

Kera gave a small smile. She had not considered that people in the criminal underworld would be so focused on doing a good job with every task, but she wasn't going to say that to Lia. Instead, she said honestly, "Well, I appreciate it."

Lia seemed genuinely pleased as she continued, laying out plans for Motorcycle Man's disappearance that would neither arouse suspicion nor leave an obvious hole that potential vigilantes or criminals would capitalize on.

Midway into Lia's informal presentation, Stephanie showed up, and Kera rose to let her in.

"Hey, Steph."

"Hey, Kera. Hi, Lia." She waved to them both as she stepped inside. "I'll have to leave by nine-thirty, but that ought to be enough time to talk about what needs to be discussed. Kera, what was it you wanted to tell me at the Mermaid? I figured it was something you didn't want to say out loud."

Kera gestured at the coffee maker and Steph nodded, heading for it to pour herself a cup.

Kera explained briefly as her friend moved. "It was about how, if at all possible, I want to use our first case as a legitimate detective agency to act as a cover for getting rid of that annoying son of a bitch known as Motorcycle Man. He's been causing me problems for far too long."

Stephanie laughed out loud. "Yeah, you may be on to something there. But how? You don't mean doing something as a counter-vigilante *against* him, do you? If the public thinks he's the bad guy and you end up getting caught someday, God forbid, that would make it tougher to get a fair trial. That's something you might have to think about. That *we* might have to think about, I mean."

Lia looked up from her laptop, frowning. "She makes a good point. If we adopt your plan to run MM out of town or whatever, we'll need to ensure that 'he' comes out looking good to the average Angeleno."

Sighing, Kera walked back to her chair and sat down. "Yeah. That's roughly what I had in mind, though I *don't* plan to ever get caught. In fact, creating the impression that MM has relocated to the Northwest Territories of Canada or something might help with that a great deal."

Moments later, Chris arrived. Kera was getting a little tired of rising to let people in, but it was worth it. "Hi," she said as she flung open the door.

Her boyfriend looked tired and haggard, but he smiled at the sight of her. "Hello." Stepping over the threshold, he landed in her arms, and they shared a quick kiss. "Glad to be here, finally. And is that coffee I smell? And taste?"

Kera poked the tip of his nose with her finger. "Yes, yes it is. Help yourself, though there may not be much left by now. We're a sleep-deprived bunch. Then come check out Lia's website for our agency."

A minute later, everyone knelt in front of the screen.

Stephanie nodded with approval. "Not bad, not bad."

Chris furrowed his brow. "It looks like a respectable lawyer's site. I'm guessing that's intentional?"

"Of course," Lia confirmed. "We wouldn't want it to look like a front for a hired-thug service, now would we? The goal is to become a company with good word of mouth among clients who are themselves respectable, while hopefully avoiding mass media attention."

They shared ideas for how to get started with cases and how

they might be able to tie MM into the whole thing. Kera liked the idea of having Johnny or Sven pretend to hire them so they could manipulate the case from the ground up.

Lia agreed that it was clever and might work, but she wasn't sure she liked the idea of exposing Johnny and Sven to scrutiny by other customers or journalists, not to mention she seemed uncomfortable with building their business on the foundation of a lie.

"Although," she conceded, "that can't entirely be helped insofar as we have been acting almost like a detective agency in our efforts against El Peluquero and aren't about to disclose that information to anyone. Still, once we incorporate, we should get off on the right foot."

Stephanie and Chris agreed. Kera frowned in annoyance but decided that they were correct.

"Fine," she grumbled. "We won't set everything up ourselves. We'll take on someone else's legitimate organic case and figure out a way to work MM into it later. What we could do, though, is pick and choose from among the headlines. Find crimes that are crying out to be solved and conveniently advertise where the victims can see or hear us. Something like that."

The others agreed.

They talked more about the boring red tape that would soon be involved in completing the process of getting their business license, setting themselves up to deal with their taxes, and so forth before Lia and Stephanie finally prepared to leave.

"Kera," said Lia, shaking her partner's hand, "I feel like we've made progress today, and I'm looking forward to the next step."

Kera smiled. "Thanks. You're already a great employee— partner—and we're not even a full company yet. Anyway, you've done enough for one day. Go home and get some rest."

Lia said goodbye and stepped out.

Stephanie was next. "Ugh. Kera, if this works out, I think I'll have to follow in your footsteps and hang up my shoes at that place. I like Cevin and Jenn, and the money's pretty good for what it is, but don't think I can keep working there full-time and have a second full-time job with you."

For some reason, Kera hadn't considered that Steph might quit to join her. "Well, it might be wise to wait and see if we're capable of turning a profit. And of course, give Cevin two weeks' notice. He deserves that much."

"Sounds like a plan." They hugged and Steph departed, leaving Kera alone with Chris.

He leaned back on the couch and folded his hands behind his head. "Soooo," he began, "looks like we have a date of sorts. I don't feel up to much of anything fancy, but you're usually not the fancy-date type...which I appreciate. I always feel awkward doing grand, romantic stuff. What do you say we order some food and watch a movie?" He raised his eyebrows, awaiting her input.

"Sure." She would have suggested something similar if he hadn't, but she liked that he was confident enough to take the initiative. "I'll drive."

They called a nearby Italian place and requested enough food for at least three, maybe four people. Magic took a toll on one's metabolism, although Kera had been casting fewer spells lately and was getting more efficient at managing her energy when she did. At her peak, she ate three or four times the amount of food that was normal for a woman her age and size, and all the while, she was gradually *losing* weight.

Kera put on her leathers and helmet, then she and Chris climbed astride Zee and drove off into the night.

I'm going to miss it, Kera admitted to herself as the wind rushed by. *Riding into battle as a vigilante against crime, doing Batman shit. But it was never tenable in the long run. No, the way we'll be doing things from now on is better. Maybe not as fun, but a hell of a lot smarter.*

CHAPTER THREE

Mick Gorsky had started his art gallery twenty years ago and had been both overjoyed and relieved when it turned out to be a success. Of course, it didn't hurt that in addition to displaying pieces as a curator, he continued to do restorations of paintings on the side, which brought in both extra money and extra prestige.

The current job all but confounded him. Not in that it was an impossible task—he was confident he could get the piece back to closely resembling its original appearance—but his mind could not let go of the overwhelming sense of weirdness surrounding the whole incident.

He stared at the sliced-up fragments of canvas on the table before him, sighed, and stood up from his seat to pace across the empty floor.

Mrs. Corvina had barged into the gallery first thing in the morning after waiting on the curb for them to open. Gorsky knew her well; she was a "grand dame" type who came in every month or so to view the pieces and occasionally purchased one to keep up her image of a gracefully aging sophisticate.

She had never asked him to repair anything, though, until today. Nor had he ever seen her so upset.

Apparently, she had, mere days ago, purchased the new piece by that kid Domingo who had begun making waves in the California art scene. The same night, someone had broken into her house and stolen the painting, then returned it to her the next night—in pieces.

Gorsky had nodded and looked her in the eye as she sobbed and railed about how anyone could do something so senselessly destructive and how the painting might never be the same even if Gorsky could repair it, et cetera. He had not voiced his suspicions and had taken the job, ever the sober professional.

He had never heard of anyone going to the trouble to steal a painting for the sole purpose of vandalism. There had to be some kind of skullduggery afoot.

Perhaps, he had speculated, someone had made a convincing fake copy, destroyed that, and sent the shreds back to Mrs. Corvina to act as a red herring while they resold the original? No, that could not be. The painting was brand new. Domingo would be the only person who could be responsible for such a plot, and that seemed highly unlikely.

Or maybe this is a ploy cooked up by Domingo and Corvina to collect insurance on the painting? But he didn't believe he had heard of that, either. It would be a ridiculous scheme that would attract too much attention from auditors and inspectors. Whoever had done this, the motive made no sense unless there was a personal vendetta at work he knew nothing about.

All he had said aloud was, "Yes, Mrs. Corvina. I will examine it closely and begin work tonight. I will call you tomorrow morning with an update on how things are going. You know my reputation for quality work, of course."

She had continued to vent her sorrows to him for another five minutes before he gently ushered her out after taking custody of the sad remains of Domingo's masterpiece.

It *was* sad. Downright tragic. He had seen the original painting at the exhibition and had a high-definition, full-color photo print of it beside him at the moment for reference. It was a remarkable work, entirely deserving of the praise its creator was increasingly garnering from critics and connoisseurs.

Something about the lifeless canvas strips seemed *wrong*, though. It was almost eerie, for lack of a better way of putting it.

First, though the painting had been cut into a random assortment of irregular shapes, it had been cut *cleanly*. The person responsible must have used an exceedingly sharp knife or razor blade and taken care not to tear the canvas or chip away the paint.

Touching the strips gingerly and with the respect of a surgeon for his patient, Gorsky had laid them out on his work table and arranged them like the pieces of a jigsaw puzzle into their proper orientation relative to one another so he could see the original and complete image more or less as it should have looked, barring the lines of the table's surface corresponding to the slices.

Everything matched his photo of the original, yet strangely, he felt as though he were looking at a completely different piece of artwork. An inferior one, and whatever was lacking in it went beyond the physical damage.

He returned to his suspicion that it was a fake and the original painting had been shipped off to the black market by the time Mrs. Corvina had finished her spiel this morning. It made sense.

But as he examined the pieces more closely, he could not find any evidence of fraud. None of the telltale signs were present, and every detail of the painting down to the tiny unintentional flaws and most minute touches appeared to be identical to his photo. He considered that the photo itself was a fraud, but that was impossible. It had been taken by a trusted friend of his at the exhibition from which Corvina had bought the damn thing.

"Weird," he muttered under his breath. "So strange."

His spine went cold. Something *was* wrong with the painting, though he couldn't pinpoint it. Another idea had formed in his head, though it was absurd, and he tried to discard it. Superstitious nonsense, but it kept popping back into his consciousness.

The painting seemed...dead, as though the blade that had slashed it to ribbons had also deprived it of life. As though a vampire had sucked the blood out of it, leaving a husk devoid of vitality, vibrancy, and the creative essence of Domingo's burgeoning genius.

It had been a profoundly emotional piece, but now it was curiously unemotive, as though traumatized, depressed, and if not deceased, at least catatonic.

Gorsky shuddered and shook his head to clear it. He had work to do. The painting could be repaired. Since the knife-wielder had done surprisingly little damage to the material, he might be able to restore it to a point where Mrs. Corvina would scarcely know the difference. And she was willing to pay for his services, after all.

"It's late," he mumbled. "That's all. My mind is more likely to slip into strange places at this hour."

But as he began the process of restoring the ravaged piece, working off the template used in the case of multiple much more famous paintings, he could not dispel the skin-crawling sensation that he had stumbled onto something he could not understand—and did not *want* to understand, either.

The Alchemist's mind wandered in tandem with the way her hand, holding the brush, wandered across the canvas. Each took its own path independent of the other, though she prided herself on her ability to maintain a proper level of control and discipline over both.

Over the course of her life—the many long years, so few of

which showed on her face—she had learned and practiced many of the arts. To be sure, painting was one of her favorites, but she also possessed a respectable degree of talent in the fields of drawing, plaster sculpture, metal sculpture, video design, graphic design, and so forth. It had been said that men were more inclined toward the visual than women, but she had always prided herself on her liking for forms of art that were appreciated primarily with the eyes.

Her studio was arranged according to that same principle. She had studied feng shui, sacred geometry, and plain old interior decorating before placing the various pieces—the complete and the half-complete, her own work and that of others—in their current configuration.

In a way, the panorama formed by the arrangement of the studio was a meta-work of art unto itself. Sadly, there was one noticeable hole that broke up the thematic cohesiveness of the spread.

The Alchemist's attention was not focused on that, though. Her attention had already returned to the violent birth of her newest work of original art.

Semi-original, anyway.

Her personal reinterpretation of Domingo's Expressionist masterwork was nearing completion. After the burst of motivation she had experienced after destroying the original, she had needed to rest and return the pieces to that fool Mrs. Corvina. But today, the creative muse once again demanded indulgence and satisfaction.

So she had indulged it, giving vent to the continuous buildup of artistic vitality within her. It reminded her so much of that possessed by the promising young Luis Domingo.

The painting's resemblance to his only increased as she worked on it. However, for each element, each section, and indeed each individual brushstroke that followed in Domingo's footsteps, the overall tendency toward distortion grew. The entire painting was being filtered through a subjective perception that was unique to the Alchemist.

Where the young man's original piece had expressed a mixture of dark tumult and joyful hope, the interpretation taking shape on the canvas before her seemed to express something different. A sequence of events, darkness followed by light that led to more darkness, which was doomed to repeat itself.

Until it ran out of energy.

The Alchemist stopped, realizing she was breathing heavily and the brush dangled from her shaking hand. She was getting...strung out. Burned out. Her movements had gone from confident and energetic to feverish and compulsive and finally had begun to flag.

And her sense of inspiration was fading. The painting was at least three-quarters completed by this point, and she felt all of a sudden that she had no idea how to finish it.

"No," she growled. "I'm so close to having this one done. I *cannot* run out now. Have I always run out this fast? It seems like it should last longer. It *should!*"

Her lower lip trembled, and she flung her head to the side to avoid having to look at the maddeningly incomplete artwork while also flipping her hair away from her face.

"I...need..." she murmured, "another dose. A stronger dose. Maybe one that comes directly from the source."

Her pulse quickened. Obtaining the creative spark straight from the central fire was a concept that both frightened and excited her. She had done it before, but it had been a long, long time. And the risks were substantial, along with the potential consequences.

She trudged away from the easel where the canvas stood and slumped over the central worktable where yesterday she had cut apart the original painting. Her ceremonial knife lay upon the surface.

The Alchemist blinked and tried to look away from the blade.

"No. That's nonsensical. I have plenty of creative ability of my own, enough to finish the piece. I do not *need* what I could get from Domingo himself. Any of it."

Her eyes returned to the hilt, and her hand itched to hold it. The edge seemed to sparkle beneath the bright fluorescent lights of the studio.

"Domingo," she said again. "Or any other healthy young artist of his caliber. Full to brimming with talent. Deep wells of potential, most of which they will waste in the pursuit of...ugh, *sales*. It is a crime against the very concept of art. Such people do not deserve the spark, let alone the entire fire. It should be..." she coughed, "*transferred* someplace where it could be of some use."

Her knife was good at making such transfers. She reached out and grasped it, feeling its familiar and comfortable weight. It was, in some ways, the most valuable of her artistic tools.

The longer the process took, she recalled, the more creative energy she was able to absorb. That was probably why she was having her current problems. She had carved up the painting too quickly in her eagerness and had not maximized the harvest.

But to use the knife not merely on a product of human creativity but on a creative human...that would provide a much bigger and more potent dose. Especially if she stretched it out, made a lengthy occasion of it. She might acquire enough artistic vitality to last her for months. Enough to complete half a dozen paintings in addition to the current one.

"Risky," she chided herself. "So, so risky. You know how other people are. And the authorities! You cannot rely upon them to understand. That's why it must only be done once in a great while and with the utmost care, caution, preparation, discretion, and so forth."

She nodded. Her mind was not entirely made up, but she knew which way the wind was blowing. Resisting the urge for much longer was not a viable prospect.

"Just once," she vowed. "If I do this, it will only be one time, and then not again for many years. And certainly not in the same place. After all, I've been in Los Angeles before, haven't I?"

She smiled with the memory, and her hand, acting independently of her conscious mind, flicked in motions much like those of a painter wielding her brush.

CHAPTER FOUR

Ezeudo had rapidly begun to suspect that the reassurance he had received from both of his teachers that they would be adhering strictly to the one-year timeline for his education had been abruptly transformed into a lie.

Not an intentional one. They had meant it when they had first said it, but circumstances had changed. The situation was evolving. Judging by how things had gone for the last two days, what they had told him no longer corresponded to reality.

At present, he was out in the vast backyard of the Lovecraft estate, admiring the twinges of color that were beginning to appear amidst the trees as summer came to an end and autumn began its encroachment upon the land. He did not much like the cold, but he enjoyed the changing of the seasons, which were much different in the northern temperate zone than they were in West Africa.

And he had time to stand there and admire the trees. James and LeBlanc had only given him the briefest outline of a lesson, teaching him one or two minor new spells per day, and then had instructed him to keep drilling in stuff he already knew.

They were busy. They wanted him out of the way while they fretted about more important things. He sighed.

"Nonsense. This is all foolishness. If the threat they received from these people, this coven from Europe, is so serious, why have they not explained it to me? Am I not to be a full member soon? It would seem that they could use my help, which means continuing my training while they enlist the aid of others to fortify themselves against the threat."

To busy himself and take his mind off his concerns and anxieties over the nightmarish and threatening message, he practiced a variety of charms for calming the mind and clarification of the senses. He could use enchantments of that sort right now and was all too happy to use himself as a subject.

First, he meditated for two or three minutes, the minimum necessary to take the initial edge off his thoughts and emotions. Then he began to employ magic, reaching deep into the pools of his memory for the necessary incantations, gestures, and other methods necessary to cast the spells correctly and with a minimum of energy expenditure.

He recalled something LeBlanc had told him about a week ago.

"Ezeudo," she had explained, "our organization strives to emphasize the importance of careful and efficient management of your personal strength while practicing thaumaturgy. Without proper self-discipline, the act of employing magic can be an enormous drain on a person's stamina."

He knew that but had played along while she got to the point. "Yes, I have always noticed that I grow more tired and hungry after I use the arts."

"Of course." She had gone on to elaborate upon the fact that many novice or apprentice thaumaturges exhausted themselves too quickly or put themselves at risk of catatonia or death by trying to pull miracles out of the ether through brute force. It was the magical equivalent of trying to earn money by robbing a bank.

"Our art," she had concluded, "is not like robbing a bank when done as it should be. It is more like negotiating a settlement from the bank and then patching up any hostilities by opening an account with them so that they might earn interest off your deposits. Reciprocity and subtlety are the hallmarks of great casters and vital skills if you wish to ascend to our level without needing to consume enough food for three to five people every single day."

He had believed her. The benefits of training and mentorship, as opposed to self-directed study, were becoming more obvious as time went on.

Which was why he was so frustrated by their outright *negligence* since the Orthodoxy had challenged them. He felt as though he might be on the verge of breaking through to a new threshold of power if only they could guide him through the next week or so.

Not that he blamed them for their concern, of course. The magnitude of threat implied by the psychic message was clear cause for alarm.

Somehow, Ezeudo had assumed that those on the council or the "Congress of American Thaumaturgy" or whatever they were currently calling themselves were the premier magic users on the planet, but his assumption might well have been wrong.

It was undeniable, based on minor things James and LeBlanc had said or things they had not said, that they considered the Orthodoxy to be at least their equals. Perhaps even their superiors.

And if *that* were the case, having war declared against them for control of the continent might be the one thing that could justify a delay in James's obsessive adherence to the one-year training program.

The calming spell took effect and Ezeudo felt his worries melt away, replaced by a serene perceptiveness, as though his mind were located not amidst the chaos of the present moment but above the stability of eternal time.

This, he thought, *is so pleasant that it could become addictive. Therefore, it is dangerous. I must not rely upon it too much.*

A minute or two later, as he returned to his practice of elemental evocation spells, James appeared from the house and strolled toward him, waving a hand to get his student's attention.

Ezeudo locked eyes with him and walked across the grass to meet him halfway. "Hello. My efforts have gone well so far today. What shall I do next? And if I may ask, what should I know about what happened the other morning?"

James grimaced as though he had bad news to deliver. "Allow me to answer both of those questions at once. What you're going to do next is come with me to a nice remote webcam meeting with the rest of the council. We're going to discuss the matter of the Orthodoxy and the crap they're pulling since unfortunately, it might affect you as well as us."

The tall Nigerian frowned. "Yes, I see."

As they ambled back into the mansion, James added, "We were going to have a proper face-to-face meeting since most of the other members live in the surrounding region anyway, but that would potentially have made it easier for you-know-who to scry on us, track us, or whatnot. Having everyone in different physical locations and broadcasting via a mixture of electronic and magical signals disperses our aura-signatures in a way that's much harder for hostile casters to get a bead on."

Ezeudo nodded and said nothing.

James led the way to his study, where his laptop and webcam were already set up and hooked into a big-screen TV he had produced and placed against the far wall. Mother LeBlanc sat off to the side in a comfortable plush chair, her face calm but grave.

"Hello, Ezeudo," she greeted him. "I hope James has explained the situation. Furthermore, I would like to apologize for our lack of attention to your teachings lately, but unforeseen events have interfered."

James coughed. "Yeah, that's one way of putting it. Have a seat. Want anything to drink? And yes, I am referring primarily to alcoholic beverages. I'll need one or more within the first sixty seconds of Lady Mitchell's appearance, after all."

Ezeudo requested a small glass of whiskey on the rocks.

LeBlanc shook her head. "Tomorrow would be an excellent first day to cut back on your drinking, James. And while Mary Mitchell has a tendency to over-focus on the letter of the law rather than the spirit, her heart is ultimately in the right place."

James poured liquor into two glasses, adding ice to both. "Heart? She has a heart?"

LeBlanc ignored the remark and waited for the men to settle in. The other members would begin the remote conference any second now.

They didn't have long to wait. The screen came to life, compartmentalized into four boxes, each of which held three or four people. Including Ezeudo, James, and LeBlanc, there were thirteen of them in all. Lauren Jones, who sometimes visited to stand in as Ezeudo's instructor for a day or three at a time, was the only one he had seen before.

LeBlanc was the first to offer her greetings. "Good day, everyone, and we're glad to see you all again. As per our previous communications, we have all agreed that the message we received was an across-the-board phenomenon intended for the entire council to see and hear at once."

Zacharia McConnell, fondling the coyote-head carving atop the large ring she wore on her left hand, replied, "Yes, indeed, Mother. It is sad that it has come to this. What could have made these people so angry? It reminds me of a dream I once had..."

Crystal Green exhaled and shook her head, and a cloud of frost appeared briefly in the air near her mouth and nose. "They clearly think we are weak, irresponsible, and illegitimate."

Amanda Moore's black cat leaped into her lap and meowed. She stroked its fur, heedless of any hairs that might get on her dress since the garment was the same sable shade as the animal's coat. "Assuming it is the Orthodoxy—an entirely realistic assumption—there have been many stories about their expansionist and aggressive tendencies."

Josiah Kane scratched the side of his gray-haired head with the top of his walking stick. "Mmm, yes, most concerning. We were aware of them, yet we never suspected they would dare to challenge us in our home territory."

Samantha Martinez looked at the camera in a way that suggested she was trying to examine one of the other people within the call. "Oh, is that Ezeudo? Hello there. You're tall, aren't you? I can tell."

Ezeudo felt a faint tingling low in his belly, but James leaned over and spoke behind in his hand in a whisper far too loud for anyone else to have failed to hear it. "Don't flatter yourself, my friend. This is how she is with *everyone*."

"I heard that," Samantha pointed out. "It's true, though." She fluffed her lovely dark hair.

Damian Diaz chuckled and flashed his white teeth. "Correction—she is like that with all the *men*. She is kind enough to leave the women to me."

Rufus Mayer adjusted his glasses and raised a dark finger. "Actually, I recall an incident in which a gentleman from Greece was, via a transmutation spell of mine, willingly sent to your chambers after—"

"Yes, yes," Damian snapped. "It happens to the best of us."

Old Hugh Buchanan, who usually allowed the other members to do most if not all the talking, intervened. "This is all terribly amusing, but might we focus on business, please? And yes, it's good to finally meet you, Ezeudo, sir. Welcome aboard."

Ezeudo nodded. "Thank you. I am pleased to be here."

Lauren Jones looked to both sides to indicate she was

speaking to the entire council. "His progress has been excellent, despite the grueling schedule James has set. Ezeudo, I'm sorry I haven't been able to show up for any lessons lately, but we've been preoccupied."

The only member who had yet to speak was Mary Carter Mitchell, who sat tight-lipped on a couch between Amanda and Josiah. One of her plants, perhaps a bean sprout, rested on the coffee table in front of her.

When she made no move to offer her two cents, James cleared his throat and took the initiative. "Well, yes, here we are. And we all understand the gravity of the situation and what sorts of fuckery it can potentially lead to. My best guess is that they suspect us of being guilty, at least according to their twisted view, of some infraction against the Elder Code."

Ezeudo squinted. "If I may ask, what is the Elder Code?"

Lauren was all too eager to answer him, and no one tried to stop her. "An armistice of sorts agreed upon many centuries past, whereby whichever coven rules over a given area has an ongoing responsibility to keep magic users safe within their domain. There is some leeway in interpretation with such things, of course, but most of us agree on the generalities."

Ezeudo tried to think of how the council, who seemed like responsible and level-headed people (mostly), could be guilty of endangering their charges. Lauren went on before he could attempt to fill in the blanks himself.

"Certainly," she elaborated, "that means each coven must ensure the physical safety of its members. It is also well-nigh universally assumed to mean that covens have an obligation to protect *the discipline of magic itself.*"

James groaned, and LeBlanc added, "Thus, the necessity of keeping the arts secret from the general public and hushing up any noisy incidents that might attract undue attention."

Lauren smiled without much mirth.

"Exactly, yes. Different covens have varying cultures and

might disagree on their approach to the craft. But it is of common interest to all thaumaturgists, witches, or whatever term is preferred that our existence be kept out of the public eye. In this way, each group is responsible for maintaining the cloak of secrecy that affects every magic-user on the planet. Should the knowledge of our powers become common in one area, word would spread across the globe, and questions would begin to be asked which other covens might have, ah, *difficulty* answering."

Ezeudo closed his eyes, processing all that had been said. It made sense. When James and LeBlanc had come for him in Switzerland, it had been on a mission to silence his activities and those of the boy Guillaume he had taken as his apprentice.

When he opened his eyes again, Mary Mitchell had raised her hand and was pointing a finger at the camera.

"James," she stated in a harsh and forceful voice, "you did this. You are the only one with any claim to responsibility for this colossal mistake. By putting out that book—that ridiculous, reckless, ill-conceived *book*, which has caused us no end of grief for months on end—you robbed us of our standing with everyone. In the minds of people like the Orthodoxy, we now represent a void of leadership that only those stronger than us can fulfill. Congratulations."

Ezeudo winced at the bitter sarcasm in her voice and sipped his whiskey, understanding why James had half-joked about needing a drink before the meeting got started.

As near as he could tell, though, Lady Mitchell was correct.

James had been slouching in his seat, but he sat bolt upright. "Bullshit," he threw back. "I asked all of your opinions before we —yes, *we*, as a collective—moved ahead with compiling and publishing the goddamn book in question. Sure, it was my idea to begin with, but each and every last one of you signed off on the project after agreeing with me that the potential rewards outweighed the risks. And since then, I have done everything in my power to lay to rest the many, many problems that have popped up."

Mitchell pointed out, "We never asked you to interfere in that bank robbery in Las Vegas, let alone to fly to Geneva."

LeBlanc butted in. "Stopping the bank robbers was necessary to cover up the incident, Mary, since they were using thaumaturgy against the police. And we mind-wiped everyone afterward. You are correct to be concerned and displeased, but if you wish to criticize something, you could find better examples than that."

Before Lady Mitchell could respond, James continued his defensive spiel.

"And none of us—none!—anticipated, or could ever have anticipated, either how successful the book would be in terms of sales or the sheer vast wealth of magical talent it revealed among the general population. We did not so much create a new problem as discovered one that had been there all along, never before unveiled."

Mitchell frowned but said, "I am willing to consider that you might be right about that."

James looked mildly surprised by Mary's words. "Wow. Well, thanks. But yes, there are many, many times more people out there who possess the gift, if only in a minor capacity, than any of us ever dreamed. Not a single coven or magical tradition worldwide had so much as half the truth of their numbers, even across centuries of consistent practice. Literally two-thirds or more of the world's magicians have been withering on the vine all this time. No wonder we thought our ways were dying out. Which, as we might all remember, was the whole reason this council agreed to give the book a shot."

Rufus Mayer tapped his lips. "Fair enough. A reasonable hypothesis."

Zacharia sighed. "This bodes ill. The spirits have grown restless. The wind speaks in hushed tones."

Amanda Moore's cat jumped out of her lap and ran somewhere off-camera. "Yes, well. How did the Orthodoxy track all of this back to us, exactly? Was it you two—or three, if we include Ezeudo—being present in Europe? They thought we were moving against their territory and decided to respond in kind?"

"Perhaps that," suggested Crystal, "or perhaps it was that business in Los Angeles that drew their attention. All those ridiculous 'superhero' rumors."

There was further debate. No one knew for sure what had led them to the brink of war, but everyone agreed the Orthodoxy had shown zero interest thus far in negotiating or reconciliation.

Mother LeBlanc swiped a slim ebony hand through the air, bringing an end to the pointless arguments. "What is done is done," she proclaimed. "Our order was dying out, we agreed to an admittedly poorly-thought-out course of action to try to save it, and now we must all work together to face what is coming. That much we can agree on, can we not? I should hope so."

There was a moment of silence, followed by slow nods or grunts of assent.

Lady Mitchell took the lead. "So be it. We are past the point of trying to assign blame. I would much rather return to my greenhouse than have to prepare fortifications, but we do not always get what we want. Beginning today, everyone should have their homes on maximum alert and take all necessary precautions. As time goes on and we discover more of how the Orthodoxy means to go about their mission, it might be advisable for several of us to lodge together to provide for the common defense."

Ezeudo sat in silence as the thaumaturges made suggestions and plotted strategy, and a feeling of deep, gnawing unease began to grow in him. The type of rhetoric they were using and the goals they seemed to pursue reminded him of things he had heard before in troubled corners of the globe.

He was sitting in on a council of war.

"Wait," he exclaimed louder than he had intended, and

everyone looked at him. "All of you are assuming you must fight. We have received but a single message from these people. Is it possible they meant only to scare us into relinquishing control of one or two areas? That they hope to gain new power but would be content with less than the entire continent? None of you seem eager to fight. I have seen war, and it is not pleasant."

James and a couple of the others on the screen appeared to be about to speak, but LeBlanc held up a hand and turned to the newcomer.

"Ezeudo," she said in a soft tone, "please come with me. It would be best to talk apart from the others so that they can continue their discussion."

He clenched his jaw but complied, irritated at being treated a bit like a child who had barged into a movie and asked for a summary of the plotline, standing up and filing out into the hallway.

LeBlanc followed, closed the study door, and guided him by the arm toward the foyer.

"There is no point," she admitted, "in mincing words. Certain conventions were set down between the great covens long ago, and even if we would prefer not to abide by them, we have no choice but to assume that the Orthodoxy means to push this thing as far as it can go."

He stared at her. "As far as it can go. *That* is mincing words, Mother. What do you mean?"

"I mean," she said, and her eyes bore sad resignation, "that this will be a battle to the death. By the end of the coming conflict, either we or the Orthodoxy will have been wiped out. A challenge of the nature they issued cannot be abandoned once in play without dishonoring the challengers. They would be the illegitimate ones, and other covens would attempt to conquer *them*. They must destroy us utterly to save face, and we must respond in kind or die."

Ezeudo's jaw dropped. People had sometimes implied with

the casual cruelty of presumptuous contempt that his home country of Nigeria was a backward and savage place, yet in his native land, there existed no tradition as awful as this one among those with the gift, which seemed almost normal to the Americans and Europeans.

"That is madness," he protested. "Barbaric and unnecessary. This is the thinking of stupid warlords and the street thugs who emulate them. I would never have suspected such idiocy from you people. I want no part of it."

LeBlanc's demeanor hardened. She was not, he intuited, angry at him, but he could tell that she had no use for anything he had just said.

"Do you think *they* care?" she snapped. "You were there when they singled us out with their threats. They will consider you one of us and have marked our order for total annihilation. They will never stop hunting any of us, including you. If you were to flee this estate and return to Europe or Africa or set out for a small island somewhere in the Pacific Ocean, they would treat you like a loose thread to be tied up and dispatch a steady stream of assassins until one of them succeeded in bringing back your head. I am sorry, Ezeudo, but that is the way of things. We must all fight or perish."

The tall man stood in shocked silence for a span of five seconds or so. Then he stormed away, leaving the woman in the multihued dress behind as he stomped up the stairs to the second floor, flung open the door to his room, and slammed it behind him, not caring if he had damaged the wood or the hinges.

He cursed and raged in his native tongue as he paced around the chamber, flinging his bedsheets onto the floor and knocking bric-a-brac off his desk. He sprinkled in a few choice obscene expressions in French for good measure before switching back to English.

He demanded of no one in particular, "Is this a fucking joke? I have to fight to the death because of choices made by others? Idiots! Barbaric, prideful, childish idiots!"

Ezeudo had not bothered to sound-screen his room, but he did not care. In fact, he hoped the entire council had heard everything he'd said.

CHAPTER FIVE

Kera draped one of her legs over the arm of the loveseat. Today was Saturday, and though she no longer had a proper job, it still seemed like the perfect gesture of laziness to emphasize that she was enjoying her weekend.

And she wasn't enjoying it alone. The four core members of her crew—her *company*, soon—were all present.

"Oh, Lia, sorry, I just remembered that we were going to meet at your place since we were at my place the other night. If I forget next time, you have my permission to remind me."

Lia gave a light shrug and turned her dark eyes to the floor. "Don't worry about it. If we're going to be running a corporation based in Los Angeles, then it would probably behoove me to move out of Long Beach, anyway. But I appreciate the offer. I have more of my tools at home, and the drive does get to be a bit much sometimes."

Chris said, "Noted. Next meeting is at Lia's. I'll take personal responsibility for clubbing Kera over the head and dragging her there if need be."

Kera spun her face toward him, pretending to be angry. He

was sitting next to and slightly behind her and had one of his arms around her shoulders.

"I'm the one with phenomenal cosmic powers, remember?" she chided him. "If you try to drag me somewhere by the hair, you might wake up as a goddamn mollusk one of these mornings. Then someone would be justified in throwing your ass into the ocean. But I mean, I *might* give you permission to pull my hair occasionally under certain circumstances."

Stephanie, who had volunteered to make lunch, burst out laughing from the kitchen.

Lia cleared her throat. "That's nice, but let's focus on business, shall we? Yes, I know I'm a stick-in-the-mud. It comes with the territory. I don't suppose anyone remembers that 'High Expectations Asian Father' meme, do they?"

Chris and Kera cracked up this time. "Lia," Kera pointed out, "you just made a successful joke, so maybe you aren't a stick-in-the-mud after all. You're probably right, though. Daylight is burning. Where were we again?"

Chris rolled his tongue around his mouth. "Umm, unsolved mysteries. Ideally, ones that are considered important and momentous but still have some present relevance. Since there aren't likely to be a lot of clients interested in paying to solve stuff that's fascinating but hasn't really affected anyone for sixty years or whatever."

"Damn," Kera replied. "I guess that rules out the Black Dahlia murder."

Chris squinted. "Didn't those guys play Anaheim last month?"

"Not the metal band, dumbass," Kera clarified. "The actual murder. This girl, Elizabeth Short, was found dead back in, um, the 1940s. I can't remember the exact year. She was badly mutilated and found cut in half. Scared the hell out of everyone, and they never caught the perpetrator. Big part of LA history."

Chris squirmed. "Ugh. Lovely."

Lia perked up. "I believe there was someone who claimed to

have solved the case five or ten years ago, but there was no way to be certain. They determined that Short was probably killed on the orders of a local nightclub owner, who may have made advances toward her, or because she knew too much about his criminal activities on the side. Then again, there are also claims that she was murdered by a serial killer from Ohio who had relocated to California. No one knows for sure."

Stephanie had wandered over while the pasta and spaghetti sauce simmered on the stove. "Damn. You guys read about stuff like that for fun? I guess I ought to get used to it if we're going into the detective business. Was kinda hoping, though, that we could find people's lost dogs, stuff like that."

Kera chortled. "That would be nice, but it wouldn't earn us the reputation we need to hit the ground running. Hmm. There's always Jimmy Hoffa, who died in the 1970s, so he might still have family who want to know what happened to him, and it's not *conclusively* tied up. But to figure it out, we'd have to go to Michigan, I think, and I'm not in the mood. Gets me too close to my parents. They might fly to Detroit and then follow me back to LA."

Her mother and father still lived on the family estate in Danbury, Connecticut, and occasionally made the switch to the townhouse in New York City, but they had recently threatened to visit her in SoCal. Though she loved them, the thought of having them breathing down her neck was too horrifying to dwell upon.

While the others tossed around half-assed ideas, Lia had begun scanning the local headlines for potential business. "There isn't exactly a shortage of crimes in the city," she pointed out. "Getting rid of El Peluquero helped reduce the worst of it, and the police got a couple of his henchmen to talk, so they're doing a fairly good job of mopping up the gangs that splintered off from his cartel. Still, there are a variety of things to choose from."

Kera leaned toward her. "Such as?"

"Let's see..." Lia's fingers glided across the pad. "An Amber Alert, but it sounds like yet another custody issue. The police suspect the abductor is taking the kids up to her mother's place in Oregon, so there probably isn't a major danger, and they'll likely intercept the woman before we could."

"Hmm." Kera thought it over. "Record all of these in a spreadsheet or something, but I agree that that one doesn't sound too promising. Better to leave it to the professionals, especially since we don't have any friends in Oregon that I'm aware of."

Lia looked up. "You have a computer of your own if I recall."

"True." Kera stretched. "I'll make a mental note for now and record the best ones myself after lunch. What else?"

Lia read off a roster of misdemeanors, felonies, and general weirdness that had occurred within the last seventy-two hours.

A man walking home from a bar had been beaten and mugged by two kids, but he hadn't seen their faces. A painting by a well-regarded local artist had been stolen and destroyed, with the owner suspecting that resale fraud may have been involved. A college girl had been found naked and unconscious in a drugstore, claiming she had been forced at gunpoint by someone else to rob the place, though the police considered her story to be highly unreliable. Three carjackings, probably by the same perps, had occurred in the vicinity of Compton and Lakewood in as many days.

Chris scratched his temple. "The thing with the painting sounds interesting, but I know jack shit about fine art fraud. Maybe the carjackings would be our best bet."

Kera removed her leg from the armrest and sat up straight. "Perhaps. We could hunt down contact info for the parties involved and at least give them our card or direct them to our website."

Stephanie commented, "I wouldn't get too involved with cases that the police are already on. They might get suspicious, especially with us being brand new on the scene."

"Yes," Lia agreed. "I think she may be right, and we should consider other ways of building up a reputation before we plunge straight into the fray. We could do a podcast."

Stephanie laughed. "I like that idea. All the cool kids have podcasts now."

Snorting, Kera observed, "Chris and I majored in Computer Science, so by definition, we're *not* the cool kids. Still, a podcast is a hell of a lot better than nothing."

The spaghetti and garlic bread were done a moment later, and Steph served them all before they settled back into place, talking between bites.

"Steph," said Chris, "why didn't you tell us before that you could cook? Wait, you're a waitress, so you probably get tired of handling food on behalf of other people."

She shrugged. "I don't mind once in a while. Lord knows Kera has cooked for all of us enough times."

Kera pointed at her while keeping her eyes on her plate. "This woman speaks the truth."

Lia kept checking her laptop as she ate. "Now this is curious," she remarked. "There's been a development in the art case. Someone on the Internet with a lot of time on their hands compared the details to a few other incidents over the last thirty years and sent his conclusions to the LAPD, who decided he was on the right track and contacted the FBI."

Slurping down her pasta as fast as she could, Kera asked, "The FBI? Why?"

"Because," Lia clarified, "the suspicion is that there has been a whole string of thefts of fine art pieces in multiple states, which, if it's all the work of the same person or group, automatically makes it a federal matter. Mostly in New York and Los Angeles, but there are a couple from other major cities with prestigious museums or thriving art scenes. They're contacting Interpol for info on similar incidents in other countries."

Stephanie, washing down a bite of garlic toast with juice,

asked, "What's the details that make them think they're all related?"

Lia smiled. "Here's where it gets weird. In each case, the pieces were stolen right after delivery to the buyer following an auction or a sale at an exhibition. And then, a day or two or three later, the pieces are returned to the new owner. And by 'pieces,' I mean the thief or thieves carve the artwork up and dump the remains in the buyer's home. Aside from that bizarre recurring detail, though, there's no unifying factor as to the type of art that's been targeted: paintings, sculptures, even a manuscript with a symphony written on it once. There do not seem to be any similarities as to the creators of the vandalized pieces either, or anything to do with who the buyer is. The pace of the thefts has picked up in the last ten years, which leads the police to suspect a single individual may be responsible."

Chris stared into space above Lia's shoulder. "Wow. So basically, it's the work of an obsessive serial killer, only they hate art instead of people. Never thought I'd hear of that. Even in California."

Stephanie furrowed her brow. "They're not selling the paintings? Just ruining them?"

"Correct, probably," said Lia. "Again, with the most recent case, there's a suggestion that someone might have faked the painting, destroyed the imitation, and then sold the original. The problem is that making an imitation painting is time-consuming and potentially expensive and usually only worth it if they're trying to steal something by one of the Renaissance masters, not an up-and-comer like this Domingo guy. So, something doesn't add up. Kera, what do you think?"

Kera had been contemplating it all, allowing the others to contribute their opinions before she offered hers.

"Well, I'm intrigued," she confessed. "I'm used to dealing with gangsters and drugs and hitmen. That's what Motorcycle Man is known for going after, so this represents a clean break. If our company could get involved with it, we wouldn't get pigeonholed as people who just dig up dirty laundry on people's extramarital affairs or what-have-you. And the nice part about stolen artwork is that there aren't any dead bodies involved."

"Right," Chris acceded. "Pretty sure we've all had our fill of dead bodies after the Battle of the Bulge against El Peluquero there. Less likely that we'll have people out for revenge if we interfere."

Kera nodded. "Exactly. And the cops tend to prioritize stuff where people are getting hurt, so they'd probably be glad to fob this one off on a private firm if they think they can get away with it without the feds intervening. Though I'm not sure how we incorporate MM's departure from the city. I suppose we can work on that later."

First, she needed a second helping of spaghetti.

Stephanie gave her a cool skeptical glance. "Hey, now. You haven't used any magic lately, have you? Do you need to eat that much?"

"Yes," said Kera. "I was underweight, remember? Mrs. Kim keeps harassing me about being too skinny. If I don't put a few more pounds back on, she'll kill me."

"Mkay." Steph shrugged. "My appetite is back down, though. I haven't been casting spells either."

"That's for the best," Lia weighed in. "With any new business, the first year is when cash tends to be shortest. The last thing our company needs is excessive expenditures on double cheese-burgers for the CEO."

Kera looked at her. "Since you kept a straight face, I can't tell. Was that a serious comment or a joke?"

For a second, it looked like Lia might have smirked. "Yes."

CHAPTER SIX

Damian Diaz stood in front of his espresso machine, thankful for it, though being alone irked him badly. Waking up next to a beautiful woman and returning to his bed with *two* espressos was vastly preferable.

But given the hazards about to befall him and his colleagues, he couldn't take the risk. He only hoped the war would arrive soon and then be *over* soon (ideally, with the council as the victors) so things could go back to normal.

"We never, ever, *ever* should have put out that stupid book," he muttered, downing the miniature cup of coffee in one steaming gulp. "James has potential, but he is a fool. We should have put out a movie instead. Or a music video. One where we hired lots of dancers."

He smiled, imagining how that would have gone. His specialty in the world of magic was illusion. The bigger and more audacious, the better, though giant spectacles of that sort created equally gigantic problems. Not unlike the ones facing them at present, albeit of lesser severity.

He wandered out of the kitchen and into the foyer of his villa, where his ferns and shag carpet greeted him with their silence as usual. The pine-forested hills outside his window were, he supposed, incongruous next to his home. He was a second-generation *Cubano* and rightfully belonged in South Florida, but with some reluctance, he had relocated to New York for the sake of being near his esteemed colleagues.

Damian had a part-time butler but had sent the man on a vacation to visit his mother in Pennsylvania. He was willing to risk his own skin but did not like the thought of innocent bystanders getting caught in the crossfire.

He expanded his mind and felt the integrity of the powerful shield he had placed around the estate. It was well within his capabilities to create a barrier and have it hold strong for a week or more. Still, one night was enough for slight atrophy to set in. He wanted both a shield against a hostile force and a tripwire that would alert him to intruders, suspicious activity, or attempts at scrying.

Everything seemed fine. He went from window to window, doing a visual scan of the property. Nothing.

"*Bueno,*" he muttered. "This is going to be boring, isn't it? These Russians are not going to show up, I would wager. They bluffed, and we called it. Everyone goes home and feels foolish."

He hoped that was the case. On the off-chance he was wrong, though, the shield around his home also contained an embedded illusion that made the villa look like a dilapidated old shack surrounded by rusted-out trucks.

Embarrassing, but if the Orthodoxy had done their homework on them, it might fool them. Damian Diaz was well-known in the world of thaumaturgy as a dapper dresser and a connoisseur of...everything, really. He would not be caught dead living in a wreck.

He ran a hand through his mop of black curls and seated himself on the couch, switching on the TV less because he wanted to watch anything in particular than for the sake of having background noise to keep him company. Some reality show came on—he didn't realize they aired those before noon—and his mind wandered into the domain of memory.

His all-time greatest enchantment. It always came back to him when he was feeling blue.

It had been in the early 1980s, a time he remembered fondly, when he was only thirty. He still *looked* thirty but had to admit he felt as though the years were finally catching up.

There had been some flare-up in the Cold War or another, an echo of the Mariel boatlift, if he recalled, which had reverberated throughout Miami. A stupid rumor began to spread that Castro might try to invade with Soviet backing.

So Damian, wanting to flex his illusionary might, had conjured up a Communist invasion and then single-handedly defeated it by manning a nonexistent heavy gun turret mounted on the beach. Hundreds of people had watched first in fear, then in jubilation and admiration and cheering triumph.

Sadly, all of them had mysteriously forgotten that they had witnessed such a spectacle. Worse yet, he hadn't yet figured out how to capture such shenanigans on film or video, which had since that time become a major obsession of his.

He sighed, gazing at the ceiling. "Those were the days. Things were so much—"

Something walked through his shield.

Damian sat upright, spinning in the direction indicated by his psionic alarm and sending out his consciousness to gather information about who or what was trespassing. It was probably a rabbit, though he had specifically tried to exclude anything smaller than a medium-sized dog.

Yes, it was likely a small, harmless animal. Otherwise, they would not have been able to pass through the barrier with such ease.

Nonetheless, Damian climbed to his feet and went to the security console next to his bar. He had never bothered to install a full camera system, but he did have two units watching the front and back of the villa.

The screens showed nothing. He nodded but went to the front door just to be safe.

He flung it open, stood on the veranda, and examined the beautifully landscaped grounds, which were peaceful and devoid of intruders.

He cast a protective shield around himself. Probably didn't need it, but...

"*Hola,*" he shouted. "If you are here, you should at least do me the courtesy of announcing yourself and fighting like a man. Or woman, though in that case, I could suggest something much more fun than fighting. What do you say?"

His voice echoed across the hills. No one answered. Something within his mind was humming and droning—a faint sense that all was *not* well—but he could detect no evidence that he was other than alone on his estate. If the Orthodoxy's lackeys had arrived so soon, they were the most skilled magicians at stealth and camouflage he had ever encountered.

Damian shrugged. "Okay, then. Guess I'm getting paranoid in my not-so-old age." Still, while the idea of shacking up (platonically) with Mary Mitchell was not something he looked forward to, her suggestion of safety in numbers was probably wise. He resolved to leave his home this evening.

As he turned to go back into the house, he saw something odd. There was a breeze blowing, and the grass in one particular area, right in front of a line of poplars, was still. As though something was standing or crouching there, blocking the wind.

Damian raised his hands, but they struck first.

A blast like a thunderclap rippled across the villa's grounds, and the air waved and distorted as an explosion of pure sonic and percussive force detonated about three inches in front of Damian's chest, right at the periphery of his personal shield.

The front of his house crumbled, along with most of the

veranda and all of the trees, bushes, fountains, and statues nearby. Damian was flung back through the collapsing wreck, his limbs flailing like those of a discarded doll. The velocity of his passage knocked over his couch, his end table, most of the bottles on the bar, and the wall separating his living room from his kitchen. He crashed into the counter beside the sink, and his espresso machine fell to the floor and broke.

Damian's mind screamed and spun and struggled not to shut down in the ensuing storm of pain, anger, and fear. No one had ever gotten the better of him like this before. No one.

His shield had protected him from the worst of the attack, but he barely clung to consciousness. He cast a moderate healing spell on himself, granting him the strength to leap back to his feet and clear his head.

Where the front of his villa had been was a jagged mass of debris, and advancing toward him across the grass were two women, both moving with a casually insulting slowness and no longer bothering to hide their presence.

Damian blinked. The healing charm had saved him from passing out, which would have ensured his death, but the fact that they had hit him with a spell that would have vaporized most people, even thaumaturgists, before he could even see them did not bode well for the immediate future.

"So, it's two ladies after all. My apologies for expecting you to fight like men," he called. His voice sounded more ragged than he would have liked.

At the same time, his brain called, too, but not to the attackers.

Mary, LeBlanc, James, Samantha, Lauren, and all the rest of you. My friends. He broadcast their names across the astral plane, knowing the assassins would probably hear, but it didn't matter. The important thing was raising the alarm. *They're here already. I will see you again if I can.*

His vision cleared, and he finally got a good look at the witches who had come to kill him.

The one out in front was an unremarkable-looking girl around twenty-eight with tawny hair and pale eyes, dressed in an equally unremarkable ensemble of blue jeans and a pink blouse. There was a vicious glint in her eye, though he sensed a tense uncertainty, as though she had no idea what came next.

The other woman was completely different. She appeared slightly older, though she was still beautiful in a strange and severe way, with milk-white skin and wavy black hair that spilled past her shoulders. She wore an old-fashioned dress—a gown, really—which was the same ebon hue as her hair, along with a bronze medallion set with a luminous green stone.

The air of total confidence that surrounded her was terrifying, and Damian was pretty sure it wasn't the result of an intimidation spell.

They did not send an amateur, I see, he concluded. *She's someone important. Well, so am I. As they are about to find out.*

"Let's talk about this," he suggested as the pair continued their approach. "For example, if you are going to drive down my property value after complaining that we are the ones failing to protect magicians, you might consider—"

He interrupted himself by striking back.

The air blazed and shimmered as a concentrated ball of heat and fire like a miniature sun erupted on the exact spot where the two women stood. Both leaped into the air the instant the spell was cast, flames trailing from the edges of their personal shields, but Damian had anticipated that and summoned a hail of howling meteors from all sides, converging on his foes.

The younger and presumably lower-ranking witch failed to dodge them. Damian saw a brief flash of her face as the meteors collided with her shield and exploded, sending her jerking and flopping through the air before crashing to the ground. Her protective barrier had held up—barely—so she was probably still alive, but the stress and impact seemed to have taken her out of the fight for the moment.

Before Damian could summon another attack, the debris from the front of his villa rose and shot toward him like a volley of spears. With augmented speed, he ducked and rolled, then leaped aside, ignoring the fragments wreaking further havoc on the interior of his home.

As he came to rest near a still-standing side wall, the pale dark-haired woman drifted closer, entering his sight again.

"You blame us for what has happened?" Damian insisted. The inflection in his voice suggested a question, but in fact, he was making a statement. "You think the explosion of new magic users around the world only happened because we allowed it? Hah! All those people were already there. They had the gift all along. We merely revealed them to the light of day. If you and your coven had any sense, you would join us in guiding these people, with you presiding over Eastern Europe and us keeping watch over North America."

Her answer was a powerful wave of fear that cut at his resolve like powerful acid eating into his bones, though he resisted the worst of it with a combination of relaxation and motivational magic. Then he reinforced his shield for good measure.

It proved to be a wise decision on his part since two bolts of lightning descending in a V shape from both the left and the right thundered against the magical barrier. He fell to his knees from the force of it, not injured but weakened from the effort it took to avoid succumbing. The woman he fought was among the most powerful magicians he had ever encountered.

Anezka moved closer, her black-nailed hands extended in front of her. Her full lips were twisted into a sneer of mockery.

"Do not make me laugh. Everyone has long suspected there were many with latent talents among the general populace, but far too few of them show enough worth to bother instructing. Your organization's arrogant and careless actions have given these people delusions of grandeur, and in so doing, you have imperiled us all. Now you prove your guilt by fighting back! If you were innocent, you would not resist."

Damian rose to his feet. "What? That is among the stupidest things I have ever heard. You're saying we should prove our point by letting you kill us and take over our territory?"

He distracted Anezka by creating a scary-looking but harmless flash of light in front of her face and then transmogrifying the ground beneath her feet into a pool of molten lava, hoping she would sink into it and never emerge.

For a second it looked as though she would, but a combination of her shield, a levitation spell, and a wave of freezing-cold air saved her. She floated above the deadly morass as it cooled back into earth. Then, glaring at him, she unleashed a cyclone of magical blades that drove him back into the ravaged house and shredded his shield.

"You had your chance," Anezka declared. "We issued our warning. You could have pleaded for mercy, and we might have allowed you to keep your lives in exchange for forfeiting this continent. But look how hard you struggle to escape justice! Is that not proof of your culpability?"

Damian felt his strength ebbing as the arcane razors sliced his shield and began tearing into his clothes, then his skin and flesh. He deflected most of them before they could do more than superficial damage, but the pain and blood loss would begin to take their toll soon, and conjuring another shield would cost him energy.

He shouted, "Your logic is beyond absurd. It reminds me of the old ways of witch-dunking, where the village idiots 'proved' someone's innocence by watching them drown in a pond. How convenient that you have no terms for—"

"*Silence!*" Anezka snapped and turned her blast of cold air away from the mostly-hardened lava pool toward Damian. He fell back, shivering as the chill tempest further sapped his strength and brought greater pain from his lacerated skin.

Anezka went on, "How dare you use such an example! You people are the ones exposing more witches to danger and persecution, not we! You are not only incompetents but traitors to our kind. May you be cursed in eternity even after your death."

Damian was expecting another projectile or wave of debilitating emotion, so he conjured another shield around himself and steeled his mind for what was to come. He had only enough stamina left for one or two counterattacks and would have to use them wisely.

His adversary responded in a way he had not anticipated; she reached out and crushed his shield against him.

He screamed in pain as gravitational pressure bore into him from all sides, collapsing his ribs and breaking his legs. He crumpled in a heap to the ground, almost passing out from the pain. A fast healing spell allowed him to remain conscious as Anezka moved in for the kill.

It's over for me, Damian concluded. *I can't beat her. But I've had a good run. And before she finishes me off, perhaps there is one thing I can do to make her victory a little more hollow...*

He was primarily an illusionist, and he had noticed that Anezka's disciple had not yet risen to her feet to rejoin the fight. Fixing the young woman's image in his mind, he created a convincing doppelganger of her, which rushed up to her superior's side.

"Anezka," the illusion asked, "what comes next after we are finished with him?"

There was a chance Anezka would recognize the deception, given how skilled she seemed to be, but no one had ever been able to outdo Damian Diaz in the field of illusion.

Anezka seemed distracted; she was focused on the broken figure of Damian. "Next," she said, "we find the others. They cannot be far. It will be more difficult since we lost our finest tracker when Pavla betrayed us, but we shall succeed. They cannot run."

Damian smirked and used the last of his magical strength to psychically beam Anezka's words to his comrades. All of them would know momentarily that the Orthodoxy was apparently short an important member and therefore not operating at full strength.

Anezka blinked when she realized what Damian had done. Her gaze snapped toward the illusory witch as it phased out of existence, then she looked at Damian again. "Clever," she snarled, "but it makes no difference."

Damian rested his head on the floor. The pain was getting worse and his vision was dimming, which suggested it would all be over soon regardless. He closed his eyes.

Thus, he did not see when Anezka stood over him and drew a black stiletto from within her dress, casting one last spell to paralyze him before, with a vicious cry of triumph, she plunged the thin blade through his throat under his chin and drove it upward. His last thought was of the adoring crowd in Miami on that legendary day in the early 80s.

Anezka stood after wiping off the dagger and returning it to its hiding place. She left Damian's body where it lay and went over to her disciple, who was only now regaining consciousness.

"Get up," she commanded, disappointed by the young woman's frailty. "One of them will no longer trouble us, but all of the remaining twelve must die as well before this continent is ours."

The junior witch rubbed her eyes, nodded, and swallowed. "I understand, Grandmistress."

CHAPTER SEVEN

Chris had opted to eat his lunch in his cubicle rather than go elsewhere, even to the break room, so that he could remain at his computer and keep up his "extracurricular" research.

He got so drawn into browsing forums, parsing through police reports and other public records, and reading up on various artists and artistic movements that he completely forgot about his friend and co-worker Ted, who worked in Human Resources and had pledged to go get food for both of them.

"Hey. You're supposed to be on break, aren't you?"

Chris half-jumped out of his chair, swiveled at the sound of the familiar voice, and saw Ted standing there with two sub sandwiches under one arm and a fountain drink in his left hand.

Exhaling, Chris said, "Hi. Thanks for bringing lunch, though we now have only, um, about ten minutes to actually eat. What is that, cold cuts? Turkey?"

Ted set one of the sandwiches in front of his friend, then pulled up a chair to begin unwrapping the other for himself. "Italian, hope that's okay. I didn't think to get you a drink since I figured you would still be guzzling coffee. Don't hate me."

Chris picked up his mug and took a sip before opening his

sub. "Nonsense. I already hate you and always will, so leaving me to subsist on breakroom coffee won't make much difference one way or another. Kudos, though."

They spent a couple minutes eating in silence, then Ted asked, "So, are you still researching that mysterious art theft? I know, I know, you can't talk about it in too much detail, but throw me a bone here. It's your fault that you actually sort of replied when I asked you thirty or forty questions about it, so now you have no choice but to fill me in on at least *some* of the rest."

"Yes," Chris confessed, "and I guess that makes a certain amount of sense. Please promise me you won't try to get involved, though. That almost certainly violates our great state's labor laws since you're not a formal employee." Considering the implications of what he'd just said, he added, "And I don't think Kera can afford to hire anyone else anytime soon."

Ted let out a half-groan, half-sigh. "Okay, fine. I promise not to meddle. But only if you keep me updated and, like, allow me to offer friendly suggestions once in a while. Deal?"

Chris agreed and updated his friend on the gist of the situation. Thus far, they didn't know much beyond what the police had stated in public or the Internet had muttered in various comments sections. The goal was to secure further information about who the art thief was, what their motivation was, and what their potential next target might be.

"Interesting," Ted mused, sipping lemonade and throwing his crumpled sandwich wrapper into the trash. The floor supervisor passed their cubicle and gave him the evil eye; their lunch break would end in the next minute or two. "Have you thought about looking into other paintings or etchings or whatever that were destroyed but not 'officially' blamed on a thief? Like, someone claimed it happened to a piece they owned by accident, but the *modus operandi* was the same as what your culprit does?"

Chris blinked. "No. That's a good idea, though. Thanks. Sadly, our break is about over, so I'll have to get back to work-work, but I will definitely look into that later."

"Don't mention it." Ted beamed with self-satisfaction. "Thanking me is redundant since my talent at basically every-thing is self-evident."

Shrugging, Chris added, "Well, everything except Human Resources."

"Right, *that.*" Ted sighed and stood up. "Before I return to the fray, how are things going with Kera? The *personal* side of your relationship, I mean, not the professional."

Chris informed his co-worker that things were mostly fine, though the amount of time and effort they had been devoting to building their agency meant neither of them had much left over for romantic evenings together. It happened occasionally, but less often than he'd like.

Ted quipped, "Understandable. From the perspective of any heterosexual or bisexual male, I doubt there is such a thing as too many romantic evenings with a girl who looks like Kera. She's the 'motivated' type, though, so you might have to remind her about stuff like that if she gets too zeroed in on business. Also, is she still living in the same place?"

"Yes," Chris replied reflexively. Then, remembering the awkward recent incident in which Ted had stopped by, added, "Please don't come over without asking first, though. Since we deal with sensitive information, Kera would not appreciate it."

"Fine," Ted grumbled. "I gotta get back to pretending to work. Talk to you later."

As he departed, Chris only hoped he would abide by his promise. When Ted had shown up, he had caught them all in the midst of some fairly intense research and preparation, which had aroused his suspicions that something weird was going on.

The last thing any of them needed was for him to stumble onto Kera or Stephanie doing certain...other things. Things that, according to most people's worldview, were not supposed to exist or be possible.

Kera pushed open the front door to Kim's Convenience Store to the familiar jangling of the bell and saw Mr. Kim behind the counter. He casually looked at her, nodding and smiling as though he had expected her, though she hadn't bothered to announce she was coming.

"Kera. Hi there," he opened and waved to her. "Did you want to visit Mrs. Kim, or are you just here to buy food? Something tells me the answer is 'both.' I figured you would show up today, or maybe tomorrow. You are extremely predictable." His eyes twinkled with amusement.

She could not help grinning as she advanced across the floor. "Both is right. Remind me to buy food before I leave, okay? After talking to you guys for a while, I might forget on my way out the door. I've been busy lately. Now that I no longer have a day job, I'm discovering how much work it is to start my own business."

As she moved toward the counter, she passed a pudgy, scruffy man in the aisle to her left. He gave her a look, half-curious about her words and half-appreciative of her ass in tight leather before turning back to the rows of bagged snack foods in front of him.

Kera leaned against the counter and shot the proverbial shit with Mr. Kim for perhaps five minutes, pausing only to stand aside when the guy from the aisle came up to pay for his purchases. It occurred to her that Mr. Kim's confidence that she would turn up today had to do with more than mere intuition or hunches.

After all, he and his wife both had the gift again. The witch Pavla had restored their powers last week after a pair of thaumaturgists had removed them months ago "for their own good."

It still made Kera's face flush with anger to think about it, even if everything had worked out for the best in the long run.

"Anyway," Mr. Kim concluded, waving his hand, "I will let you go now. I have a store to watch since unfortunately, Sam has things to deal with and can't do all of my work for me. Ye-Jin is upstairs. She will not complain about getting to see you again."

Kera gave the older man a quick hug, then stepped past him, behind the counter, and into the short but dark hallway that led from the store into the Kims' semi-hidden living quarters.

Beyond the hall was a stairwell, and past it lay a door on the first floor that led out to the well-concealed courtyard and a small outbuilding. The actual living area was on the second floor. Kera got halfway up the steps when a small woman about the same age as Mr. Kim leaned out of a doorway.

"Kera. Welcome." She dried her hands on a towel, indicating that she had probably been washing the dishes from lunch in preparation for dinner. She enjoyed cooking and insisted on preparing most of the family's meals. "I expected you."

As Kera finished ascending the stairs, she took an instant to appreciate the vibe of the Kims' modest home with its neatness, sparse yet homey decorating, and potted plants. Then she crossed the floor to embrace Mrs. Kim, and they stood holding each other for a good half-minute.

"I suppose," Kera began, "that if you have the time, it would be nice to talk. But honestly, if you think we could go out to the dojang to train, even if it's only for twenty or thirty minutes, I could use it. Practicing on my own isn't the same."

The older woman made a "hmm" sound in her throat, then said, "Need five minutes. Then we can train for little while." She had never achieved full fluency in English like her husband had, but she and Kera were still able to communicate effectively. It helped that their connection went beyond what words alone could express.

Kera sat as Mrs. Kim finished up a couple of minor chores in the kitchen and asked how Sam was doing. The boy was not home right now. He was off with a friend somewhere and would be busy with schoolwork when he got back.

Once Ye-Jin was ready, the pair descended to the back door and crossed the neat little courtyard to the outbuilding that served them as a makeshift dojang. Within, Kera took off her boots and leathers, retaining her shorts and tank-top, and bowed before positioning the training dummy at the edge of the mat while Mrs. Kim watched and offered commentary.

Kera had studied Shotokan karate for a couple years as a teenager, and since she had moved to LA, Mrs. Kim had begun teaching her elements of taekwondo, hapkido, and judo to supplement her skills. Though Kera could not train with the Kims as often as she wanted, she felt that their sessions were moving her toward developing a well-rounded fighting style.

After all, it was dangerous to rely upon magic alone. It helped for a woman to know how to knock heads if she had to.

Kera attacked the dummy with a sequence of kicks, punches, aggressive blocks, sweeps, and takedowns while her instructor watched and offered commentary. Occasionally Mrs. Kim stepped onto the mat to demonstrate how moves should be performed.

In the past, they had spent hours in the dojang, working to bring Kera's skills up to par despite Mrs. Kim's limited strength, but today they called it quits after about half an hour. It was enough for Kera to work up a sweat, and she felt limber, energized, and refreshed in her abilities.

When they returned to the house, Mr. Kim was waiting for them. He had closed the shop for a short break and made a pot of tea.

"Thanks," Kera told him. "If we'd have been out there longer, I'd probably ask for iced tea, but hot sounds surprisingly good right now."

He waved a finger at her as they sat down in the living room, the pot and cups on the coffee table between the Kims' couch and Kera's usual chair. "Hot tea is always good. Now, tell us about what you have been doing. This agency of yours. We have both been itching with curiosity for days."

Kera took a long sip from her teacup, then breathed in and began telling them the story. They listened patiently and nodded every minute or so.

"...so, while it was tempting to go after the carjackers since they're posing more of a threat to ordinary people, not to mention I have more experience in dealing with that type of crime," Kera concluded, "we ended up deciding to try to solve the case with the stolen and destroyed painting. It captured everyone's interest, and it moves us away from shady, scary stuff. Makes it easier to rebrand ourselves as legitimate businesspeople and attract higher-class customers, you might say."

Both the Kims nodded and seemed to be chewing on her words.

Mr. Kim rubbed his chin. "Well, this is good. You will be staying with things you are good at and that you think are interesting and important. It will still feel like it's worth doing, and that matters. At the same time, it sounds much less dangerous than what you were doing before. Waging war against drug cartels...that is not something you should do for long, though the city is better off for your having done it."

Ye-Jin added, "We worried much. Do not make us worry more. But do what you must. Less dangerous is good."

Kera gave a sardonic chuckle. "Well, it's less dangerous so far, anyway. Who knows what the future holds? If anyone finds out who I am—or, um, you know, who I used to be—I could be in trouble no matter what. But yes, for the time being, we chose an art-theft case for that exact reason. Not as many bullets flying around."

Mr. Kim grunted his approval, then blinked. "Who you used to be? You mean, Motorcycle Woman?"

"Yes," Kera confirmed. "I think I told you, but I'm trying to leave that identity behind. It is a liability if I'm going into legitimate detective work."

The old couple glanced into each other's eyes, communicating without words (as they often did) before looking at their guest again.

Speaking for both of them, Mr. Kim asked, "How do you plan to put her to rest? Your alter ego. As you say, you might be done with her, but other people, enemies you made in the past, may not feel the same way."

Kera cleared her throat. In a way, she felt put-upon, but she had expected this question and was prepared for it.

"Well, originally, we wanted to incorporate it into our first case. Like, we would create a scenario where Motorcycle Woman shows up and announces she's leaving LA to go wander the earth or whatever. But we're not sure how to do that with this painting case, so Lia had another, more low-key idea. I mentioned Lia, didn't I?"

The Kims nodded.

"Good," said Kera. "She's going to spread the word, slowly but steadily, that MW is no longer active so all the talk about her just eventually fizzles out. No longer active, or was never real. That sort of thing."

Mr. Kim cocked an eyebrow. "Oh? How will she do that?"

Kera finished drinking her tea and set the cup on the table between them. "Posting stuff on various Internet forums. Talking to people she knows and having her friends Johnny and Sven speak to people they know, making it sound like they know what they're talking about and are passing on the 'word on the street.'"

Mrs. Kim commented, "People love to talk."

"True that," agreed Kera. "The plan is to keep suggesting there never was a real Motorcycle Man, or Woman, whatever. That it was an assortment of random people helping others where they could, some of whom happened to be bikers. Or by being the 'voice of reason' and pointing out all the ways in which my so-called superhero activities are scientifically impossible. At least, according to science as most people understand it. It's no fun to be 'that guy,' the buzzkill who screws up other people's myths, but many humans are capable enough of being realistic that I think they'll listen."

Again, the old couple paused to reflect on what she'd said, then Mr. Kim inquired, "Is it working?"

Kera shrugged. "We only started a couple days ago. Based on what Lia is saying, it probably will work, especially if there are no new stories of Motorcycle Woman doing crazy stuff to cause the urban legend to flare back up."

She thought but did not say aloud, *We can probably win by attrition as long as some asshole doesn't try to be a copycat vigilante in my stead. Ugh, I hope I didn't jinx myself by allowing that idea into my head.*

With the conversation drawing to a close, Kera and Mrs. Kim returned to training, and Mr. Kim went back to watching the shop. The women agreed that rather than going back out to the dojang for more fight practice, they would remain in the house and work on meditation, breathing, and visualization tactics, which were good for the clarity of mind necessary for effective self-discipline in both hand-to-hand combat and magic.

It was easier on Mrs. Kim as well. Her cancer treatments were going well; she was stronger and sprier than Kera had seen her in a long time. But the combination of her illness and her advancing age nonetheless had left her weakened, and she could not keep up with the girl in terms of stamina.

As they finished up, Kera ruminated on her teacher's fate and what she might be able to expect in the decades down the road.

Everyone had heard of elderly people who are still downright formidable in the martial arts. Mrs. Kim was only middle-aged, in all honesty. If she made a full recovery, could she regain the level of badassitude she used to have? Kera hoped so. She was not going to be young forever either, but she wanted to do as much as possible physically and otherwise, regardless of age.

Kera stood, and Mrs. Kim did likewise. They had both sensed it was time for them to part ways since Kera had work to do at home, furthering the goals of her new business, and Mrs. Kim had to get dinner started and keep caring for her family. They embraced, communicating in their own way without bothering to speak.

But as they drew apart and descended the stairs, Mrs. Kim asked, "Is there anything else?" She meant that she had sensed other concerns on her student's mind.

Kera grimaced. "I suppose there is one thing." They were in the hall now, and Mr. Kim could probably hear them. She trusted him but didn't want to waste their time by opening a new line of conversation.

"Oh?" Mrs. Kim never *demanded* that anyone talk about anything, but it was hard to refuse her gentle suggestions.

Sighing, Kera admitted, "My mom. She keeps threatening to come out to the West Coast, despite my best efforts to convince her otherwise. Now that I'm dating, she *has* to meet Chris. Maybe I'll get lucky and she will just wait in Connecticut until we visit her, but my luck can't last forever, can it?"

They emerged from behind the counter, and Mr. Kim turned to them. "Ha. That is how mothers are. Resistance is futile. Perhaps you should invite her on your own terms and get it over with? Or go see her soon in the East. You could probably use a vacation."

Since Mrs. Kim did not say anything, Kera assumed she agreed with her husband.

Kera gave them both a hug and before departing the store, she mumbled, "I'll think it over."

CHAPTER EIGHT

The Alchemist gazed at the photograph of Luis Domingo. She had been sitting, immobile and transfixed, with her eyes on the picture for a good fifteen minutes. She did not so much as blink more than was necessary. She wanted to ensure she would know him on sight.

With all the other information she had collected on him that had fattened the dossier over the course of the last few days, she was confident that she knew him as well as if she were his girlfriend, his longtime co-worker, or perhaps his sister.

She knew where he lived. That had been relatively easy to find out. It had been a simple matter of haunting the art-oriented locales where he had been seen until he showed up and then following him home.

He rented a loft in Silver Lake, a hipster neighborhood wholly appropriate to an artist, she felt. Not far from the Reservoir. Once the Alchemist had pinpointed the location, she had spent much of her time staking it out, observing when Domingo came and went and following him to and from his destinations.

Like many creative persons, he did not stick to a strict schedule. However, humans were creatures of habit, and soon the

Alchemist had a good idea about how often the young man went shopping, where he went, which places he went to for recreation or business, who his agent was, and so forth.

Just as useful, he often seemed to have his head in the clouds. He had never noticed her shadowing him. The poor man would be easy prey, she concluded, for a mugger or kidnapper or another vicious criminal.

Additionally, the Alchemist had used a combination of the limited tech skills she had acquired and contacts she had made in the telecommunications industry to figure out who most of Domingo's phone and Internet contacts were. He had family and friends elsewhere in California and a smattering of others across the United States. A couple lived in foreign countries as well.

She knew which TV shows and movies he liked and what his reading habits were, thanks to the access she had gained to his Amazon account. She could not examine his shopping habits in as much detail as she would have liked, but poking through his garbage made it clear what he ate and how fastidious he was with his hygiene.

Within a week, it was as though she lived with him, all without him being any the wiser. The information she had gleaned had gone into her special folder, the one with Domingo written on the front in bold black marker.

The dossier lay on the table to the right of the photograph. The Alchemist closed it, then adjusted her position a tad, moving to the left of the photo, where another item lay—an ancient book bound in dark brown leather with yellowed vellum pages. One section was marked with a strip of scarlet silk. The Alchemist opened the tome.

The bookmark lay over a diagram on the left page and a set of instructions in Latin on the right. The drawing depicted a crude human figure, the front and back side by side, with lines and markings on different parts of the body.

In the lower right corner of the page was a depiction of a

knife that looked exactly like the ceremonial blade the Alchemist used when carving up paintings. Or other things.

She ran the tips of her middle and index fingers over the lines. To gain the maximum benefit from the process, the cuts had to be performed in the right sequence. While death was unfortunately a necessary side effect of the process, it was not the goal. Quite the opposite, in fact.

The cuts were made according to the collected knowledge of many ancient traditions spanning multiple civilizations across the centuries, anywhere humans had learned that nothing brought existence to a heightened state of life and drew out the vital essence within the living being like the combination of pain and fear. The body and the soul never wanted to live more than when their continued existence was threatened with harm and suffering.

Artists were special people, as the Alchemist well knew. They specialized in channeling that life force into their work, where it could be appreciated (and harvested) by others. But even the greatest works of art, the ones that were most "alive," fell short of the vitality possessed by living entities, especially those who also created art.

The lines began with the extremities. They moved on to the face and the torso and only targeted the vital organs at the end of the process when the drained husk was consigned to oblivion. Whoever had drawn the diagram had understood the necessity of drawing blood, and with it pain and fear, without killing the subject too quickly.

Though exciting and sometimes necessary, the Alchemist had to admit it could be an ugly business. And risky. The subject would have to be restrained since a living body would naturally struggle against such harsh treatment.

"Sad," she murmured, fixing the procedure in her mind. It had been a long time since she had given it much thought. "A tragedy that it must sometimes be done. Though tragedy is full of vitality, too. It is crucial to remember that. Like that saying about dying young and leaving a beautiful corpse. The sad, sad death of the afflicted takes on a life of its own as myth, and the extracted survival-essence can be put to better use elsewhere."

She raised a hand and touched her face. Then, nodding, she closed the book and walked out of the room, heading for a small chamber beside her studio.

Within, a crude, homemade medical dummy lay strapped to a table. On a nightstand next to it was the beautiful ceremonial knife, which the Alchemist had cleaned and sharpened since she had employed it on Domingo's lovely painting.

She took a deep breath and closed her eyes, recalling every detail of the diagram and the instructions. Then, picking up the blade, she set to work, practicing her routine. When—no, *if*, since she had not made up her mind yet—she performed the real procedure, there must be no mistakes.

If she was going to do it, it must be done right.

James Lovecraft wanted a drink. That was part of the problem. Everyone including him was well aware that he was developing honest-to-gosh alcoholism since returning to the US and leaning upon his liquor to deal with the constant stresses and uncertainties of their burgeoning situation.

As of today, though, he had not drunk liquor for four days. The time for such stupid indulgences had passed.

He exhaled and wiped the sweat from his brow, thankful for the cool breeze that indicated autumn was right around the corner as Lauren Jones brought their practice session to a halt. In addition to her and him, their group included Mother LeBlanc, Ezeudo, and old Hugh Buchanon. The day's classes had been held in James' backyard.

"All right," Lauren announced, clapping her hands. "That is

enough for now. I suppose we've done enough damage to poor James's landscaping by this point, but we should remember that being well-practiced in battle magic is our only hope of avoiding far worse damage to more than the landscaping. There is no point in kidding ourselves about the gravity of our situation."

Everyone nodded and murmured their assent.

They had been training in thaumaturgic combat since half an hour past dawn, and it was now early afternoon. In addition to them all needing a refresher course in martial casting, there were other things that still had to be done before the day was spent.

"Okay," James called, addressing everyone at once, "if Lauren has no objections since she's our semi-official master of cere-monies or whatever, I propose we take a lunch break and work on our presentation to the minor covens before we plunge back into boot camp. How does everyone else feel about that?"

Mother LeBlanc was the first to respond. "Yes, we could do with a short rest, and the sooner we are able to speak to the other covens, the better. They likely received word at much the same time we did, but since the challenge was not issued to them, they might not be preparing themselves accordingly. They might be hoping the whole matter will pass them by."

Hugh added, "They are not the main targets. I would wager money that the Orthodoxy intends to wipe us out and rule the minor covens as vassals once we are out of the way."

It was unusual for him to speak with that degree of bold conviction, given his policy of keeping his mouth shut to avoid looking foolish. For him to have spoken, he must have been confident about his words.

"Probably," James agreed. "But I don't think they would like that much better than being exterminated, so let's give them the chance to make up their own minds—notwithstanding us using every trick in the book to ensure that they make up their minds to help us."

Ezeudo frowned, flexed his hands, and asked, "Does that

mean you intend to influence them into coming to our aid by magic? If so, that would not be the work of their free will, would it?"

Mother LeBlanc raised her eyebrows and looked at each of them in turn. Lauren and Hugh hung back and did not get involved.

Clearing his throat to disguise his mild annoyance, James responded, "Not exactly. We are not going to *compel* them for the reasons you mention. That would be tantamount to enslaving them and using them as human shields. But allow me to remind you that I majored in advertising, and I intend to use every dirty trick in my non-magical arsenal to show them that we are *all* under threat and would do well to respond as a unified collective, whatever our petty differences."

"Very well," Ezeudo muttered, though it still seemed that something was troubling him. "You did not give *me* a choice to ignore your 'advertisement,' and I have even less knowledge of this world of covens than they do."

James thought, *I need one drink. Just one. A single, solitary drink that will not be followed by any others for at least, say, another three or four days. That's reasonable.*

Out loud, he said, "Yeah, sorry. You did, however, choose to commit yourself totally to our order. Granted, you didn't know we'd be under siege soon—none of us did—but it's a bit late to back out now. Besides, like I told you before, the Orthodoxy won't care that you're a new recruit. As far as they're concerned, you are one of us and will have the honor of sharing our fate."

No one, least of all Ezeudo, spoke again as the group filed back into James's mansion. His staff had anticipated them taking a break around this time of day and had prepared an expansive lunch spread plus coffee to help them recharge their energy.

As everyone prepared to settle in and eat, James told them, "Let's head into the study. I'm not overly concerned with a couple of crumbs on the carpet, and it will make it easier for us to dive straight into the presentation while we finish eating."

No one objected, so they took their plates and cups with them and sat down in easy chairs or around the central meeting table beyond James's desk. He gazed longingly at his liquor cabinet, which he had locked, and decided not to bother with it after all. It would be embarrassing if they all saw his resolve weaken.

Once everyone had made themselves comfortable and had a few bites, James went through the motions of setting up the discussions to come, summarizing the need to make a convincing pitch to the minor covens throughout the United States, Canada, Mexico, and Central America (and the one in Greenland) and persuade them to pledge themselves to the common defense.

Concluding his opening spiel, James turned the proverbial floor over to Lauren Jones. They had agreed this morning that she would handle the mundane task of reviewing the structure of the North American magical establishment and go over the strength and specialties of each small group. That was partly for Ezeudo's benefit, but it would be good for them all since the council largely left the lesser covens to their own devices and was not always up to date on their affairs.

"So," Lauren began, standing up and automatically switching into Teacher Mode, which came so easily to her, "we, the Council of Thaumaturgy, represent those with what might be called a 'global' talent for the highest and most sophisticated forms of magic. However, it has always been the case that certain other individuals have demonstrated small amounts of magical aptitude, usually only in one or two highly specific areas. Or, perhaps, they might be able to sense magic in others but cannot perform it themselves."

The man in Geneva, James recalled. *The British guy who pointed us toward Ezeudo and Guillaume. He fell into one or both of those categories since his power was faint but his perception was significant.*

Lauren continued. "These sorts of people constitute the

membership of the lesser covens. There are, as of the most up-to-date information we possess, forty-four of them across the continent, though it is not unheard of for one to disband or two to merge or a new one to crop up in an area that has had a recent population boom, and so forth."

She went on to explain how some of the minor covens had formed around a common aptitude. For example, green mages, whose skills lay in helping plants grow, might self-select into a community where a group of dedicated gardeners would not attract undue attention.

Other groups were more heterogeneous, congregating in large cities as small, loose networks of people who did not practice collective spells in any meaningful capacity but simply looked out for one another and protected people who were unaware that they possessed the gift.

After all, many would never have enough magic to become true thaumaturges and tended to get in over their heads when they tried to overuse their talents.

"Each of the lesser covens," Lauren concluded, "is required to contact us once every seven years with an update on their membership, their whereabouts, and any problems they have encountered. They also are encouraged to get in touch if any substantial problems arise."

Ezeudo asked, "Do they know the Orthodoxy is coming for us?"

"Most likely," Lauren stated. "Such challenges are usually made as public declarations. We do not know for certain, but it's possible the Orthodoxy informed the minor groups *before* they challenged us and threatened them to stay out of the way, which would explain their silence thus far. Or worse yet, they might have recruited some of them to their cause."

Ezeudo rubbed his face with both hands. James wondered if he wanted a drink too. When the Nigerian's eyes were visible again, they glowered with resentment.

James reached over and put a hand atop Ezeudo's. "It's okay," he pointed out. "If I was in your position, I'd be pissed off, too. It *is* unfair, but it's not like we were the ones who started it."

Unless you consider the book to be what started it, but everyone who isn't a moron knows that the Orthodoxy is just capitalizing on the opportunity to fuck us over and steal our turf. He contemplated saying as much aloud but decided against it.

Next, James took the floor and outlined the sales pitch he would send to all the lesser covens. It would emphasize horror stories about the Orthodoxy's ruthless and unethical ways of doing business contrasted with the relative benevolence of the council, with a dash of appeal to the patriotic urge to resist foreign invasion.

Partway into the presentation, he was interrupted.

A sound appeared in all of their minds at once: the unmistakable alarm of a psionic message being sent. It was from someone they knew and trusted since outsiders were currently behind a powerful filter.

James recognized it immediately as a tinkling bell, accompanied by the flashing mental image of a flower opening its petals to receive water and sunlight.

"Lady Mitchell." He sighed. "Okay, let's hear what she has to say. Probably wants us all to promise to die defending her greenhouse or hydroponic lab or whatever she has from the Orthodoxy lest her plants fall under the jackboot of tyranny."

Be quiet, James. Mitchell's voice spoke in his head. *I have something important of which you all must be informed. Gather in the study, as I am going to manifest via an avatar-aspect to make things simpler.*

Everyone was already gathered there, and they fell silent and turned to the table in the center of the room. A moment later, white light tinged with pale green began to shimmer on the surface, and it coalesced into the shining and translucent form of Mary Mitchell.

LeBlanc said, "Greetings. I take it this has to do with the

garbled signal we received yesterday?" She was calm and polite, but there was a tense edge to her voice. All the thaumaturgists present knew the coming news might be exceedingly bad.

In a voice tinged with a faint echo, the ghostly astral projection of Mitchell replied, "Yes. Most of us thought we heard something, and those of us who could discern the details through the magical distortion thought it might be coming from Damian. I have investigated the matter, and I regret to inform you that our worst fears have been confirmed."

James let out a long, rattling sigh and looked down at the surface of the table, his shoulders slumping. Around him, he heard LeBlanc and Buchanon draw sharp breaths as half-formed gasps. Ezeudo remained silent. He was puzzled but smart enough to guess what Mitchell meant.

The avatar went on. "Damian is dead. His house was largely destroyed by what looks like a large-scale elemental battle, and he was severely battered. It appeared that in the end, he was ritualistically executed with a knife or a dagger. There were no other bodies present. The magical residues at the place suggest that whoever attacked him possessed enormous power."

While she said all this, Mary's face was controlled, but she failed to hide her feelings. Her lower lip trembled, and her eyes looked heavy with dammed-up tears.

When James glanced sidelong at LeBlanc, he saw her covering her eyes with her right hand and shaking her head.

Mary continued, "I suppose some of you—I will politely refrain from naming names—view me as a killjoy, a martinet schoolmarm who cares more for her begonias than she does for your lives, but I never wanted this to happen, nor for it to happen to any of the rest of you. Damian was a good friend as well as a good thaumaturge and we should mourn him as we see fit, but there is not much time. We must also prepare to defend ourselves against the next strike."

Well, she's not wrong, James admitted to himself. *Maybe I've been a bit too harsh on the old gal. Damian, though? Somehow I would have expected his wily ass to be the last of us to go if something like this happened. God. I still can't believe it.*

LeBlanc took her hand away from her eyes and raised it before interjecting, "Yes, and though I would imagine you've already thought of this, none of us should stay alone at any time. Groups of no fewer than three would be wise, and we would do well to remain in places that are either difficult to find or easy to defend. I am tempted to suggest going to the city to hide amidst the general public, but there is a chance the Orthodoxy might be willing to risk collateral damage among civilians for the sake of wiping us out."

The others agreed and began to discuss further plans and tactics for fighting a defensive campaign. Going on the offensive might have allowed them to defeat some of their foes' agents, but it would also make it look as though they were fleeing or going underground, which might reinforce the Eurasian coven's claim to the mantle of legitimacy over America.

Over the talking hung a pall of grief heavy as a winter fog. Later, each of them would need time to come to emotional terms with the loss their fellowship had suffered.

Ezeudo just listened. He rarely contributed since he did not feel entirely qualified. His charitable work had taken him into many warzones, but this was different. As far as he had known at the time, he was always the only person who possessed the gift. A battle between many different magicians was beyond him.

And still he smoldered over the apparent necessity that he fight to the death beside these people he barely knew. He did not understand why it was impossible for them to call a summit with the Orthodoxy and negotiate a course of action other than war.

Of course, first blood had been drawn. They had killed Damian Diaz, and he doubted the cycle of violence could be averted now that there had been casualties.

Madness, he thought, trying to keep his feelings off his face.

This is complete and utter madness. I had no idea my new friends would succumb to it so quickly.

After all, he was here because James and LeBlanc had assured him this was the better, more civilized way to organize magic. If there were vigilantes and renegades, they had said, things could go badly wrong.

What does this count as if not going badly wrong? he wondered.

CHAPTER NINE

Kera, Lia, and Johnny were going to have a long evening ahead of them, but at least it would be one in which they got some exercise and fresh air. Kera was looking forward to it. For a brief period, she had begun to fear that becoming a legitimate detective would mean being cooped up indoors all the time.

She reassured herself, *This is like venturing out on the town back in the olden days of a couple weeks ago when I was still a vigilante, minus all the danger of being arrested, injured, or killed. Well, minus most of it, anyway.*

They had agreed to meet near Barrington Plaza in West Los Angeles. It was a pedestrian-friendly area, and, more importantly, it was close to the wealthy estates of Beverly Hills, Pacific Palisades, and Bel Air, which was where the bulk of the homes they needed to look at were located.

Kera had been the first to arrive. It was only about a twenty-minute drive for her, whereas Lia and Johnny, whom she assumed would be riding together, had to come a good thirty-five minutes from eastern Long Beach in Lia's case and twenty-five from Torrance in Johnny's.

I feel bad for Lia at this point, Kera thought as she pulled into an available parking spot and texted her friends her exact location. *She keeps having to drive too damn far anytime we need to do anything. Then again, she did say something about wanting to move closer to the middle of the metropolitan area, which would make things easier for all of us.*

It was dusk when Kera arrived, and as she lounged near her bike, watching the various passersby and hoping parking enforcement or a beat cop wouldn't show up to tell her not to loiter, the last of the day's light faded and died.

Perhaps five minutes after darkness fell and the city was re-illuminated by vast arrays of electric lights, Johnny's familiar Mustang pulled up.

"Hey," Kera called, waving to them. "Somehow I thought you'd bring Lia's car since it's less conspicuous, but whatever. I saved you a space." She gestured at one that lay two down from her own, and Johnny pulled in.

When he and Lia stepped out, Kera was surprised to see them dressed in snappy-casual clothes. Johnny had worn a suit when he'd worked for Pauline but had been dressing like a common LA schmuck since he'd (mostly) transitioned to honest work. Lia had *always* dressed formally. Seeing her in a nice blouse and trousers, she looked like a different person.

"You look good," Kera complimented her. "You both do. It would appear that you have located the fabled Goldilocks Zone in terms of how to dress. Not that there was anything wrong with how you dressed previously, but just saying. This is probably best for where we're going."

Then she frowned. "Me looking like a biker, which I technically am, might be a bit, um, incongruous."

Lia waved a hand. "Don't worry about it. It's not as though there is a shortage of motorcycle enthusiasts in this city. Also, I located another theft victim within the same area we'll be scoping out, so that makes three in this region alone. There are also the two in San Fernando and West Covina, but we might not have time for those tonight."

Kera shrugged. "We'll see. Johnny, what do you say?"

"I say," he began and put his hands in his pockets, "we play it by ear. Walking around town always takes longer than you think it will. LA is a motor city, but with traffic, driving might take just about as long, heh." He was wearing an open-fronted button-down shirt over a good-quality t-shirt, along with well-pressed khaki trousers. Alongside Lia, they looked like a respectable young upper-middle-class couple.

Or perhaps rich people trying not to look too rich. As such, they would not be overly suspicious if they were seen wandering around the Hills, provided they didn't get too nosy with people's camera-equipped private gates and so forth.

Kera gloated, *I have the ability to surpass minor inconveniences like that if I have to.*

Earlier today, she had been to a half-dozen art galleries and auction houses where the stolen and destroyed pieces had last been seen in public before they met their cruel fates. She had found nothing aside from confirmation of the stuff that was already in the news, the police reports, and so forth.

The trio wandered north, then east, chatting casually to give off the appropriate air of tourists or daytrippers checking out the most glamorous parts of the city on a beautiful night. It took them about twenty minutes to arrive in front of the first house on their list, the residence of one Mr. Pavlovsky, who'd had a mezzotint stolen and sliced to ribbons a few years ago.

Kera's spirits sank as they neared the place. They could not see the house from the street, given that it was hidden behind a wall, a gate, and a hedge, and since the theft had occurred long ago, it was unlikely any evidence would remain. Still, it was worth a look.

Johnny and Lia covered for her by pretending to ooh and ahh over the white marble wall and impressive security setup while

Kera sat on the curb and adjusted her boots. Meanwhile, she sent out her consciousness, seeking anything she could find that might be related to the unsolved art theft.

To her surprise, something came to her almost immediately—a string of intense feelings following the path of the mezzotint. The burglary of the piece had been a momentous experience for both the owner and the thief. But the chain was twisted; Kera could not yet distinguish the emotions of the one from another, though the overall impression was of pain and unpleasantness.

She fixed it in her mind, then stood up. "Okay, boots are better. Nice place, or I assume it's nice behind the moat and bailey." She stared at the wall. "Let's go."

They moved in the direction of the place that was most likely to bear investigative fruit—the residence of Mrs. Corvina, owner of the Domingo piece stolen and wrecked mere days ago.

The old lady lived in a house that was less palatial and less private than Pavlovsky's. It was only about fifty yards from the sidewalk and was surrounded by a wrought iron fence with no obvious security gear outside, though Kera supposed there might be some on the porch. The house was a borderline Victorian pile, likely dating back to the early days of Los Angeles a century ago —swanky enough but a cut or two below the city's most elite mansions. Ivy grew up the walls. It was the dwelling of someone who came from old money that was gradually running out.

Interesting. Kera stared at the place; it was sufficiently unusual that she could justify doing so as innocent curiosity.

It would have been easier to break in. Hell, I could probably do it right now without using magic if I could find a rope or something to climb the fence. Makes me wonder if Chateau Pavlovsky's fortress-like setup was directly caused by the mezzotint theft in the previous decade. I don't think Mrs. Corvina could afford anything on that level, however. She strikes me as the type who spends most of her dwindling fortune on art and cat food.

Once again, Johnny and Lia provided cover while Kera

pretended to fish around in her satchel for something. As her hands fumbled amidst her meager possessions, her mind expanded and sought the psychic traces left by the business with the Domingo painting.

What Kera felt was shockingly similar to what she had encountered at the Pavlovsky estate, only far stronger, given how much more recent the events were. For a moment she paused, staring dumbly into space with jaw agape, as her brain tried to sort through all the emotional noise.

"Uhh," she half-groaned, "I'm, um, not feeling so well, guys. Let's head to the Palisades, shall we?"

Johnny and Lia stared at her in concern, then shrugged and took her by the arms to help her back the way they had come.

It was a long walk, then drive, and by the time they were halfway to the third and final house they needed to investigate, Kera was feeling better. Her thoughts were still clouded, however. A couple of homeless people asked for change, and to her embarrassment, Kera did not even register that they had done so until they were past. She usually gave a few coins, if nothing else. Lia and Johnny did not seem to share her philosophy on the matter.

"Sure," Johnny remarked, "some of them are just people with a run of bad luck, but some are professional panhandlers, seriously. I used to know a few guys who did that shit all the time."

Frowning, Kera muttered, "I'd rather have given them something anyway, but we don't have time to go back."

Chris was set to join them in a matter of minutes. He had gotten out of work at five o'clock as usual and had needed a nap since he had unwisely stayed up too late last night. After waking up, he had texted Kera to get her approximate location in fifteen minutes and hopped into his Jeep.

The big dark vehicle pulled ahead of the three at an intersection as they continued their lengthy amble. Kera waved at Chris and directed him to park up ahead. After he found a space, he joined them on foot, embracing Kera and asking where they were going next.

Lia informed him, "A mansion near the Palisades, where there was a crime similar to the one we're investigating some twenty years ago. That is a long time to be looking for evidence, but Kera has her ways. We'll have to drive."

Her words proved true as they neared the estate in question. Based on the reports Lia and Kera had studied, the police had thoroughly examined the crime scene, yet there were things that they would never have been able to notice. None of them, it seemed, had the gift, or if they did, they had no idea how to use it.

The gift told her, as they passed the third mansion, that the person responsible for stealing a statue from within it was behind the crimes involving the mezzotint and the painting.

As Kera's skill in the arts of magic and her immersion in the hidden world of all things thaumaturgic, arcane, and miraculous had increased, her perceptions had altered and grown. Not only could she see, hear, smell, taste, and even touch things that would have been invisible to most people, but she could also "read between the lines" of new information, intuitively grasping the meaning of obscure phenomena.

She supposed—and hoped—it would be a good talent for a detective to have.

For the moment, picking up the threads of emotional energy left behind by their probable art thief, Kera found her mind semi-voluntarily weaving the threads into a pattern that made sense to her. The nature of the residues became comprehensible, identifiable.

This person, whoever they were, was *hungry*. Hungry and angry. It was not a perfect way of thinking about it, but it was the best Kera could come up with on short notice. The burglar was driven by a desperate and strangely bitter desire to *consume* something. It was difficult to say what.

Chris asked, "Kera, is something wrong? You're getting that

look you sometimes get when you're on the verge of blurting out something either important or inadvisable. No offense."

Kera raised a hand and shook it stiffly, an awkward gesture for conveying that she did not want to be bothered. Not yet. She felt as though a revelation was seconds away if only she could maintain her train of thought.

It doesn't make any sense. Her brow furrowed and her eyes narrowed in frustration as the gears within her head continued to turn. *They certainly aren't eating the works of art. That would be nonsensical, and in each case, the owner had all the pieces returned to them. Could it be someone with, uhh, an eating disorder who desperately needs money to feed their habit? No, that's stupid.*

Her pace had slowed to a trudge and her eyes glazed over. Chris and Johnny and Lia had pulled far ahead of her on the sidewalk, but they stopped and waited for their friend to catch up. Kera appreciated it, but she could not hurry. She had other priorities.

It almost feels like this person is leaking magic. A little bit, not much. But intense human emotions can sometimes be indistinguishable from spellcasting, at least in terms of the traces they leave. Could it be someone with vestigial thaumaturgic capabilities who needs to eat to replenish themselves the way Steph and I do? No, that doesn't make much sense either. Again, I'm not sure how they'd make money by stealing a painting, only to destroy it.

Kera came abreast of her partners, who started walking again, albeit at a far more languid pace to allow her to keep up.

Ugh, Kera's mind spun on. *For some reason, I'm thinking of vampires, which is even sillier than everything else that's popped into my consciousness. I think. Is it? If vampires were real, I would imagine that I would have heard about it by now. Maybe from Pavla. She's from Eastern Europe, for fuck's sake.* She mentioned nothing of the sort.

Wait, what about psychic vampires? People who supposedly feed on other people's energy? I heard about that somewhere. Seemed like another woo-woo urban legend. But now I'm not so sure. I myself am an urban legend, technically.

As she considered the possibility, the volume and brightness of the vision in her mind's eye increased like she had ripped aside the first of several veils cloaking it from identification. Though the truth remained partially hidden, she did not like what she saw.

There was something ugly about the whole matter. She didn't know what it was, but her pulse and heart rate increased, and clammy sweat broke out on her skin under her leathers despite the relative warmth of the evening.

Perhaps I'm overthinking it, but whatever lurks behind that veil has got to be disturbing as hell. I'm not sure I want to see it.

Did we make a mistake? Now I'm wondering if this case is really as simple, or for that matter, as nonviolent as we'd thought. Fuck.

With that notion, her brain stopped working. It had shifted into neutral, idling in front of a roadblock and refusing to go any farther. She shook her head, rubbed her eyes, and resolved to come back to it later. She had made progress, but not enough.

Lia asked, "Is everything all right?"

"Yeah," Kera answered her, "mostly. There's something creepy about all this, but I can't figure it out or put it into words yet. Maybe it will come to me later when I'm in the shower."

Johnny nodded. "Probably. Sounds like we need to get this girl to a shower."

She laughed. "That's not a bad idea. I'm overdressed for the weather anyway, and I don't think we're going to find anything else in Beverly Hills, at least not without recreating the burglaries, which would be a poor idea for people trying to establish ourselves on the right side of the law. Let's go home and get something to eat."

Lia pointed out, "Your place is closer than mine or Johnny's, so I'll recommend we eat there, although technically it's my turn to host a gathering."

Kera shrugged. "Well, if it's okay with you, it's okay with me."

They headed back to Chris's Jeep, which was the closest of the three vehicles to their current location. As they strolled down the sidewalks, Kera asked, "Hey, did you find anything? Probably not if you've been at work all day."

Chris coughed. "Actually, I got some research done on my lunch break, plus during random five-minute intervals when I thought no one was watching."

"Impressive." She took his hand and squeezed it. "Once again, though, don't work too hard. Anyway, let's hear it."

Chris went on to elaborate on how he had turned up another art theft that had been reported to a private investigator rather than to the police, though it took place ten years ago and seemed to be a "conventional" theft. The painting had not been destroyed and returned, so it probably wasn't part of the same pattern.

"However," he added, "Ted, of all people, had an idea that I think is worth looking into. He said we should seek out incidents where expensive works of art were destroyed but supposedly not stolen since you'd have the weird common element of them being ripped apart but without the legal cover of the theft story. So if it is someone running an elaborate insurance racket, that could point us in the right direction."

Lia perked up. "Yes, that makes sense. I'll make a note of it and get on that tomorrow. Possibly tonight, if we have time."

Kera wasn't sure, though. The unsettling notions she had come up with while sniffing around the crime sites didn't suggest a financial motive.

Lia and Johnny went ahead to the latter's Mustang, waving goodbye and promising to meet Kera and Chris back at her warehouse. For the moment, the couple lingered beside Chris's Jeep.

"So." Kera pressed against her boyfriend. "Is Ted warming up to me? I mean, to us being together. You mentioned before that he was half-assedly suggesting that maybe I wasn't the right girl for you."

He kissed her. "Yeah, he's coming around. We've been together without any major fights for, um, multiple weeks now, after all. And I know he seems abrasive or obnoxious at times, but he's not a bad guy. A good one, in fact. And a good friend."

Kera rested her head on his shoulder. If the dark implications she had picked up upon tonight were legitimate, she suddenly disliked the thought of Chris being involved.

"I know." She kissed him back. "He wasn't trying to talk you out of dating me to tear you down out of jealousy or because he hates me or anything. He was doing it to protect you."

CHAPTER TEN

Chris, who possessed the largest vehicle of the group, took it upon himself to buy several buckets of fried chicken along with some biscuits and green beans, which he distributed once they arrived back at Kera's place. Kera got the largest share, though she insisted she didn't need that much food.

"Hey," she pointed out, "I barely used any magic out there. It's not like when we attacked El Peluquero's satellite warehouses and I was emptying my strength reserves within ten or fifteen minutes. Fried chicken *is* good, though."

Chris shrugged. "Eat what you can, and we'll deal with the rest. Leftovers are always an option."

As they tore into their late supper, Lia hooked up her laptop to Kera's TV and displayed pictures of the various pieces of stolen and destroyed artwork she had gleaned from gallery archives, art websites, and the police's incident reports.

"Okay," she began, "this is the Domingo piece, which was the most recent of them. An Expressionist sort of painting. Reminds me of Munch or a Van Gogh."

Johnny nodded. "I like it. Too bad it got cut up."

"Indeed." Lia clicked something on her laptop. "And on that

note, this is what it looks like now." The image shifted to the cops' photograph of the painting's remains.

Kera was struck by the oddity of it, once the initial dismay at seeing a fine piece of art in pieces subsided. The painting had been slashed apart in a haphazard way. There was no identifiable pattern the vandal had been trying to create, and yet, they must have used an extremely sharp blade and a curious degree of what looked like...*care*.

Domingo's masterpiece had not been torn asunder as if by a rabid animal. It had been dissected.

Or butchered, Kera surmised, *by a skilled meat-cutter*. She shuddered, wondering where the hell such a morbid thought had come from. Her mind wanted to turn back to the psychic residues she had analyzed, but Lia had more to show them.

"Next up," the small woman continued, "we have the mezzotint that belonged to Mr. Pavlovsky and the sculpture purchased by the third victim, the now-deceased Mr. Sarkisian. You will notice a similar pattern." She clicked through the images, giving the others about ten seconds to study each before moving on. "All three were carved into random pieces, albeit with a bizarre, laser-like precision, such that they were all considered good candidates for restoration. As you can imagine, the police are baffled."

Chris commented, "They don't have any suspects yet, from what I read. I believe they had one or two 'persons of interest,' but they've been cleared."

"Correct," said Lia.

Kera, tapping her lips, offered in a low, hesitant tone, "It's as though the culprit wants to show off what they're doing. 'Look how creative and talented I am at destroying these things.' Not a single ragged edge."

Lia gave a nod. "I agree. Some personality types, malignant narcissists and sadists, mostly, get off on displaying their acts of wrongdoing as blatantly as possible. It's a way of grandstanding and driving home the point of how powerless their victims are."

"Cute," said Johnny. "But the victims are, like, *objects*. Not people. What the hell, man?"

Lia raised a finger. "Unless the intended victim is the piece's owner rather than the piece itself. Since none of the works have been resold, the police have thus far been assuming revenge is the motive. The person of interest they were questioning in the Domingo-Corvina case was one of the other art aficionados Mrs. Corvina outbid at the auction. He had a good alibi, though, and so far, there isn't any evidence to suggest he hired someone to do the deed, either."

She clicked back through all the pictures, allowing everyone to review them.

"What's strange to me, though," Lia concluded, her voice lowering to a near-whisper, "is how *impersonal* it seems. Revenge is by definition a personal matter. Ridiculous as it might sound, the idea we mentioned before that our culprit is the equivalent of a showboating serial killer who happens to target paintings and such instead of human beings is the only thing that even comes close to making sense. For a given value of 'sense,' anyway, since I've never heard of anything like that."

"Yeah," said Johnny. "Whoever did this, it's not about the person they stole it from. It's some other crazy shit."

Chris looked at his girlfriend. "Kera, you got anything? I don't. Stuff like this is why I went into computer programming. The right-brained subjects are full of nutcases. No offense to anyone with an artistic streak, I guess."

Kera had been turning things over in her mind, allowing her thoughts and the emotional impressions she had received earlier to percolate while letting the others do most of the talking. She still hadn't made the desired breakthrough, but once again, she felt as though it was within her grasp. Or barely outside it, taunting her.

"When we walked past those houses," she intoned, her eyes half-glazed though she realized that everyone was watching her and nearly holding their breath, "there was this particular weird sensation I kept getting, which I'm almost positive was left there by the perp. And by the way, I think it was the same person. Or if it was different people in each case, they were awfully similar and had the same, um, issues."

Her friends leaned closer.

Kera sighed. "There's no way to say this that won't sound either creepy or absurd, but it was this sensation of...hunger. I don't think it was greed for money. More like a vampire needing blood. Best analogy I can come up with."

Johnny stiffened. "Wait, wait. Do *not* fucking tell me vampires are real. I'm still getting used to witches, okay?"

Kera shrugged. "I don't think it was a literal vampire. I just mean that I got this sense that whoever did this was fulfilling a compulsive need, and there was something carnivorous, or maybe parasitic, about it."

Chris shuddered. "Maybe we should be having this conversation in the light of day."

"Maybe," Lia conceded, "but our time is not unlimited. Kera, do you suspect this has anything to do with magic? At this point, supernatural explanations would make about as much sense as mundane ones. We've basically exhausted the rational possibilities."

Kera shook her head. "I'm not sure yet. When it comes to psychic residues, I can't always discern between magical ones from those that are the result of strong emotions. I'm wondering, though, if we could talk to this Corvina woman. We technically want her as a client anyway, and she might let us examine the remains of the painting. If it's cursed or enchanted, I should be able to tell."

They all agreed it was worth a shot, though Lia wanted to wait until they had more information to go on before they risked approaching Corvina since she might become suspicious of them and alert the police.

As Lia disconnected her laptop from the television, the picture switched to the local news channel. Apparently, there had just been a homicide in Silver Lake.

"...locals are still horrified by the brutality of the murder, with police refusing to disclose the details to the public yet and recommending that the eyewitness refrain from speaking to the press until more is known."

The newscaster's concerned face switched to a jerky camera scene of someone approaching a residence while other people screamed and called for help in the background. There was a visible bloodstain on the door, which hung open, but the picture cut away before any of the gory details came into view.

"Law enforcement has also refused to disclose the name of the victim so far but have mentioned that—"

Kera picked up her remote control and switched off the TV. "No," she stated. "Not in the mood to see stuff like that right now. Ugh."

No one challenged her. They seemed to have lost their stomach for such things at the same time she had.

It also occurred to her that, whoever had been killed, Motorcycle Woman might have stopped it.

But Motorcycle Woman was always half a step away from getting murdered herself, wasn't she? *I have Chris to think about, and my parents, and the Kims, and my future—*

Chris interrupted her thoughts by clapping his hands. "I'll get the extra food into the fridge."

Kera went to kiss him, glad of the distraction. "I'll help."

Ezeudo polished, rehearsed, and refurbished his speech in his head as the other and more senior thaumaturgists took their places near the podium James had set up in his vast sitting room.

The chamber was crowded with dozens of people, many of them standing, the rest sitting in whatever chairs or couches fit into the available space. Stragglers were crammed into doorways, craning their necks to get a view of the conference. According to Lady Mitchell, the attendees represented around half the total members of the minor covens within the US and excluded those in Canada and Latin America since they could not get here that fast.

Never would Ezeudo have dreamed that so many people possessed the gift of magic, if only in a limited capacity in their cases.

James stood behind the podium and flicked the microphone, which screeched obnoxiously through the speakers. "Testing, testing, one-two-three. Okay, clearly this thing is on. We can all celebrate knowing that something is going right so far. Boost my volume, though. Check? Check?"

The guy running the audio-visual setup turned up the necessary dials, and James's voice grew louder as the generalized murmur of the crowd softened, then died. Everyone's attention was focused on the speakers up front.

"Right," James concluded and breathed in, straightening as he looked the lesser magicians over. He seemed to be having difficulty adjusting to sobriety, but he was managing. Still, the lack of alcohol was not doing his temper any favors.

Once total silence set in, he began his formal introduction. "Welcome, everyone. Thank you all for coming on such short notice, but obviously, we are dealing with an emergency here. Everyone present, as well as those who aren't present for whatever reasons, received the same psionic message from the Moscow-based coven known as the Orthodoxy. Correct?"

The sea of heads nodded, and their murmurs of assent

sounded like rolling waves breaking on a beach. Once it was clear that everyone was in agreement, James shut them up by tapping the mic again and subjecting them to the unpleasant squealing sound.

"Good," he stated. "Well, *bad*, actually, but you know what I mean. Based on the emails I received from some of you, our Slavic friends did—as we would have guessed—message you before us and include a nice little addendum that you were to stay away from us and let things take their course. In other words, let them kill us, or they would kill you too. About what we expected from such charming people.

"And now they have struck first. Damian Diaz, an esteemed member of our council, was killed at his home three days ago. Since then, we have not seen or heard anything from the Orthodoxy, which suggests they are plotting their next move."

The crowd shifted in fear and confusion, and Ezeudo winced. James's cynical and sardonic way of speaking, no doubt exacerbated by trying to remain sober after such a lengthy bender, was not the right tone to take to either rouse these people to action or reassure them that all would be well. He was further alarming them and perhaps inducing depression. He hoped James would finish his piece soon and turn the microphone over to LeBlanc, Jones, Buchanan, or even Mary Mitchell.

Fortunately, he did, after describing the horrifying circumstances of Damian's death and implying that some of the invitees who *hadn't* shown up might be working with the enemy. As he left the podium, someone shouted, "The Kansas City coven would never work with those people. They only accept Americans, and they refuse to ever be ruled by foreigners."

James leaned back toward the podium and said into the mic, "Good." Then he wandered off to the rear corner as Mother LeBlanc took center stage.

"Friends, welcome," she began, and her pleasant tone of voice, possibly augmented by a minor soothing spell, immediately improved the mood within the hall. "It must be addressed that what is happening now is happening *in part* because of our actions. We, the council, by trying to provide for the general welfare of our discipline and its followers, made a mistake, and now our rivals seek to capitalize upon it."

The room was silent, everyone listening for what came next.

LeBlanc went on. "It is true that we inadvertently exposed the entire hidden world of thaumaturgy and enchantment to more public scrutiny than has ever occurred in known history. However, we were successful in containing the majority of it. And it is a bald-faced lie that we knowingly exposed any magic users to harm, let alone that any of our actions were taken with malign intent. Our goal was only to recruit new apprentices. Little did anyone realize how widespread the gift truly is..."

She spoke on in a similar vein for around five minutes, calming the assembly's jangled nerves, explaining and justifying the council's actions, and emphasizing that the Orthodoxy was known for behaving like an organized crime ring, demanding tribute payments from smaller covens in exchange for "protection" and enforcing their will through the threat of merciless violence.

Ezeudo reflected on the irony at work in the presentation. Much of what LeBlanc was saying and what the others *would* say had been scripted by James, yet he had seemingly improvised his own introduction and had not done a good job of it. It was up to the rest of them to soothe and persuade the members of the lesser covens through a mixture of their talents and wisdom and the outline that Lovecraft had provided them.

Each member of the council, the eleven who still lived, spoke in turn, though their speeches grew shorter as time went on since it was unnecessary for all of them to repeat the same information. Instead, they approached the issue from different angles and offered personal or idiosyncratic examples illustrating why the entire North American magical community should band together against the common foe.

And, Ezeudo noted, not a single person suggested suing for peace. Whatever bizarre tradition the American and Eurasian magicians followed, it did not seem to include the possibility of making a treaty once war had been declared. Annihilation of one side or the other was apparently the only possible outcome.

It weighed upon him like cold rain dragging down his clothes and dampening his spirits.

If this is how they insist on approaching a disagreement, he wondered, *does either side deserve to win? Would the council's victory be anything less than a horror for the Orthodoxy? Surely not every member of their organization is evil.*

When it came time for his speech, he struggled to stay on script. He wanted to blurt out that they were all fools to treat the burgeoning conflict as a zero-sum game. That was how conflicts spun out of control and into blood-drenched chaos.

He glossed over most of what James wanted him to say, focusing instead on describing how he had been recruited in Switzerland and on his inner conflict about the council's mission. He had a fair amount of experience as a public speaker and considered himself good at it despite occasionally struggling to choose the right English word or phrase or garbling it with his accent when he did.

Still, the assembled individuals—a truly motley band representing every type of human found on the American continent, minus those with zero magical ability—listened to all he said with brightening eyes.

"The council convinced me," he declared with full honesty, "that their mission was just. Their methods were strange to me at first, and I needed a great deal of instruction, but I see now that their goal is to maintain the peace and well-being of us all."

That part was on script and caused him no inner conflict. He was supposed to deliver a rousing battle cry next, but he did not.

Instead, he continued, "I strongly feel that violence should not be the answer to our problems. I have seen enough violence already, and nothing good ever comes of it. If—*if*—it should come to pass that we have no other option, then so be it; we will defend our lives. But first, we might consider the alternatives. We must talk to one another, even our enemies. Aggressive people may seem impossible to argue with at first, but sometimes, for such people, it is a matter of saving face more than a true commitment to destruction. It is possible the Orthodoxy will retreat if we allow them a way out, a means by which they can preserve their honor without having to avenge it."

With that, he nodded and stepped away from the podium.

There was cautious applause, but some of the faces looked confused. As Ezeudo glanced at the council, he saw that half of them—the polite ones, notably LeBlanc, Hugh, and Lauren—were stony-faced. The others were glaring at him. In their eyes, he had done something wrong.

Well, he thought as he took his place in the rear and let James step up to finish the presentation, *the feeling is mutual.*

CHAPTER ELEVEN

Kera had her place to herself for the day, which did not happen very often anymore. Until further notice, her de facto apartment was also their de facto office. She had temporarily converted it into a studio to boot.

Everyone had gone home after their unsettling and inconclusive brainstorming session last night. Kera had summarized their findings in an email to Stephanie, who had been working, and asked her to come over later if possible so they could talk about it in person. Then she had passed out.

She'd found it difficult to sleep, arising after barely six hours. Her brain refused to leave the mystery they had been studying alone.

"So," she had said to the empty warehouse as she drank her coffee and ate a bowl of cereal, "if I were an insane art thief who is possibly also a psychic vampire and/or a serial killer of paintings, what sort of personal gratification would I get from cutting up other people's works of art? What hunger would that feed?"

Her mind turned over a variety of prospects. It might be someone who had been screwed out of an art career and was lashing back at those more fortunate. It could be someone with magical perceptiveness or who at least *thought* they could perceive magic, trying to exorcise demons from "possessed" works of art.

She even went back to the age-old motive of profit, considering the notion that their culprit might be a professional "art assassin" hired by someone behind the scenes to destroy valuable pieces in the hopes of manipulating the market in some way, but that struck her as such an overelaborate scheme that the demonic possession story was arguably more sensible.

After finishing her breakfast and showering, Kera had gone to an art supplies store and purchased an easel, two canvases, paint, and brushes.

She stood in front of her attempt at a masterpiece. Lacking the inclination to try anything too challenging, she had attempted to recreate her childhood home from memory. It was not particularly inspiring, looking like an aborted cross between a kindergartner's crayon drawing and a highly abstract work of modernism. It was not magnificently shitty enough to be "so bad it's good," as some pieces were. It was merely bad.

"Oh, well." She sighed. "Nobody's perfect. Anyway, it's not like I planned on letting the thing live."

Chuckling to herself, she went into the kitchen, retrieved a large steak knife, and ran it over her whetstone until it was keen enough to shave the fine hairs on her forearm. There was no reason investigations couldn't be fun.

But any sense of levity evaporated as she sat with the knife on her lap, reviewing the photos of the destroyed pieces Lia had sent to her overnight. In each case, their perp had used a knife or a razor, including with the sculpture—which suggested a very patient regimen of sawing through the plaster—and had disassembled their inanimate victim with a strange combination of passionate violence and targeted precision.

Kera's spine went cold. No living thing had been killed, but some people attached enormous importance to art, and *that* had been destroyed with the utmost ruthlessness. She wasn't sure she wanted to get into the head of someone who was compelled to do such a thing.

"Damn." She exhaled, got up, and walked over toward her terrible attempt at a masterwork. Since the paint was still drying, she instead picked up the second canvas, still blank, and set to work.

As sharp as the knife was, carving it into seemingly random pieces without tearing the material and ruining the "cleanliness" of the cuts was surprisingly difficult. Whoever the Art Slasher was, they either had the best knife in human history, or they were highly skilled and experienced, or both.

Forty minutes later, Kera sat on the floor, knife in hand and fragments of canvas scattered in front of her. She had acquired no insights from the task and had achieved no sense of gratification. It was simply an arduous, pointless process of destruction, comparable to tearing up old carpets.

But, she realized, *that was a blank canvas. My "art" isn't much, but will it somehow feel different if I destroy a completed painting?*

There was only one way to find out. After resharpening her knife and reflecting with some consternation that the blade might be ground halfway into oblivion by the time she was done, she went back to her abomination of a childhood house.

Kera examined it. *I suck horribly, but I recognize it as the old house in Danbury, even if no one else would. Is that important? Does the artist's ability to express their intent matter to this wacko?*

She reached out with her right hand, holding the knife, and touched the blade gently to a blank spot on the canvas. Without thinking about what she was doing, the tip of the blade seemed to naturally move across certain paths along the image's surface. It had something to do with the way the elements of the painting were composed and the flow of them.

Maybe the cuts aren't random after all. What if there's a pattern, but it's one that only makes sense in the head of our perp? Do they dissect a piece according to their subjective perception of how the image "flows?" Hell if I know.

The knifepoint had made ridges in the paint, which was still soft. Following them, Kera began to slice it apart.

And this time, it was different.

But how? It's more fun and also more unpleasant in a perverse way since I'm not only dismantling an object, I'm wrecking a creation. A low-quality, half-assed one, but a creation all the same. It's like the difference between junking an old pile of car parts and crashing an Italian sports car.

Partway into the process, the doorbell rang. Kera blinked and started. She was not expecting anyone at this hour, nor had she ordered any deliveries. It was probably the Kims, or Lia, or a Jehovah's Witness. She walked over to the window and peered out. A delivery guy was holding a parcel about a foot square, wrapped in brown paper.

Kera readied a defensive shielding charm on the off-chance the man was delivering a gun or a bomb, compliments of one of the many influential criminals she had pissed off, who had finally figured out her identity.

But as she opened the door, she had no premonition of threat.

"Hi," the young man said. "Package for you." He showed her the label. The return address was a nearby bakery, but they had included a note saying, "To Kera, from your mother."

Kera accepted it. "Ah, I see. Thanks."

As the man drove away, she closed the door with her foot and tore open the paper. As soon as it parted, she saw an aluminum tin beneath, and her nose picked up the unmistakable aroma of freshly baked peanut butter cookies.

She slumped against the wall. "Dammit, Mom. Here I am, trying to dodge your phone calls and stonewall you, and you go and send my favorite from when I was a kid. And I'm hungry. Lumberjacking canvases is hard work."

Not bothering to get a glass of milk or a cup of coffee to go with them, Kera opened the tin and devoured two of the cookies, hoping she didn't have any paint residue on her hands. Though not identical to the way her mother made them, they were delicious.

In an oddly bittersweet mood that mixed sentimentality, contentment, and guilt, Kera paused and stared into space, the tin between her hands. Her eyes focused directly on the half-destroyed painting.

Ironic. I painted the house I grew up in, and along comes this blast from the past. Now I'm craving Mom's mac 'n cheese, too. Shit. What if—

She blinked and dropped the tin. Fortunately, the lid was on securely and it landed flat on its bottom, saving the remaining cookies from spilling out. But she barely noticed.

It was almost clear—the nature of the mystery she had begun to perceive with her mind's eye. The one she had visualized as concealed by a series of veils. Another veil had been torn away. She almost had it. So close.

The Art Slasher is getting something out of this. It's both emotional and physical. Ugh, I hope it's not sexual, but I could see that, too. I think it's something else, though. Cookies. Works of art as acts of creation. Cutting with the "flow" of the painting. Hunger. Sentimentality. It's right on the tip of my tongue. Goddammit. It's coming together, but I still can't see it all in focus.

When her mind tried to go over it in a purely rational fashion, the connections fell apart. It all seemed absurd, and she wondered if she was crazy. But when she approached it from a less logical perspective, combining a childlike worldview, her female intuition, and the things she had learned from her misadventures in thaumaturgy...

There had to be something there. Either there was a connection, or she was going crazy.

Her phone buzzed once. When she checked the screen,

assuming it was her mother asking if she had received the cookies, she was half-surprised to see that it was Lia.

I'm coming over, the text message began. **Sorry for the lack of notice, but this is big. We need to talk immediately. Details when I arrive.**

Kera frowned and returned the device to her pocket. She hated it when people were vague with her, but she trusted Lia's judgment. If she was hustling over even though Kera should by rights be driving to Long Beach, it must legitimately be important.

While waiting for her business partner to show up, Kera sat at her computer and tried to compose an email to her mom. The cookies were a nice gesture, and her neck tingled and her face flushed red when she thought about how crappy a daughter she had been lately.

Her mother used to call her at least once a week, but Kera had finally made it clear that she wanted more breathing room, more independence. She suspected her dad had stepped in as well, urging the woman to lay off. Right about now, though, Kera wished her mother would call so she could thank her in person. Still, an email would be far better than nothing. Why couldn't she bring herself to just call? Well, that was a matter for another time.

She got halfway into it after deleting eight or nine prospective sentences for being either too stilted, too sarcastic, or too emotional when Lia knocked on the door.

"Shit," Kera muttered. "Sorry, Mom. I'll get back to you soon, though. I promise."

When she pulled open the door, Lia was pale and jittery. "Hello, Kera," she said. "I apologize for intruding, but this really can't wait. We need to... What were you doing? Trying to recreate the scene of the crime?"

Her eyes had drifted to the deranged mess on the open part of the warehouse's floor, where one and a half canvases lay in mangled shreds. Part of the painting of her childhood home was still intact, with its bright, cheery colors, and it occurred to Kera how creepy it must look. If she had burst in on such a scene in the house of someone she didn't know well, she might have turned around and walked out.

"Yes," she admitted. "I was trying to see if I, you know, *felt* anything in particular when doing, um, *that*." She gestured vaguely at the canvases. "Anyway, tell me the bad news. No point in delaying."

Lia swallowed and looked at the floor. "I'm sorry, but you should not have switched off the TV when you did last night."

Oh, fuck. Kera did not know what to expect, but if it had to do with a homicide, then...

"The victim," Lia pronounced, "was Luis Domingo, the author of the piece Mrs. Corvina purchased before it was stolen. They don't know who did it yet, but the rumors are running wild."

Kera felt herself growing cold. "How did he die? I probably don't want to know, but I'm pretty sure I have to."

Lia sat down on the couch. "He was, they're pretty sure, tortured to death. It...it was awful. They found him strapped to a table, mutilated, and his blood was almost completely drained. Someone worked him over with a series of cuts from a well-sharpened knife. Like, well..."

Her voice trailed off. It was unnecessary for her to finish the comparison. No wonder she'd been so disturbed by the sight of what Kera had spent her day doing.

Kera put a hand over her eyes and groaned. The only thing that could have made the news any worse was if the victim had been someone she had known personally. She gave thanks that the universe had spared her that.

"Well, shit," she muttered and tried not to shudder. "We had to go and pick *this* case out of all the ones in the city. It just got a hell of a lot less quirky and respectable and non-dangerous, didn't it?"

CHAPTER TWELVE

Lia had remained at Kera's place all day, and the two had been working diligently since the former had broken the news to the latter.

Chris was on his way, and Stephanie would be arriving about the same time since she was working the early shift today. Better still, she had tomorrow off, so they could work late if necessary.

"Lia," Kera said, "please take a break. You realize you're a clinical workaholic, right? You and my boyfriend both. I suppose that's better than being lazy, but neither of you is going to be much good to my agency if you end up dead of exhaustion or have a psychotic episode or something."

Kera had done quite a bit as well, but she'd rested sporadically. Lia's monomaniacal commitment to whatever task she took on was borderline frightening at times.

Her partner waved a hand in dismissal. "Don't worry about it. You offered to cook, which frees me from having to worry about food for the rest of the day, especially given the *amounts* of food you always make. Furthermore, I almost have it."

The petite Korean woman was hunched over her laptop,

which she'd set up on Kera's desk, and sat plinking on her keyboard.

Kera leaned over her shoulder. "Have what?"

"The crime scene photos," replied Lia. "I imagine they will be, well, highly unpleasant, but examining them could tell us a few things about the M.O. of the killer since I think we're in agreement that Domingo's murder is related to what happened to his painting."

Kera's stomach curdled at the thought of seeing what had happened to the poor man. "We are in agreement on that, yes. And it's nice that we'll probably get to see the pics right before dinner."

As per her earlier craving, she had made a massive pot of macaroni and cheese, albeit with steamed vegetables added to give it flavor, nutrition, and fiber. The water was boiling steadily, and Kera stirred the pasta, estimating that it needed another two minutes to reach *al dente*.

She had drained the macaroni and was stirring in the milk, butter, and cheese sauce (and adding the veggies) when Lia exclaimed, "Got it! Oh, God. Give me a minute. I've seen people killed before, but..."

"Yeah," Kera muttered in a dark tone. She had never met Luis Domingo, but there was something especially cruel about his fate. A young man bursting with talent had been put on the map by his most recent painting, only to have it destroyed days before he himself met an unspeakable fate. The world would never get to see his next masterpiece.

She was in no hurry to examine the photographs, leaving the task to Lia while she finished making food. The mac was ready to serve when Chris and Stephanie arrived. Unbeknownst to Kera, they had met somewhere along the way and carpooled to Kera's place in the Jeep.

"*Hola*," said Chris. "What fun-filled hijinks are we getting into today?"

Kera frowned. "Don't ask. Let's eat first, though." She considered adding a disclaimer that it wasn't her fault if they ended up throwing up later but opted not to.

Stephanie sniffed the air. "Is that mac n' cheese? It might be budget food, but it's also comfort food. Haven't had that stuff in way too long."

Kera shrugged. "Well, it mostly consists of fat and carbohydrates, so it's perfect for us in case we need to cast any spells. Anyway, I'll let Lia deliver the not-so-good news of what we get to deal with tonight."

Lia, still sitting at the computer desk, told them.

"Jesus," Chris remarked. "That was not what I was hoping to hear."

Stephanie shook her head. "That's damn sad. We thought we were taking on a case where we *wouldn't* have to deal with terrible things happening to innocent people, right? Though I guess we don't have no cause to complain about our luck compared to Domingo."

"Aye," Kera agreed. "Have some macaroni. If anyone doesn't feel up to examining the pictures, Lia and I can handle it, I suppose."

Lia pointed out, "I've already studied them in detail. I can describe the pertinent elements if you three would rather abstain."

They ate in silence for a moment. "No," Kera said after the first several mouthfuls. "You've been doing enough of the work, and I'm pretty sure I've killed more people than anyone else here. Not that I'm proud of it, but I can stand to look at a couple of goddamn photographs."

Twenty minutes later, she did so and almost immediately regretted it. The crime scene, with Domingo's body at the center, looked like something from the sort of horror film that would be banned in more conservative countries, yet it was real. Her gorge rose. She wished she had looked at the pics *before* eating since if she lost her appetite, the mac could be saved for later.

"Well, this is terrible," she stated. Her mind was forcing itself to grow desensitized, though, for the purpose of gleaning information. If she had to look at such vileness, it at least ought to help them solve the crime. And something about the manner in which the young man had been mutilated looked weirdly familiar.

She turned to Lia. "Does this ring any bells? I feel like it's reminding me of something we saw or talked about recently, but I can't think of what."

Lia reacted with a slow nod. "Elizabeth Short. The Black Dahlia."

Chris, who had passed on viewing the photos, exclaimed, "Holy shit. No way. A copycat killer?"

Stephanie put her hands on her face again. "Oh, Lord. What did we get ourselves into this time? This is even worse than dealing with drug dealers. What the hell does it have to do with the painting, though?"

Kera barely heard either of them. When Lia had mentioned the Black Dahlia murder, something like a bomb had gone off in her brain. The final veil had been half-drawn away from the core of the mystery. She wanted to reach out and rip it off, but there was some final component of the truth that remained hidden.

As if sensing her frustration while also responding to Chris and Steph, Lia suggested, "Yes, the nature of the murder was almost *exactly* the same, so it's fairly safe to assume, I would wager, that it is indeed a copycat incident. As for how it relates to the painting, I'm not sure. It seems as though there's another crime behind all this, somehow. As though the culprit used the murder to distract attention from the destruction of the painting. But that makes no sense. Kera, what do you think?"

Kera had hastened to her computer and was frantically performing searches, trying to pull up as many results as she could that might be helpful to her. Her mind, at the same time, was repeatedly going back through the psychic impressions she had received last night.

The strange mixture of anger and voracious desperation at each of the crime scenes. One contemporary, one from six or seven years ago, one from about twenty years ago.

Are there others? she wondered. *I would not be shocked if there were. But how far back do they go?*

Her friends waited for her commentary, but she ignored them, knowing she was being rude but unwilling to interrupt the powerful mental processes that had been set in motion. She began comparing her search results to the reams of data Lia had dug up over the last several days.

The others discussed possibilities among themselves as Kera worked, their voices seeming like distant echoes. Finally, after about ten minutes of cross-referencing the info and letting her intuition run wild, Kera had it. It was insane, but there it was. She spun around in her chair, and everyone stopped talking and looked at her.

"Hi," her boyfriend said. "I'm Chris. What's your name?"

Kera cleared her throat. "It's the same person."

Her friends blinked in confusion, and Lia asked, "Do you mean the murderer is the same person who stole the—"

"I mean yes to that, *and* it's the same person who killed Elizabeth Short." She took a deep breath, waiting for the inevitable pushback.

Chris and Steph squinted and tried to remember the dates, but Lia beat them to the punch. "Um, pardon me, Kera, but Elizabeth Short died in 1947. It is now the year 2022. You do the math."

"Yeah." Kera sighed, "I have. But my stupid little hunches have gotten me just as far as math has. I know it sounds ridiculous, but somehow I know it's true, okay? We are dealing with someone who has been around for a *long* time. These incidents, suspiciously similar art thefts *and* murders, go back to the goddamn 1940s. Remember Pavla? Well, she's only been gone a week or two, so of course you do. She looked about thirty, but she told me that she was closer to sixty. More things in heaven and earth..."

Everyone was silent for a couple of heartbeats. Stephanie was the first to speak.

"So," she surmised, "this case involves magic after all."

Kera could not see any possibility that didn't. "Yes."

Chris rubbed his eyes. "I mean, by now, I'll believe almost anything, but it's still a stretch. Are you sure, Kera? I trust you, but maybe you've been immersed in this kind of stuff for too long. Like, a 'when all you have is a hammer, everything looks like a nail' situation."

Kera paused and considered that he might have a point. Then she shook her head. "No, I'm certain. It's like when I was doing my vigilante rides. Sometimes I followed the police scanner, but other times, all I had to go on was a hunch, for lack of a better way of putting it, that something was going on in such-and-such neighborhood. It might be miles away, but it never steered me wrong."

Her boyfriend shrugged. "You're the expert. So, what the hell do we do now?"

While Kera thought it over, Lia piped up. "This is not exactly what we signed up for. It's true, we've dealt with things that are similar or perhaps even worse, but we wanted our agency to get off on the right foot. Less dirty, less dangerous cases that will distance us from our pasts. A magically-empowered murderer fails to tick those boxes."

They all fell into glum silence for a moment, and Kera sensed that her friends were as conflicted as she was.

But the horrible crime scene photos flashed again in her mind. She imagined something like that happening *again* because she'd allowed it to.

"No," she stated, setting her jaw. "We have the power to stop this. I can find clues and details the police can't. I cannot and will not allow myself to stand by while this...person gets away with murder."

Chris and Stephanie were the first to nod. Lia joined them a couple of seconds later.

"Okay," Steph said. "I guess that settles it. We're still doing, um, *exciting* stuff after all."

The majority of the council—the *surviving* council—had remained at James's estate throughout the week. The various members of the lesser covens had gone home to see to their own affairs and also to think about their coming course of action. Half the council was at Lady Mitchell's place, and the two residences had set up a conference call after James had hooked up his large-screen plasma TV to the internet.

At the moment, the call was well underway. James sat front and center within his study (which still hadn't fully recovered from the mess created by all the recent guests), with Mother LeBlanc, Amanda Moore, Rufus Mayer, and Crystal Green spread out to his sides. Ezeudo was there too, hovering in the rear of the room.

Everyone else was at the Mitchell estate, the six of them staring into the screen, with Lady Mitchell presiding over the group. Two of her begonias rested on the mantelpiece behind her.

"Okay," James began, "I think all the votes are in now. Shall we go straight to counting them, or should we include a preamble or something?"

Josiah Kane suggested, "Let's tally the votes. That way, we will have more time to discuss the results after the fact. Much more important than formalities. Besides, after James's performance at the recent congress, I'd say we don't particularly need to hear his introduction."

A few people tittered; others frowned in disapproval at the barb. Hands clenched and unclenched nervously. Bodies were held rigid. Eyes darted about. The tension was thick enough that it filtered through the cameras in both directions. None of them had slept too well. Their sense of unity was growing frayed.

"Cute," James quipped. "I already apologized for not scripting my own words as well as I did everyone else's. Anyway, yeah, I agree that we might as well get right down to business."

Mary Mitchell added, "Yes. I remain hopeful that our friends will do the right thing. At the same time, though, we cannot *depend* upon them. They lack the ability to deal with the current situation that we have. The bulk of this fight will be up to us."

Mother LeBlanc nodded. "Seconded. They are at best our auxiliaries."

James took a deep breath and moved the cursor toward the third of the three windows he had open. In addition to the two cameras for the conference call, there was a third showing the email account the council collectively used for official business. All the messages from the lesser covens had come in.

LeBlanc is acting dismissive, James thought, *though earlier she all but confided in me that she did not have much confidence in them, since despite all our well-presented evidence that they would suffer under the Orthodoxy's rule, they are inclined to regard it as not their problem. Not worth dying for. So, it will be a question if we end up with a quarter, a half, two-thirds of them, or however many agreeing to help us. Hoping for one hundred percent is unrealistic.*

He clicked open the first message. It was nearly a full page's worth of rambling, so he skipped to the important part. The prattle could be reviewed in detail later.

"No," he stated. "That's a no from New Orleans."

LeBlanc, who was from NOLA, could not stop herself from

frowning. Meanwhile, Rufus recorded the results on a spreadsheet program he had open on his tablet.

On they went, opening vote after vote from the chiefs of each of the minor covens. As per their agreement, everyone had submitted their decision within the same one-hour period, but otherwise, they were not in any particular order. Covens that ran semi-major operations in large cities appeared next to others based in obscure outposts deep in the rustic hinterlands of Canada, the United States, and Mexico.

They had one thing in common, though. A trend emerged.

"No," James declared. "*Another* no. Next up, Portland, Maine. And...they're a no. Our good friends have been remarkably consistent so far, haven't they? And we're halfway into the list."

He wanted to laugh, albeit in a way that nobody would have found funny.

As they neared the final quarter of the messages, Mitchell interjected, "Are you sure you're reading those correctly, James? Some of them might be couched in overly vague language." He could see the desperation in her eyes and suspected his own looked about the same.

"Quite sure," he responded. The others on his end of the call nodded, backing him up. They had all seen the same things he had. Rufus continued to punch keys, tallying the uniform stream of rejections.

James announced, "Final message from none other than Los Angeles. Aaaaand...it's a negative. One hundred percent! Or rather, *zero* percent. We have been unanimously hung out to dry. Total party kill."

He so wanted to get drunk. Instead, he rubbed his forehead.

Rufus asked, "What about the Orthodoxy? Did any of the covens vote to back *them*, or are they all remaining neutral?" He had missed being able to read the surrounding details of each message since he had been busy with the spreadsheet.

James already knew the answer, but for the sake of politeness and decorum, he went back and did a fast scan of the results, making a show of ensuring that his response was correct.

He pushed his glasses up his nose with his forefinger. "Mmm, no. There is not a single vote of support either way. Every last one of them voted to stay out of it and let the chips fall where they may."

Amanda shook her head. "The heads of the lesser covens must have had their own meeting among themselves after they left us and agreed to impose non-intervention on everyone in their purview. The newer and lower-ranking members have little power within the small grottoes they occupy. I'm sure at least a smattering of them would have supported us after all we have tried to do for them, but the leaders clearly do not want to risk retaliation. They assume we will not punish them if we come out on top, whereas they *know* that the Orthodoxy will kill them for resisting. They are taking the safest course of action."

Samantha Martinez pouted. "They have no feelings for us? I have fond memories of some of *them*. Did someone tamper with their email accounts?"

James furrowed his brow. "I don't think so. I probably would have noticed something amiss if the Orthodoxy were trying to screw with us, but who knows? As it stands, though, I think we have to assume that we are on our own."

Brooding quiet set in, the members of the council at first trying to look at nothing. Gradually, their eyes were drawn toward the only people they could trust.

Zacharia McConnell speculated, "What did we do wrong? Should we have been more involved with their affairs? Our traditional position was that they ought to be allowed maximum freedom to manage their lives. Is this a protest against what they saw as us being callous and not caring about them?"

Mitchell waved a hand in a surprisingly violent motion. "*No.* Blaming ourselves while gazing into our navels is pointless. They are frightened, that is all. Most of them probably hope we win.

They simply are not willing to risk themselves to make it happen so they can hope to beg for scraps if our foes emerge victorious. We must accept things as they are and move on with plans to take care of business without counting on outside aid. It is only the eleven of us. Excuse me, twelve."

Until now, Ezeudo had remained silent. He spoke up. "Perhaps you mean, eleven and a half. I do not possess your level of training."

James looked at him. "You possess enough, and we'll get you as much more as we can before the proverbial shit hits the fan." Glancing again at the screen, he declared, "If the rest of you would like to come back to my house to plan things out and possibly stay here indefinitely, I won't refuse you."

It took a few seconds before he noticed that LeBlanc had put a gentle hand on his forearm. Without meeting her eyes, he put his hand atop hers. It had been a long time since he'd been so glad to have her by his side.

CHAPTER THIRTEEN

The brush, still moist and glistening with the last residue of oil paint, trembled in the Alchemist's hand. Her eyes stared at the canvas, intense and unblinking.

Is it finished? she wondered. Her mind had been afire with the buzzing, whirling, maddened process of creation, channeling the surplus of artistic life energy she had accumulated into the completion of the work.

I think it might be done at last. It is so close to perfect, but would one final stroke bring it to absolute perfection? Two strokes? Or would that be too much? It takes only a single unnecessary addition to ruin a work of art that would have been truly great without such a mistake. I must pause and think.

She breathed in and out again, keeping the brush in her hand, but stepping away from the canvas. She closed her eyes, counting to fifty. When she opened them again, her mind had calmed, and she was able to perceive the painting afresh.

It was done. It was as close to perfect as she could make it. Her hand, which had ceased trembling around thirty seconds ago, slowly lowered the brush.

"Good," she stated. She advanced toward the canvas once

more, reexamining it up close, and confirmed that her painting—her beautiful tribute to the talent and genius of Luis Domingo—had passed through the birthing process and was now fit to call itself alive.

The Alchemist put the brush down next to her other tools. In a minute, she would have to think about what came next, but first, she would congratulate herself and consider the magnitude of her achievement.

She had recreated the *spirit* of Domingo's classic of modern Expressionism. The explicit visual details were slightly different. The central figure was clearly female after leaning toward looking masculine in the original. The blues were less indigo and more turquoise. The patterns in which the energy flowed were not *quite* the same.

But with Domingo's help, she had transferred the soul of his painting into another. One that would never be degraded by being bartered at an auction like a chest of drawers or an old car.

He should have known better than to sell it. She smirked, recalling that she had made him pay for his ignorance. The main purpose of what she had done to him, of course, was to ensure that his genius would be passed on and put to good use. However, punishing him for defiling his own vision, as with so many of the others, was a nice added bonus, even if it had taken her a while to get the knife clean again afterward.

The Alchemist sighed and turned away. She had never been as talented an artist as she'd always wanted to be. The passion was there, and the dedication, and apparently a small modicum of inborn ability, but it had been apparent to her since her adolescence that she lacked the potential for true greatness.

What she *did* have above and beyond what most people possessed was the ability to *appreciate* art. Even many of the masters seemed unable, as she saw it, to grasp the importance of their own work. And the philistines willing to *pay* for their art were worse still.

For that reason, the Alchemist had vowed that she would survive until such time as she could gather all the finest talent the world had to offer and preside over the greatest artistic achievements in known history. Through sheer force of will, combined with health consciousness and a few minor tricks, she had stopped herself from aging beyond the point at which she would no longer be able to pursue her ambitions.

She walked into the bathroom to wash her face and hands and admired herself in the mirror. She did not have many friends or close acquaintances, but when she spoke to other women, they marveled at how well-preserved she was. Often, she lied about her true age to avoid embarrassing them or inspiring too much envy and resentment. Still, they always wanted to know what her secret was.

"Oh," she would say, "rest, hydration, good diet, exercise. Staying out of the sun, mostly. A few creams and whatnot. The occasional peel. Otherwise, I suppose I'm just lucky."

Drying herself off, she returned to the studio. This time she stood near the center of the back wall so she could examine everything at once.

Domingo's new painting represented the second-to-last piece of the overall arrangement. The ultimate work, the meta-work which would tie together all the fine pieces she had created, still had one hole in it, and *that* was the next thing on her agenda.

In fact, it was part of why she had returned to Los Angeles after spending the last several years mostly in New York. The final artist she sought was unlike any she had pursued before.

An artist who did not work in a visual medium that had a *physical* existence. One whose genius was manifested only on the canvas of the human imagination. One whose work had inspired a whole city and given birth to a genre of rumors and fancies all its own. The Alchemist shuddered, imagining the vitality that must surely overflow from such an incredible person.

She had been trying to find him—or her, since there was some debate as to their gender—for a shorter time than was usual—mere weeks. But she had known that she *must* succeed, no matter what.

And time was running out because the rumors were beginning to suggest Motorcycle Man had disappeared. Or worse, that he had never existed and was simply an urban legend that had attached itself to a number of mundane individuals found helping their fellow citizens.

"No," the Alchemist told herself, looking at the central void in her arrangement. "That can't be true. It has too much of the stench of a coordinated campaign to get people to either believe that which is not true or stop paying attention and asking questions. Perhaps it's the work of someone in power trying to shut up the speculation, or it might be Motorcycle Man's own doing if he's decided to retire in peace. It doesn't matter either way."

Beyond logical thought, a primitive intuition, a hunch that drew from nothing but instinct, informed her that the wildest rumors were the ones closest to the truth. He was real, he was a single individual, and he possessed extraordinary courage and abilities.

Which the Alchemist could put to better use than he could.

She breathed out, brushing her hair away from her face. "Now I only need to find him."

It was a jumbled mixture of feelings, notions, and ideas that had led Kera back to her old place of employment. The Mermaid had been a pretty good business to work for, and she missed it.

More pertinently, though, she needed to talk to Stephanie as soon as possible, and it wasn't fair to keep making everyone come over to her place.

She pushed open the front doors. It was about nine o'clock at night, and the place was busy. Half the tables on the dining floor as well as two-thirds or so of the bar were occupied by a wide range of chattering customers.

Damn. She had removed her helmet outside and now unzipped the front of her leather jacket since it was surprisingly warm and stuffy in the room. *Steph might not have time to talk, but maybe I'll get lucky and catch her for five minutes between tables.*

Five seconds later, Stephanie appeared in person, rushing toward a table with a tray piled with three drinks. Their eyes met and they nodded, and Kera stood back to let her do her job until she could spare a second to say hello properly.

As Kera waited, her gaze absently drifted around. Then it stopped, fixated on a table near the edge of the dining area before one got to the bar. Two familiar individuals sat there with a half-eaten tray of mozzarella sticks between them.

Crap, Kera thought. *It's those two reporters who were always trailing me and trying to write puff pieces about me. Which I guess was nice of them, but...wait, what am I saying? They never saw me without the helmet on, and usually I had a cloaking spell in effect, too. They won't recognize me. It's Motorcycle Woman they were obsessed with, not Kera MacDonagh.*

Briefly, the woman glanced at Kera. For a second she squinted at her as though trying to remember something, then she returned to her food, drink, and conversation with her partner. The man had his back to Kera and did not notice.

She sighed in relief.

Stephanie hastened to her side, pausing and wiping the sweat from her hands on the edges of her apron. "Hey, girl. You had to come on a night when we're doing good business. I got a sec, though. You okay?"

"Yeah, mostly." Kera scanned their surroundings to ensure no one was paying close attention to them. "I want to ask your opinion about how to, um, go about something. It might take a couple of minutes."

She could tell that Steph, who seemed to be on the verge of

bursting into motion at any second, did not have entire minutes to spare just yet. "I dunno about all that. Might have to wait till my shift's over, but we'll see, okay?"

Kera smiled. "Okay. I'll hang out for an hour-ish."

As her friend hustled back toward the kitchen, Kera sauntered up to one of the free places at the bar. Jennifer appeared. "Welcome back, stranger." She grinned. "What'll it be?"

"Hi," Kera replied. "And, uh, a short glass of whatever cheap stuff you have on tap right now. I'm not feeling too picky this evening."

Jenn, who didn't have much time to talk either, produced the beer, asked her briefly how she was doing, and then went back to her other customers.

To Kera's surprise, Cevin appeared a moment later. He noticed her and walked over while she sat sipping her drink.

"Hello again. Good to see you. I'll be right back, okay?"

She nodded, reflecting on her poor luck. None of her friends had time for her, but then again, they all had bills to pay and a business to run. Same as her.

Cevin moved past her to the table where the two reporters were sitting. Kera heard most of their conversation through the general buzzing din with the aid of a minor focus and amplification charm she surreptitiously cast while staring vacantly at the wall.

"Hi, Doug. Hi, Mia. So happy to see you here again. You two have been a godsend as far as getting my books back in the black. I was afraid I'd have to declare bankruptcy for a while there after we got all that negative press about the gangsters fighting in the parking lots and stuff."

Ah, yes, Kera ruminated. *The reporters came in here looking for my alter ego and must have gotten attached to the place.*

"No problem!" Doug threw back, his tone jovial. "You guys seriously have the best mozz sticks in town. I don't know what your cooks do with them, but they're incredible. Or maybe it's the marinara rather than the sticks themselves. Whatever."

Mia added, "And the drinks aren't half bad either. But yeah, we're always willing to help out a deserving local business. Now that the whole Motorcycle Man situation is settling down, we're being shuffled back to 'local interest' stuff. It isn't as exciting, but if it means we get to check out bars and restaurants as part of 'work,' I'm not about to complain."

Kera wasn't looking at them, but in her mind's eye, she could see Cevin blushing with half-embarrassed gratitude. "Thanks so much. We had someone from a magazine in here two days ago, and he mentioned that he was here on your recommendation."

They talked for another minute about mundane things, then Mia inquired if Cevin had seen or heard anything about "mysterious characters" operating around the property.

Kera's abdominal muscles tightened. *Nothing to worry about,* she assured herself. *Of course journalists are going to ask stuff like that. I'm not sensing a suspicious vibe from them, or nothing directed at me, anyway.*

"Nah," said Cevin. "Things have been normal and peaceful lately."

He took his leave and moved back toward Kera at the same moment some guy next to her began asking if she rode a motorcycle.

She looked up; the man was halfway drunk but was seemingly just being friendly. "Oh, yeah," she confessed. "My usual ride. Like, I don't see the point in bothering with a car. A bike will get me to work and back as easily as anything else will, and it's not like we get snow here, ha."

The man made a couple of banal comments, and Kera did not notice Doug or Mia paying any renewed attention to her. She relaxed.

Finally, Stephanie got a short break and motioned her over.

The two of them circled around the bar into the hall that led to the small employee lounge and locker area in the back.

"Okay," said Steph, "what's up? I can guess the basic idea, of course."

Kera let out a ragged-edged sigh. "We have a murderer to catch, and I have no idea where to start. From what I'm reading, we probably won't be able to simply walk up to the morgue and demand they show us Domingo's body. Not that I *want* to see that in real life anyway. But without being able to examine the...evidence, I have no idea what other leads we might be able to pursue."

She let her shoulders slump. After how confident she had felt in her conclusions about *who* the culprit was, it made her cheeks burn with shame to admit that she was stumped about where to go from here.

Stephanie narrowed her eyes as her brain raced. "Wait a minute. I think I got it. Since we started the agency, you've been trying to turn over a new leaf, right? Well, okay, we're doing what we do mostly out in the open now, but that doesn't mean you or I have changed, like, in terms of what we can *do*. You're going about this like a normal person would."

Kera blinked. Oddly, that hadn't occurred to her.

"So," her friend went on, "you ought to be using the same powers you used before to find things out. Cast a scrying spell to get the information you need, something like that. I can maybe help you later, but I'll have to get back to work in a minute here."

The invisible weight lifted from Kera's shoulders, at least in part. There were still questions about how to go about it, but she no longer felt as lost as she had.

"Yeah, you're right," she conceded, putting her hands on her hips. "Thanks, Steph. I only wish I'd have come in sooner since I want to talk to the Kims about it before I jump into anything, and they're probably in bed now."

They began wandering back toward the main floor. "Well," Steph quipped, "might be better for you to sleep on it anyway."

"Perhaps." Kera frowned. "As long as the Art Slasher doesn't strike again overnight."

She somehow doubted it. Their culprit struck her as a meticulous person who would be unlikely to leap into multiple serious crimes in such a short period. Then again, they had murdered Domingo less than a week after stealing the painting.

Dammit, Kera lamented. *I suppose I could drive by the convenience store and see if there's still a light on upstairs.*

CHAPTER FOURTEEN

Kera had, to her disappointment, overslept and missed her opportunity to catch the Kims in the early morning. There had been no light on at their place last night, so she had resolved to rest and think. She succeeded a little too well.

After dragging herself out of bed at eleven, she figured the next best thing would be to visit the convenience store during the half-hour when Mr. Kim usually closed the place for lunch. That would be a better option than waiting until evening.

She pulled Zee into the side lot at 12:58 p.m. The store typically stayed open from noon until one to cater to business people on *their* lunch hour, with the Kims taking their own break afterward.

She congratulated herself as she left Zee in his usual parking space. "Hey, at least I'm still punctual."

When she entered the shop, Mr. Kim greeted her at once. "Hi, Kera. I am preparing to close up for lunch. If you want to see Mrs. Kim, I am sorry to say she's not feeling very well. There was a complication with her cancer treatments the other day, and she has started chemotherapy."

Kera's heart tried to jump into her throat, and her eyes widened. "Oh, no. Is she okay?"

Though she knew it was stupid, she wanted to blame herself. *I could have continued with my own healing spells in addition to the other treatments she is receiving. Maybe she would have been fully recovered by now if I had.*

Mr. Kim flapped a hand. "She is mostly fine, but she will have to continue her treatments for some time yet. I suppose you can read the report from the doctors if you want to. Anyway, you may have lunch with us. Soup, if that's okay."

"Yeah, that sounds great." Since no other customers were in the store and none were on the verge of barging in at the last minute, she took the initiative of flipping the Yes, We're Open! Sign to Sorry, We're Closed, then locked the door and followed Mr. Kim back to the family's living quarters.

"Well," Kera commented, "I was going to stop over this morning, but I guess that wouldn't have worked if you were at the clinic or hospital or wherever. I've been free of working at the bar for a few weeks now, but my sleep schedule refuses to adjust to the whole nine-to-five thing."

Mr. Kim chuckled. "Give it time. But yes, if you are running a legitimate business, it is better to be awake at the same times your customers probably are."

"I'll keep that in mind. Though I suppose Lia—and Chris in the long run—could handle the daytime stuff if needed and leave the nights to me."

The older man shrugged. "That might also work."

They found Mrs. Kim lying on the couch in the living room, as she used to do when the cancer was on the verge of killing her, and the sight made Kera want to cry. She looked healthier on the whole than she had then, though.

"Oh," the woman said, stirring. "Hello, Kera. I am not feeling good for training, but we can talk."

"That's fine." Kera, along with Mr. Kim, helped her into a

sitting position. "I didn't want to go out to the dojang today anyway. I just, um, wanted to ask a few things."

Is it right of me to ask them for help with a scrying spell? Mr. Kim will have to get back to work shortly, and Mrs. Kim is sick. But someone might get killed if I can't pull this off. Fuck it, I'll just tell them everything upfront.

While Mr. Kim reheated the soup, she explained the situation —that she and her friends had inadvertently stumbled into a murder case, and she was feeling a strange lack of confidence in her ability to solve it. And she needed help, or advice if nothing else.

They sat down at the table and dug into their soup.

"Huh," Mr. Kim remarked. "Your luck is ridiculously terrible. Sorry. But it seems as though the universe will not let you get away from dangerous things. We worry about you, but we also know that you can handle yourself. What do you need help with?"

Though Mrs. Kim didn't speak much, she was clearly paying attention to the conversation. Kera addressed them both.

"Scrying," she stated. "It might be the only way to find this person before they strike again. Call it a hunch, but I have a bad feeling they're going to escalate what they're doing. I wanted to talk to you last night, but I got here too late, and you were already in bed."

The Kims exchanged glances. Ye-Jin was the one who answered her. "We can try."

Mr. Kim nodded. "I can stay closed for an extra half-hour if we must, but no more than that. And Ye-Jin is tougher than she looks, haha. We will see what we can do..."

They finished lunch ten minutes later and left the bowls in the sink for the time being. Then Mrs. Kim sat on the couch, and her husband and their guest in chairs facing her at angles so the three of them formed a rough triangle.

Their hands locked together, completing the chain. "Oof," said

Mr. Kim. "I have not done magic lately. Like I told you before, we don't use it much and didn't particularly want it back, but maybe it's for the best that we have it when we need it."

Smiling but otherwise ignoring the comment, Kera expanded her mind and allowed it to link with the consciousness of her mentors. She felt Mr. Kim's mixture of good humor and deep concern for his family—his wife, his son, and Kera. She also felt Mrs. Kim's serene pool of wisdom and sensed that, though she was feeling somewhat ill, she was not as weak as Kera had feared.

"Kera," Mr. Kim asked, "are we trying to see where this person is, or are we trying to see into their head? And do you have anything that could help us focus on them?"

Grimacing, Kera pulled a folded-up piece of paper out of her pocket. "We don't have anything that could tie us to their location, but they're probably still in LA, so we'll have to try to find their mental signature and locate ourselves inside it. I'm really sorry about this, but the only thing that can help us with that is," she gulped, "a picture of one of the victims."

It wasn't the photo of Domingo. Instead, she had printed a photo of Elizabeth Short.

As soon as they saw it, the Kims' doubts entered their shared consciousness. *Please, trust me,* Kera responded, and they relaxed.

They all focused on the hideous image of the young woman, dead for nearly eighty years. Much had been taken from her, certainly her life, but somehow it seemed like more than that. What remained of her innocence, her spirit, her potential?

Who took it? Kera asked. *He's still alive, whoever he is. Who? Where? Is he still using what he took from her for something?* She recalled that the body had been drained of blood and forced herself not to think about that.

She felt the Kims' thoughts and emotions at the periphery of her mind and absorbed the trickle of their magical stamina that kept her own from ebbing too low. They were assisting, but the main thrust of the spell would be on her.

The inner eye was open, and Kera barely saw what was in front of her face. Her thoughts raced through both space and time, following what seemed like a trail of blood that led from the Los Angeles of 1947 halfway around the world, only to circle back to LA in 2022.

Kera went cold. Despite her best efforts to avoid thinking about blood, it was almost impossible to conceptualize the theft of Short's life force as anything else. Her half-assed notion that they might be hunting a vampire popped back into her head. The psychic blood trail led to something that had never gone away over the decades; it had been consumed but not truly digested. Whatever the killer had stolen from the victim, they were still holding onto it.

Confusion was about to set in when the haze over her mind's eye cleared and she saw a room somewhere in the city as clearly as though she were standing in it. In fact, she momentarily believed she *was* standing in it.

The room was an artist's studio. That failed to shock Kera, though the half-glimpsed paintings, etchings, and statues chilled her. Each looked similar to the ones that had been stolen over the years but had been altered in subtle yet unmistakable ways.

There was something else. Kera was, to some extent, seeing through the culprit's eyes. She was almost positive, based on minor intuitive clues that were sensed rather than seen, that the person she sought was a woman.

She suppressed her pang of surprise, not wanting to cause an emotional echo that the subject of the scry might notice. Most serial killers were male, she recalled, and she had more or less assumed she was seeking a man.

Kera felt the Kims add more of their own strength to steady her. The depth of her sight grew, and the thoughts of the mysterious artist began to unveil themselves.

No. The killer was angry but was tempering her anger with a kind of gloating satisfaction over something she had recently done.

Oh, God, no, Kera thought, but she didn't dare break the spell. *Please, don't make me have to remember what she remembers when she—*

The woman had murdered someone else last night. Last night, while Kera had hesitated to act and had gone home to sleep.

No!

The screams were echoing through her mind, but they were not happening at that moment. The murderer was reliving what she'd done and taking enjoyment out of it but was furious that she had killed the wrong person.

Kera saw the victim, a man in his late twenties or early thirties, slender and athletic. She had never seen or met him. He was a biker, and the woman had ambushed him, immobilized him with chloroform, and strapped him to a table, then cut up his black leather outfit before turning her knife on him.

Mercifully, the details of the slaying itself phased out as the murderer's anger returned. She had gone to a great deal of trouble to stalk and capture her victim, only to discover that he was entirely normal and unremarkable. She had been seeking...someone else. Someone with powers she wanted to possess. Her hand descended toward a table and gripped the hilt of the knife she would soon use to—

Kera slammed her mind's eye shut and the spell shattered. The Kims gasped and started as Kera fell out of her chair, landing hard on her knees on the floor. She was going to be sick. Before the Kims could stop her, she rushed to the bathroom and threw up.

Her friends let her be for a couple minutes. She cleaned up and came out to speak to them, still shaken and queasy but steeling herself and ready to deal with the reality of what they'd witnessed.

I've killed people, she reflected. *More than I would have liked, but some of those were accidents that happened during a struggle, and others were acts of necessity. I did what I had to do to survive or to stop other people from being hurt. That was all. I never did anything like what this person has done, and I sure as hell never enjoyed it. This monster likes cutting people up.*

Kera sat between the Kims, who each put a hand on her shoulders. "It's okay," said Ye-Jin.

"We're here," said Mr. Kim. "We saw most of what you saw, though from a greater distance. I imagine you were too close for comfort. Not pleasant, but did you learn anything? It seems like you saw much of what this person is doing. If so, it was worth it."

Nodding and taking a deep breath, Kera sorted through the new information that had lodged itself in her brain. There were other hints amid the impressions she'd received, things that had only clarified themselves after she had detached from the scry and had a few moments to think.

She answered Mr. Kim's question. "Yes, I know what she was trying to do and failed at. She was trying to kill a particular individual but got the wrong person, and the poor guy's body hasn't been found yet. She dumped his remains in Turnbull Canyon, though I doubt that's anywhere close to her lair. I'm not sure where she lives, but..."

The awful truth of the killer's current fixation could no longer be denied.

"Oh, God," Kera moaned, putting a hand over her face. "She's after *me*. I don't know why, but she wants Motorcycle Man dead. She thought that biker was him. *Me*. He died because he resembled the popular image I created."

Mrs. Kim stared at her with deep, dark eyes and Mr. Kim tensed, tightening his hand on her shoulder. "That is bad," he observed, "but you are not an easy person to kill. Still, we are worried. Do you think someone hired her? You have made a lot of enemies this year, after all."

Kera shook her head. "No. She doesn't seem to care about

MICHAEL ANDERLE

money. Makes me think she must be independently wealthy or something. But she has a compulsion to do this to people as well as works of art. Like a serial killer who gets…ugh…gratification from it. Whatever she gets, it's personal."

Her hands curled into fists as the phrase repeated in her mind. *It's personal.*

Mr. Kim let out a half-groan, half-sigh. "I am sorry your efforts to get away from bloody, dangerous stuff have failed. We want you to be safe, but you know we will not tell you that you *can't* stop people like this."

"Yeah." She squeezed Mrs. Kim's hand. "And stopping her is exactly what I'm going to do. She's not going to kill anyone else, especially not someone she mistakes for *me*. Goddammit."

She stood up. "For starters, someone has to find that poor man's body. I'll, um, have Lia tell the police. She probably knows how to safely place an anonymous tip. It seems like the kind of thing people with criminal backgrounds would be wise to."

"Probably," Mr. Kim agreed. "I will have to reopen the store soon. I would like to stay here and talk to you, but we have bills to pay. Will you be all right?"

Kera's instinct was to say "yes," but that would have been a lie. She hesitated, hoping she didn't look too much like she was going to burst into tears or be sick again. What she had been through five or ten minutes ago was, in its way, one of the worst experiences of her life so far.

Ye-Jin spoke. "Tell Chris."

Blinking, Kera turned to Mr. Kim, who was nodding. "Yes, that's a good idea," he affirmed in a gentle voice. His eyes were full of sympathy. "Text him, and talk to him in person later. You don't like to rely upon other people. It's good to be able to take care of yourself, yes, but he will want to be there for you."

With no further words, he left to perform his duties to his family and his customers. Kera stayed behind for a moment, standing next to Mrs. Kim and holding her hand.

Finally, she decided it was time to leave. "Thank you," she told the other woman. "And I'm sorry."

Mrs. Kim gave a rueful smile. She looked like she wanted to lie down and take a nap. "It's okay. Be safe."

CHAPTER FIFTEEN

Hugh Buchanan had been the one to suggest they abide by an old canard of military strategy: "Never divide your force." When James had asked him who had originally said that, Hugh had merely shrugged.

"I can't remember them all," he'd grumbled. "I suppose I should have looked it up before I opened my mouth, but time is limited."

James had not bothered to argue. The hammer stroke might fall upon them at any moment.

Nonetheless, he obtusely resented that the council had decided to make their stand at the place they usually gathered for important meetings. His house. His home. The estate his family has passed down to him with the admonition that he keep things tidy and in order.

Taking a short break from his labors, he stood up and looked around the broad expanse of his property. The place was "in order" after a fashion, but not in the way his antecedents had intended, he was pretty sure.

To the untrained eye, there were only a smattering of things that looked the slightest bit unusual. Landscaping that had been dug up or blasted out and the earth moved elsewhere to reshape the overall lay of the land in ways that made it less convenient to traverse. A couple of mirrors lay in plain sight on the lawn. And there was a noticeable profusion of new plant life, mostly thanks to Mary Mitchell.

An average person would have seen the estate and concluded that something unusual was going on, but then they'd have scratched their head, shrugged their shoulders, and concluded that the owner had odd taste in decorating before moving on.

To an experienced magician, though, the place looked exactly like what it was—a no man's land. A war zone. A place where nearly every available square foot of space was being transformed into either a barrier, a trap, or a flow point designed to funnel attackers into a chokepoint where they could be more easily destroyed.

There was no innocence left here, James realized. His beautiful home no longer existed for its own sake. Rather, it existed to defend him and his friends and colleagues from people who were coming to kill them.

The entire council, plus Ezeudo, plus James's servants, had been hard at work all day. Night would fall in about two hours.

Mother LeBlanc came up. "How are you doing, James? Do you need any help with that?"

He had been setting up an immobilization trap, a delayed-action spell that, while relatively high-level, was subtle enough that *some* of the Orthodoxy's soldiers might not notice it until it was too late.

It functioned via an invisible trigger disguised as ambient magical residue of the type associated with spots where old trees had grown and so forth. When sprung, it would encase the intruders in a powerful barrier wrapped around a field of pressurized air. It could crush a person to death, but he assumed most of their enemies possessed sufficient magical capabilities to protect themselves. However, unless they were exceedingly good, they would be trapped as surely as if they had been turned to stone.

For a minute anyway, until they figured out how to get around it or someone else freed them. But a minute in the midst of a battle was enough time to make a difference.

"Eh," James said to LeBlanc. "I should be fine. The actual spell is up and running, though it will wear off in about two days. The annoying part is shifting the ground around in a way so that our friends will naturally want to take the path that leads straight into the trap without being too obvious about it."

"Of course." LeBlanc walked past him, observing the area where he worked from ten, fifty, and a hundred yards and various angles. She strolled back to his side. "If I may offer a suggestion, narrow that space beside the tree there so it will be harder to creep around the tree on the ledge and descending into this little ravine becomes a more attractive option. Or, instead of narrowing the earth, you could have Mary add a cluster of roots to the ledge to make it even more hostile."

James decided she had a point. However...

"Mary has done enough for one day without foisting another task on her," he pointed out. "I think she's accomplished as much single-handedly as half of the rest of us have today. What's gotten into her?"

LeBlanc shrugged. "Her inner decent person must be emerging in response to the situation. Crisis sometimes brings out the best in people."

James looked across the field and down the hill, where Lady Mitchell was adding strangler vines to virtually all his trees. "I guess so. She could have done something to, like, *prepare* us for the revelation that she's not all bad, though. I'm still in low-level shock."

LeBlanc tittered. "She can probably hear you."

"Well, that's half the fun." James telekinetically blasted a six-foot-long section of earth away from the ridge beside the tree, transforming the gentle slope into a low cliff. The dislodged earth spilled in all directions except toward the immobilization trap lest a piece of debris trigger it. James held it in midair and then diverted it toward a large pile of random dirt and rock that everyone had been using as their communal trash heap.

"That's a start." He swiped his hands off on each other. "And in a minute, I'll *ask* Mary if she would *like* to add some roots to what's left."

LeBlanc moved her hand over the ground, smoothing out some of the damage James had done to make it look more natural. "Good. We've all had a long day and your staff has not had much time to cook, so I will see what I can produce out of my dress for supper once we're done."

James had no objections.

As LeBlanc turned to help Crystal Green with a couple of tree-mounted invisible "turrets" that would freeze atmospheric moisture into large icicles and launch them at attackers, James approached Lady Mitchell.

"Mary," he opened, "thanks for doing so much today. LeBlanc suggested that you add some strangler vines to my ridge over there, next to the immobilization trap. If you would be so kind..." His voice trailed off.

Mitchell was on her hands and knees, nurturing the last of the deadly plants and coaxing it to grow around a tree near the western edge of his property. She turned her head sideways and up to look at him. "Yes, just a moment, please."

He waited for her to finish, then she accompanied him to the site in question. After examining the layout and making several calculations in her mind, she set to conjuring up the seeds and planting them along the narrow ridge as well as in the grass on the other side of the little ridge where the trap lay.

"Nice," he commented and helped summon the necessary water, nutrition, and general healing and life-affirming energy that could be used to fast-track the growth process.

As he performed the auxiliary channeling, offering some of his strength to her, he admired Mary's care and expertise. Her almost Druidic mastery of the plant kingdom and the joy she clearly took in nursing green things were clear.

In this case, though, the "green things" in question were semi-sentient plants that attacked moving living creatures with their vines, which acted like the bodies of boa constrictors and could be every bit as fatal. As with James's immobilization spell, they could be resisted by talented magicians but would still provide a nice impediment. The Orthodoxy might win in the end, but they would not do so easily.

"There," Mitchell said, standing up as the emerald vines curled around the base of the tree and slithered their way under the grass. "Anyone who comes close enough to your delayed-action trap to sense it and tries to escape will run afoul of these dear things. Aren't they precious? It's better not to see them when they're in action, but when things are peaceful, they're quite pleasant to look at."

James offered her his arm. "Agreed. And if you plan to conjure any more, I'll help."

She linked elbows with him, and they walked back to the main tree line.

Halfway down the other side of the estate grounds, while the rest of the council members cast spells of their own or worked alongside James's servants at the mundane tasks of laying wires or setting up cameras, Lauren Jones and Ezeudo stood apart from the others.

"Now," Lauren resumed while her pupil followed along, "this next spell was developed by none other than our own Rufus Mayer, who is a noted master of transmutation magic. You have already learned several procedures within that school, so this one will build on past knowledge. It's a rather nasty spell, but under the circumstances, you would benefit greatly from learning it."

Ezeudo nodded. "Yes, I understand. I do not like the thought of harming anyone, but I will not allow myself or my friends to be harmed either."

"Of course." Lauren raised her hands into the appropriate positions, which Ezeudo mimicked, but she held off on reciting the incantation. "It involves transmuting the iron in a living thing's bloodstream into lead, which will poison them and cause death."

Ezeudo balked. "Yes, 'nasty' is a good word for it, but perhaps it is necessary." His eyes darkened. "Perhaps..."

Lauren lowered her arms, and her demeanor changed. She had shifted out of "teacher mode" and was now addressing him as one person to another.

"Ezeudo," she began, "I see your ambivalence toward this whole business, and I understand it. Truly, I do. We all feel the same way on some level. Having met us, you know that our usual pursuits, hobbies, and passions have nothing to do with violence. There are very few people in the world who truly *want* to kill. Even those who pretend they do, when speaking abstractly, often find themselves far more hesitant when facing a potential enemy."

The tall Nigerian nodded. "I know this. I have been in war zones. When I was in Yemen, someone gave me a pistol for protection, and a *guerilla* with a rifle startled me. We drew our guns at the same moment and stood facing each other. He was little more than a boy and did not want to shoot me. Neither of us fired. Then a bomb went off somewhere nearby, and he fled. I let him go and fled in the other direction. I am glad that I did not shoot him."

Lauren's smile was soft and held a trace of sadness. "I don't blame you. And in this case, as in the civil war in Yemen, the fight is not yours. But you agreed to go into that conflict, and now you find yourself in this one, too. And once again, you will encounter people who might try to kill you, and you may have to defend yourself. No, not might. They *will*. I am sorry, but that is the way it is. We cannot escape from the ancient traditions that govern feuds between covens."

Ezeudo turned away from her, flinging out his hands and uttering a brief stream of oaths and curses in his native tongue as all of his pent-up exasperation flowed out of him at once. He wanted to kick something. Instead, he spun back toward her and demanded, "Can we not negotiate a truce with them? It is not as though you people are entirely without fault! James and LeBlanc had to make a great many *promises* in order to get me to accompany them back to America."

His tone made it obvious that he questioned his own judgment for having listened to them.

The small woman shook her head. "I'm afraid we cannot negotiate unless you consider surrendering our lives without a fight to be a 'truce.' Which leads back to my main point. Yes, our council is not blameless. Some of our actions were perhaps misguided. That is clearer than ever now. But the Orthodoxy are not people any sane person would want as masters."

Ezeudo squinted. "Why? I know little about them. They killed Damian Diaz, which tells me that they are not friendly. And the council seems to dislike them, but I hear only rumors and generalities. Where is the hard proof that they are as bad as you say?"

"Later," said Lauren. "After dinner, I will show you."

They went through the routine so that Ezeudo had a basic grasp of how to perform Rufus's iron-to-lead spell, though he would likely need more practice to cast it properly under pressure. Then James, Mitchell, and LeBlanc called a halt to the day's labors and urged them all inside to rest and eat.

A couple of the servants had put together a nice vegetable tray, and LeBlanc somehow pulled no fewer than six large pizzas in blank white cardboard boxes sporting a variety of toppings from her dress. They enjoyed the meal but spoke little. Everyone was tired. And afraid.

Following the repast, Lauren asked James for permission to

use his computer to enlighten Ezeudo as to the nature of their adversaries.

He blinked and rubbed his eyes. "Why? We just *ate*. Wait, I get it; our word isn't good enough, and you want to see for yourself, right? Well, don't say I didn't warn you."

James pulled up a set of files with photographs next to excerpts from news stories with the text blown up to make the pertinent details more legible. Ezeudo leaned in, immediately feeling his gut clench.

Most of the incidents took place in Eastern Europe, mainly Russia, plus a couple each in the former Soviet republics of Central Asia or the coastal region along the Sea of Japan near the land borders with Korea and Manchuria. Ezeudo's frown deepened as he read the text and James gradually clicked through the images.

"There," James said. "The headless bodies hanging upside-down by their legs. I wonder if they learned that from the Mexican cartels? Well, probably not; it's not as though the Russian Mafia isn't bad enough as is. The Orthodoxy claim to be a sort of anti-church that exists to protect witches from persecution by religious authorities, but for all intents and purposes, they *are* the Russian Mafia, only, like, with magic. Charming people. Oh, and it looks like the extended families of another coven they wiped out got sold into slavery in the Middle East and North Africa. I missed that part before."

Ezeudo closed his eyes. "And these are the people we have inadvertently angered and who have vowed to wipe us out? Why has it come to this?"

Lauren said, "Poor luck, mostly. But they've been aggressively expanding their sphere of influence since the end of the Cold War. The Communists sent them into remission, it seems. But under their current leadership, it was perhaps inevitable that they would find an excuse to challenge a group of our standing."

There was a knock, and Samantha let herself in. "Hi," she said, fluffing her hair. "I made a new potion that turns to gas as soon as it encounters oxygen and makes a nice cloud. Distracts anyone who sniffs it, makes them totally obsessed with erotic fantasies about the first person they see. I need a test subject. Any volunteers?"

James got up and shoved her out the door as she whined in protest. "Nice try, but we don't have time for anyone to be 'distracted' right now. Maybe later, though."

"Fine." She pouted as she walked away.

CHAPTER SIXTEEN

At long last, Kera and Lia set together working, at Lia's desk. The ride had been a tad long and tedious, but Kera had nonetheless enjoyed the change in scenery that Long Beach provided.

"See?" Kera quipped. "I promised you I'd do the driving one of these times."

Lia was unfazed. "It's appreciated occasionally. I suppose it helps that Chris and Stephanie are busy since it's a longer drive for them to come here than to your place. I will have to legitimately begin looking at moving back to the core of LA. By now, the worst of the heat related to my former, um, employment with Pauline ought to have died down."

Kera hoped she was correct. Though if anyone tried to threaten Lia, she would be happy to step in to defend her new business partner.

After Kera had spoken to Chris yesterday evening about the horrible experience of getting inside the Art Slasher's head and all but witnessing the death of the unfortunate biker, she found herself feeling a little better, though only a little. Chris was a good listener, as usual. Simply being able to tell him how she felt had helped. The awful guilt and nausea and desire to separate her own past desperation-killings from the cruel and intentional murders committed by the woman with the strange art studio had faded.

Still, there was another thing she had needed to do. Now, with Lia's help, it was done.

"It's truly weird," Lia had confessed, "to be helping the police find evidence. I did call in an anonymous tip once before, using an encrypted program, of course, for the purpose of sabotaging a rival gang after they screwed something up and left a few too many unintentional calling cards at the scene. Otherwise, I was more likely to be doing the opposite. I did a fair amount of it to our operation after you, um, shut us down."

By that, she had meant Pauline's criminal enterprise.

"Well, I'm just glad that it's done. Thanks so much, really. If the guy was going to be murdered for no reason except that he looks like me with riding gear on and has a similar bike, then the least we can do is make sure he gets a proper burial, his family is informed, and the cops can start looking into it."

"Of course." Lia had, typically, remained cool and professional through the whole thing.

Kera's guilt extended further, though. Feeling awkward, she'd queried, "You're not, like, offended that I immediately came to you about this? I know you're trying to start over and get away from your past. It's not like I asked you to launder money or buy illegal contraband, after all."

Lia had shrugged. "No, it's fine. If we are going to be successful both in a business sense and in the bigger picture of stopping crime in the city and trying to do the right thing, it makes sense for both of us to get the most out of our respective skill sets."

At present, they were working on narrowing down the areas where the Art Slasher might live, work, or have recently been. It was difficult since there was so little to go on. Kera had not been able to determine a damn thing about where the madwoman's studio was located from her vision.

And while they both figured she probably hadn't dared go *too* far with a dead body before dumping it in Turnbull Canyon—it was unlikely that she was based in, say, Sacramento or Tucson or Las Vegas—that did not help them much, given the vast and sprawling nature of the Greater Los Angeles megalopolis.

Still, they considered it a safe bet that the killer resided somewhere east of downtown, west of the Inland Empire, and north of Long Beach and Anaheim. Lia had further begun plotting the fastest routes to the canyon that would avoid the areas most likely to be swarming with cops.

Kera had an idea. "Speaking of which, it's been a good hour and a half since we sent in the tip. You think the press has noticed yet?"

"Quite possibly," Lia agreed. "I'm in the middle of running another postulate, but feel free to check a news website. Or turn on the TV."

Kera had always found something oddly relaxing about local television news. It had an old-fashioned quality that reminded her of mornings with her parents as a kid. She found Lia's all-but-forgotten remote control and switched on the set, flipping to the appropriate station.

Her jaw dropped. "Speak of the devil," she muttered. Lia glanced over her shoulder.

Standing near the trailhead on Turnbull Canyon Road in front of a news van and near four different police cruisers and a medical vehicle were Doug Lopez and Mia Angel, the reporters Kera had seen at the Mermaid who in the recent past had so diligently followed her career as a vigilante.

"...and we'd like to thank Officer Barnes for agreeing to speak with us," Mia said to the camera. "Officer, can you tell us, is the individual the so-called 'Motorcycle Man,' as some have suspected?"

The cop paused, trying to think of how to answer an unexpected question, and in the ensuing silence, Kera failed to keep her mouth shut. "Son of a bitch! I bet those two jumped back on the MM train immediately. What if this gives them ideas?"

Lia tried to reassure her. "Doubtful. It's the crime, not you."

Officer Barnes finally responded to the reporter's inquiry. "We can't comment on that. We're still confirming the victim's identity, and since the investigation is still ongoing, we won't be able to divulge the information right away. But, uh, we encourage the public *not* to spread crazy rumors, but instead to come to us with any useful tips you might have."

Mia's eyes hardened with annoyance, but she nodded. "Yes, thank you for your commentary, Officer, and we'll have contact information for our viewers at the end of this segment. Doug?"

They cut to her co-worker, who had gone partway up the trail to where the body had been found. By now, the paramedics had removed the man's remains.

"Speculation," Doug began, "is ongoing. Once again, murder has become the norm in Southern California. Officers have refused thus far to remark on whether this incident is related either to the Motorcycle Man incidents of recent months or the murder of renowned artist Luis Domingo mere days ago. Authorities estimate the victim was killed two nights ago before being brought here in the early hours of yesterday morning."

Once more, Kera cringed. She should have called in the tip sooner, even if she had to do it herself.

"Lia," she mumbled, "I know it's stupid, but I can't stop thinking that this is my fault. That guy died because of me. Sure, it's not like I contributed *directly*, but if I hadn't gone out and become an underground celebrity, this crazy person might never have thought to target bikers." She paused, squinting as her mind raced. "Then again, I suppose she would have kept targeting artists no matter what."

"I agree," replied Lia. "We are dealing with a disturbed individual with a compulsion that goes way beyond anything you have or have not done. Also, I recall that we were lamenting that we would not be able to use the Domingo-Corvina art theft to incorporate our plan of getting rid of Motorcycle Man ourselves, so to speak."

Kera spun.

Holding up a hand, Lia went on. "Not to sound too callous or opportunistic, but, well, if there's any good to come from this terrible incident, it's that MM is now, as far as *everyone* is concerned, involved in the situation. So, in the process of stopping our killer, we might be able to put the mythology behind your alter ego to rest once and for all."

In her emotional turmoil over the general awfulness of the murder, Kera had not thought of that. Something within her revolted as the idea of capitalizing on a tragedy, but...

"You have a point," she admitted. "I don't like it. Not that it's your fault, but frankly, it *does* sound callous and opportunistic. Still, maybe it's our best bet. I'll think it over."

Lia's nostrils flared, though otherwise, she maintained her unflappable demeanor. "We can discuss it more later. For now, come and have a look at what I've come up with on areas within an hour's drive of the canyon, where privacy is easier than in more densely populated neighborhoods and where there seem to be art scenes of note. I could be wrong, but I would imagine that this individual prefers to be somewhere close to places artists frequent."

Kera peered over Lia's shoulder, examining the possibilities. "Yeah, could be. Oh, I don't know if this is relevant, but there's something else I remembered from being inside her head. She occasionally, in her thoughts, refers to herself in the third person."

Lia looked at her partner, and her eyes widened. "A name? Or is that too much to hope for."

Kera sighed. "No name but a title. She calls herself 'the

Alchemist.' Weird, since I didn't notice anything to do with chemicals or lead or gold, so I guess it has something to do with her art obsession. Or just being grandiose."

Shrugging, Lia quipped, "Did you expect a maniac who cuts people up and drains their blood to be *subtle?*"

It was date night. Kera had needed one. *They* had needed one, her and Chris.

"Mkay," Chris had announced as he opened the passenger side door of his Jeep. "Hop in. We're not going too far from here, so you can leave your bike if you want. I don't mind bringing you back to it."

She considered it, having been too distracted to think about that earlier. About an hour after seeing the news report at Lia's, she could not stand to work on the case any longer and had begged off. Lia seemingly wanted to keep plunking away all night and grumbled something about how she didn't mind doing most of the work.

"I promise I'll make it up to you, but Chris has some problems I need to help him deal with, okay?"

In point of fact, it was the other way around. She couldn't wait to see him and had ridden Zee to Gardena, browsing around a mall while she waited for him to get out of work and head down to pick her up. Fearful that Lia might try to call or text her, she'd switched her phone off.

This isn't right, she'd scolded herself. *I'm acting like an angsty teenage girl, whereas Lia is being an adult. But she wasn't the one who had to see what happened to the biker. She didn't feel the Alchemist's batshit-insane emotions about the incident as though the feelings were her own. I'm going to be useless and messed up until I can get over the worst of it. If this date helps me, when I get back to work, I'll be in much better shape and able to pick up the slack.*

Chris snapped her out of her reflections. "Well, if you want, I can open up the back, and we can probably fit Zee in there and take him with us. In fact, I was thinking of suggesting that for some other time, like we could take the Jeep out to the desert, then ride around on your bike, stuff like that. Not tonight, sadly. But soon."

Kera smiled and planted a quick kiss on his lips. "I like that idea. Loading the bike up now, I mean, *and* our next date being something out in the boonies. Better to buy a bike carrier, though. Won't be dignified otherwise. We'll come back and get him. Where are we going tonight, though?"

She had left it up to him. Not that she was picky, but she was hoping to be pleasantly surprised.

"Oh, you'll find out." He smirked as though he was keeping a diabolical secret, and her curiosity burned brightly enough to blot out her thoughts of the awful scrying session.

They climbed into their seats and headed north. It was dark by now, and Kera didn't bother paying enough attention to all the turns and streets to keep track of exactly where they were going. Instead, she asked Chris how his day had gone and prodded him for the details, listening intently as he answered.

"...so now they want everything to be in compliance with that stupid new telecommunications law, so people like me get to basically overhaul the entire email system despite it being a California-only law and most of our customers being from out of state. Your tax dollars at work, but I guess you could say they're creating jobs insofar as I'm swamped, and they might have to hire someone to help with all the bullshit that needs to be done."

Kera laughed. "Sounds about right. I swear, most jobs exist for the purpose of making work. Like, if everything was perfect, there would be a company dedicated to wrecking things when people got bored just so another company could be hired to fix them again."

Chris snapped his fingers. "There's a name for that. Um, the

Broken Window Fallacy. It was in that movie, *The Fifth Element,* Gary Oldman's character. I can't remember the specifics, but it was pretty close to what you said there."

"Really?" Kera was fascinated. "I only studied computer shit, aside from the minimal prerequisite stuff in other subjects, so I never got the chance to delve too deep into philosophy and so forth."

They took another turn, and Chris began to slow down. "That would be a good subject to discuss another time. But for tonight's entertainment," he coughed, "we have something a smidgeon more lowbrow."

Kera looked through the windshield as they pulled into a parking lot. The building in the lot had a neon sign that featured the symbols for Mars and Venus. "What?" she inquired as ideas popped into her head.

Chris shrugged. "New place that Ted mentioned since he would hear about stuff like this. It's a coed strip club oriented toward couples. Things are strategically arranged, apparently, so that anywhere we sit, each person can look in a given direction and see a stripper of their choice. Both male and female every night."

Kera stared at him, her jaw dropping. She was amused, but the angsty teenager side of her, having come out earlier, refused to go away completely.

"So," she began in a low, coy tone, "you wanted to look at other women and figured you could get away with it if there were other men for me to look at, is that it?" It came out sounding sharper and more confrontational than she had intended, but she was suddenly self-conscious and could not help it.

Chris pouted. "Well, mostly I thought you would think it's hilarious. It's so different from our usual food dates that I figured it would shock you out of your depression. Plus, of course, they have booze."

Kera burst out laughing. "Okay, fine, you convinced me, but only on the condition that I get to make fun of you for taking me here next time we have a group date with Ted and Steph's sister. Actually, we've never had a group date with them. We should do that sometime. Maybe here!"

He chuckled. "We'll see."

As they climbed out of the Jeep, Kera retained her doubts but was determined to have a good time. Even if the experience proved awkward, it would be superior to dwelling on the morbid crap put into her head by the Alchemist.

They went in and quickly found that couples received a small discount on their cover charge, which was a good start. Once they entered the main floor, the place was too dark for them to feel obvious and exposed as long as they didn't sit right next to any of the strippers.

Both glanced around. "Mmm, yep," Chris remarked. "This reminds me of the other reason I chose this place. I knew it would inspire me to work out more. Those guys are *ripped.*"

Kera too examined her surroundings. "Fuck. I'm pretty sure I have the smallest boobs of any female in this building."

"Well," Chris assured her, "I can't speak for everyone, but I like skinny girls with small breasts."

"I noticed," she said and bumped his hips with her own. "Let's sit over there. Oh, and since you're driving, stick to one drink. I think I'll have two."

Chris didn't object. They took their seats and immediately ordered the most ridiculous margaritas the place had available: a bright pink one flavored with cherry and watermelon for Kera and a bright blue one, raspberry- and coconut-tinged, for Chris.

They talked about anything they could think of except the murder, such as recent hilariously dumb shit Ted had said or Kera's mom's recipe for the cookies she used to make. Between discussions, their gazes drifted to the eye candy.

Chris, marveling, wondered, "How do those dudes get that,

like, rippling effect along their sides? Is there a way to lift barbells with your ribs or something that I haven't heard of? Or, wait, no. It's probably one of those exercises where they hang suspended by a bunch of straps and contort themselves in midair a hundred times. Sounds like fun."

Absentmindedly, Kera muttered, "I dunno" while she studied a different stripper. "Man, that chick over there is as skinny as I am, but her ass is about twice the size of mine. I mean, mine is *okay*, but it got kind of flat after I lost all that weight. There has to be a way to do extra squats to add muscle-bulge to the gluteals. Right?"

A guy at the table next to them got up and stumbled past, pausing to turn toward them. However many drinks he'd had, it was a lot more than one.

"Pfffft, hahahaha." He guffawed. "Ever since you two came in, you done nothing but look at the strippers who are the *same* sex you are. Like, are you both bi or what?"

Kera, feeling relaxed as the alcohol worked its way through her system, gave a half-scowl, half-smile. "No, but I'll think it over."

"He has a point," Chris observed. "I wonder why that is? *There's* something to bring up when we get the chance to discuss philosophy. Maybe he…oh, crap, never mind."

He had been about to ask their new friend something, but the man had slipped toward the bathrooms.

Kera nudged Chris's leg with her foot. "Well, if you want to work out more, I won't stop you, but I don't think you need rippling side-muscles. It's just ornamentation, really."

To her surprise, Chris blushed. "Thanks. I like to think I have a *somewhat* better body than most computer programmers. And I think your ass is fine the way it is."

"Aw." She leaned across the table and kissed him.

The drunk guy passed them again, having finished his business and hopefully washed his hands. "Nice!" he remarked, watching them smooch, then fell into his chair and ordered another beer.

After Kera's and Chris's mouths parted, she pressed her forehead against his, allowing her thoughts to drift.

This hadn't been such a weird date idea after all, she concluded. Going out to the desert to do some off-roading and generalized riding around might be more fun, though.

Then her thoughts darkened.

If we get the chance, that is. If the Alchemist doesn't catch the real Motorcycle Woman next time.

CHAPTER SEVENTEEN

Kera hadn't bothered to set an alarm and was surprised to find herself awake at 9:32, which was early by her standards. She had, to the best of her memory, passed out around 1:00 a.m.

"Damn." She groaned. "Chris will pay for this. He should have stopped me from having the third margarita. It's all his fault." She kicked off the sheet, sat on the edge of the bed, and rubbed the sleep crusts from her eyes.

"Whatever," she muttered. "Still a fun night. I needed that shit. Which probably means that today is going to be a rude awakening by way of contrast."

She glanced at her phone, which was lying next to the alarm. Having a traditional alarm clock was technically pointless since the phone could serve the same function, but she liked the classics.

A flashing light indicated she had received at least one text message overnight. She didn't feel like checking them yet, though, and went into the kitchen to make herself a cup of coffee. It wasn't until after she had sat on the bed again and was midway into her second sip that she examined the device.

Kera's eyes bulged at the same time that her cheeks did, and she forced the coffee down her throat, partially choking on it to keep from spitting it out. Once she had swallowed, she burst into a fit of coughing.

"What the goddamn hell?" she exclaimed. "No way. Just, *no*."

Assuming that today would suck had, as it turned out, been an understatement.

According to the four messages from Lia, the city was abuzz with rumors of the challenge that had been issued and the possibility of an ultimate showdown within the city. In three separate neighborhoods, all of which lay around the periphery of downtown, large, obvious, threatening notes had been posted. The means used by the vandal had been different each time, but the essential message was the same in all of them.

There was one in Pico Gardens, consisting of red paint slathered across the entire wall of an arts and crafts shop. There was another in the northern reaches of Historic South Central, made from lines burned into the grass so the dark patches spelled out letters that were only visible from a distance, like from a second-story window or from the air. The third was in Angelino Heights not far from Dodger Stadium, where someone had taken over an electronic billboard and reprogrammed it to display the basic message in the previous two notices.

Motorcycle Man, they all read, must show himself again. He was a coward, allowing innocents to be killed while he remained in hiding. Besides that, he was wasting his potential.

It was time to come out and fight. The messages were generally interpreted as not only a chastisement but a threat.

Kera read on in horror, hoping no one else had died on her behalf. The challenger seemingly wanted her and only her, so it would not make sense to kill anyone else. But some of the chatter on the Internet suggested the murderer on the loose (since everyone seemed to assume that the person who had killed the biker was responsible) was implying that more bodies would pile up if their demands were not met.

Worse yet, as Lia's lengthy multi-part missive explained, at all three of the vandalized sites, the perpetrator had left a piece of paper with a printed photograph of the dead man found in the canyon, with a caption that read, *I know this wasn't you.*

Kera felt as though her blood had turned to Connecticut-winter sleet. Reflexively, she glanced at her doors and windows as though she half-expected to see someone watching her or there was a spider or some other unpleasant vermin on the loose in her apartment.

"How the hell," she muttered, "did she know the guy she cut up *isn't* Motorcycle Man? She wouldn't have targeted him if she hadn't felt confident he was the right person. Would she?"

Her thoughts returned to the night she had tied the Domingo case to the Black Dahlia. She had come to the well-nigh inescapable conclusion that magic of some sort had to be involved.

She wondered aloud, "Can the Alchemist tell when someone *else* has magic? Did she expect something to happen when she carved that poor schmuck up?" Her skin crawled at the hideous notion that there might exist a type of spellcraft that could only be practiced concurrently with the act of murder. *How to Be a Badass Witch* had not so much as alluded to anything that abominable.

There might not be another night to wait and see what happened. The case had to be solved posthaste. Kera guzzled the rest of her coffee and took the fastest shower she could, pinning her hair up to avoid having to wash it and sticking to the basics. She had procrastinated long enough.

Once out of the shower, she texted Lia back, apologizing for having run off, explaining that she was emotionally messed up over the whole situation and vowing to deal with everything *right now.*

A minute later, as she was getting dressed, the phone rang. It wasn't Lia, however. It was Stephanie.

"Hi," Kera said after swiping the green icon. "I heard the news from Lia already. Looks like we've got our work cut out for us. Are you okay?"

Steph responded, "Yeah, I'm fine…so far, anyway. Lia sent all that stuff to me too, so I won't repeat it. But there's something she didn't know about that I got to add."

"Uh-oh." Kera toughened her mind, bracing for what was likely something even worse than what she'd heard so far. "What is it?"

Her friend explained that last night, someone had come into the Mermaid, slipped unnoticed into the employee break room, and posted a note on the board that everyone used to barter for shifts. She and Cevin had kept it to themselves, so it wasn't all over the media the way the other three were.

Kera nodded. "So, it was the same message as what Lia was talking about?

"Yeah." Stephanie hesitated, and it sounded like she was taking a deep breath. "But it had a phone number. And I think I know who it was, too. This strange-ass woman came in right at midnight and stayed until exactly one o'clock."

The witching hour, Kera thought, but she refrained from saying it out loud. *Does this mean the Alchemist is affiliated with the Orthodoxy? I didn't get any sense of that when I was inside her mind, but they seem like the kind of people who hold a grudge for a long, long time, so I can't discount the possibility.*

Steph went on. "She was creepy as hell, to be honest. Had this really 'off' vibe, like every once in a while, you meet someone who you just *know* is crazy. Not like 'cat lady who does Tarot readings' crazy, but, like, something's really flat-out *wrong* with them. She kept talking about random stuff, but it seemed like everything she said had a double meaning, or it didn't make any sense. Like, about how much life the place had, but there wasn't hardly anyone in there. It was a quiet night. Kinda dead."

Kera's thoughts raced. "Okay, I'm glad you told me. What did she look like? Did she say what her name was? Probably lied if so, but still. Did she do anything but talk?"

"Yeah, that's the thing," Steph answered her. "She was flirting really hard with TJ, this new guy who works the bar now. Have you met TJ? No, don't think so. He's okay, but he's like, twenty-five and super good-looking, and this lady wasn't all *that* much to look at. She was okay, I guess, but didn't seem like TJ would go for her. Wasn't a gorgeous young thing, wasn't old and decrepit either. Maybe forty? White people age weirdly, to be honest, so I don't claim to know. She had blue hair, though, which you don't see much on females past thirty or so."

"I see," said Kera. "How did TJ react to her? He didn't, like, go home with her, did he?"

"He was going to," Steph pointed out, "but we talked him out of it. Me and Jenn. Men are blind as hell sometimes, I swear. But it was more than that. She was...doing *something* to him. It felt like it might be magic, but if so, it's a type that didn't make any sense to me. Maybe it was just psychology, hypnosis, something like that, but he was way more excited about her than I would've thought he'd be. I could tell that she wanted his ass, too, but it wasn't like she wanted the D. More like..."

She trailed off, not wanting to say it, but Kera guessed the rest.

"Like she was hungry," she stated.

Stephanie made an "ugh" sound in the back of her throat. "Exactly."

Over the course of the conversation, Kera had felt her mind sharpening. The coffee had undoubtedly helped, but it was more than that. Her fear was beginning to melt, and she had stopped dwelling on the horror she had personally experienced. She'd ceased feeling sorry for herself.

Instead, her view of the scenario playing out around her had expanded. What was happening to the city affected everyone, even if it now involved her in a central capacity. And since she was at the center of it, the author of their recent troubles had begun to seek out connections to her prey.

It was bad enough that the Alchemist was willing to commit murder and that she wanted to kill Kera for whatever twisted reason. The notion that the madwoman would start targeting people Kera knew and cared about had pushed aside all of her mushy, chaotic feelings, replacing them with the intense focus of cold rage and disciplined fury.

I don't even know this TJ guy, Kera reflected, *but he's an innocent bystander in all this. He works with Steph and Cevin and Jenn. The Alchemist doesn't know I've never met him. She deliberately tried to lure him back to her lair because she figured it was a way to have some fun by getting to me.*

What if she had followed Steph home? What if she had found out about the Kims? Hell, what if she flew to the East Coast and hunted down her parents or her dumbass brother?

Kera said in a soft yet firm voice, "All right, Steph, I appreciate you calling. We need to talk this over in person and soon. Are you working today?"

"Nope. In fact, I was gonna ask if I could come over directly, but I wasn't sure if you were home or busy or what."

"Yeah, come over as soon as you reasonably can. I'm going to text Chris and Lia too. We need to deal with this. I don't want to endanger anyone, but the time for fucking around has passed. I'll bear the brunt of it since it's me this bitch wants, but, well, as usual, I might need your help."

Stephanie laughed. "Yeah, I know you will. I'll be over in an hour tops, okay? Maybe sooner."

"Great. See you then." Kera hung up and tossed the phone on her bed, rolling over on her back as another tremor of anger went through her.

Dammit. We thought that by getting into the legitimate detective business, we would be able to pull everyone out of the line of fire. We'd still be doing good, helping people, but we wouldn't be sticking our necks

*out where crazy bastards could slash them. So much for that. Like Mr.
Kim said, my luck isn't the best when it comes to staying out of trouble.
It always finds me, regardless.*

Inhaling deeply through her nose, she sat back up, grabbed
her phone, and group-texted Lia, Chris, and Steph. For
Stephanie, it would mostly be redundant, but she liked the idea of
everyone getting the same message to ensure there were no
discrepancies in what she was about to say.

She typed slowly, choosing her words with care, and reviewed
the text message before she sent it.

**The Alchemist, the Art Slasher, has made it clear that
she's willing to kill anyone and everyone she wants to
or thinks she has to. Well, that's not going to happen.
We couldn't find her, but she's willing to come to me if I
show myself. I'll walk straight into her little trap if
that's what it takes to stop her from murdering again,
but we can still be smart about this. Everyone meet at
my place ASAP. We are doing this tonight before anyone
else gets hurt.**

Confident that her meaning was clear, she tapped the Send
button and waited.

Lia was the first to reply, saying curtly that she understood
and would be there in eighty or ninety minutes. Steph was next,
simply typing "OK," since she knew most of Kera's intentions
already and was probably in the process of getting dressed.

Kera figured Chris would take longer to respond since he was
at work. While she waited to hear from him, she logged onto her
computer and, out of morbid curiosity, searched for updates on
the murder case: the biker, the guy who had unwittingly taken
her place under the Alchemist's knife.

The police had released the name of the victim: Randall
Barnes, aged twenty-nine, resident of Montebello. Mechanic. He

wasn't married, and to Kera's relief, did not have children, but he did have friends, a brother and sister, parents. People left behind.

Well, Randall Barnes, Kera thought, and some of the sadness and uncertainty came back to her, *I'm sorry for what happened. You should still be alive right now, just like Luis Domingo and Elizabeth Short. But for what little it is worth, you'll be the last. She will not claim another life. I promise.*

CHAPTER EIGHTEEN

Lia, ever the ideal businesswoman, had brought a massive flat box of two dozen donuts, along with a couple of cappuccinos. "You have a coffee maker," she had told Kera, "but I figure the extra sugar might come in handy for the amount of work we probably have to do."

"Great," Kera had told her, eyeing the donuts. "I'll make, like, half a pot, then you can dump those into it to distribute it a little more equally."

"So be it." Lia had set the cappuccinos on the counter while Kera manned the drip machine.

Stephanie was already there. "What kind of donuts are those? I've been eating halfway healthy again since I haven't been doing too much magic, but like you said, that might change now, so might as well stock up on calories."

Lia gave a small smile. "I selected a sampler tray of everything they had available. Feel free to browse, but we can't waste much time. We need to narrow down our locations. First and foremost, we need a place to lay the trap to meet the Alchemist, somewhere that will hopefully minimize collateral damage. I've also made progress on potential locales where our killer might have sequestered herself."

Steph stood up and opened the box. "Oh, nice. I'm out of the loop as far as the research you guys have done, but I'll help any way I can. I'm the only one who's seen this lady in person, after all. That's got to count for something. Then again, there isn't a shortage of weird-looking people around the city, so I got no idea where she'd fit in best."

She pondered the question as she ate. "Maybe Hollywood."

Kera had wandered toward her workout area. Though she wanted to help with the planning, she needed to get her mind and body working on the same page and be in the best possible condition when the moment of truth came.

Sure, she thought as she stretched and began moving her limbs in basic warm-up exercises, *we're dealing with a crazy older woman who thinks she's an artist and might have latent magical ability. That isn't the same thing as a coven of powerful sorceresses or a major drug cartel, or even Pauline's gang, but it's always unwise to underestimate an opponent. I barely came out on top against garden-variety gangsters a couple of times. Whoever this person truly is, she has been killing people, not to mention stealing expensive and well-guarded works of art, for nearly a century and getting away with it. She might be nuts, but she's not incompetent or stupid.*

Contemplating the terrible fact that her foe had devoted such meticulous care and passion to something as cruel and ugly as a campaign of theft and murder, Kera felt her rage rising again. It wasn't as cold this time; it was hot and nearing the point of explosion.

She charged at her bag and drove a straight punch, piston-like, into its center, knocking it back so it flew almost horizontal, then advanced again and hit it with her elbow before it could swing back. When it did, she circled around and push-kicked it in the opposite direction so it picked up speed when it swung toward her again.

She crushed it with her foot, impaled it with her fists, collapsed it around her knee. The blood, the life essence within her, flowed, and her magical potential swelled and asked to be used. She denied it. Magic might be required, but she wanted her natural fighting skills honed before she turned to thaumaturgy.

Five minutes into her workout, Chris arrived. Stephanie got up to let him in.

"Hey there. Kera's in the zone; you know how she gets sometimes. We didn't expect you for a couple hours, at least.

Chris chortled. "I begged off by pretending to have diarrhea. I'll pay for it in the next couple days in terms of being backed up with work, but this is important. And yeah, I heard the distinctive sound of her beating the shit out of that poor sack. You'd think the neighbors would call the cops and say there's a domestic dispute or something."

Kera snapped, "I heard that. I don't *have* neighbors in the conventional sense, you prick." She side-kicked the bag, then pantomimed a defensive wristlock as it swung past her.

Chris stepped in. "You call me a prick now, but little do you realize I stopped for chicken tenders on the way here." He hoisted a bag, then took it over to the table. Kera nodded but otherwise remained focused on assaulting and battering her equipment.

Looking around, Lia said, "Hi, Chris. Thank you for the food. Please sit down with Steph and me and help us with the location work. We'll want to have more information to sum up for Kera once she, um, becomes rational again."

Chris poured himself a cup of coffee, then loaded a plate with donuts, chicken, and coleslaw before sitting down to Lia's left at the computer desk. Steph sat to the right. "Okay, what do we know so far? I'm sorry I haven't been available to help much with the data-crunching lately."

"It's all right," Lia replied with a brusque gesture. "You still have a day job. This is all I do nowadays. Anyhow, if we go with the plan of responding to the Alchemist's challenge and agree to meet her somewhere, the place I'm proposing is the Bandini area, far south of East LA by the railroad tracks. It's enough of a no-man's-land in places that it will allow us to confront her without risking too much attention or innocent bystanders getting hurt."

Steph remarked, "As long as they don't get into a fight in front of a train and accidentally derail the damn thing."

"True," Lia conceded. "We'll have to run it by Kera and then hash out the details of how to do it as safely as possible. But it's within the range we established for places the killer might live or work and might be our best bet. Speaking of which..."

She opened a map of the city with notes she'd added to parts of it. "Between analysis of the info we have available combined with a couple of Kera's famous hunches, we've narrowed down the enemy's probable lair to three locations. One is, fittingly, the Arts District, though that almost seems too easy and obvious."

Chris scratched his nose. "That's, like, practically next door. Might be close enough for Kera to just drive around and see if she senses anything."

"Right." Lia paused to drink some of the mixture of cappuccino and regular coffee. "For that reason, I'm putting it at the bottom of the likelihood list out of the three. If the Alchemist was that close by, Kera might have already stumbled onto her. Sure, the city hides more things in seemingly small areas than people think, but still."

Stephanie laughed. "People used to say LA was all spread out compared to, like, New York and other cities back east, but it seems pretty dense to me these days."

"Aye," Chris agreed. "What are the other two?"

Lia zoomed in on the map. "Montebello, where the recent victim Barnes lived. Granted, if she's from the same community as her victim, that increases the likelihood that she might fall under police suspicion. Still, it means she would have bumped into the man more easily, and it's not far from Turnbull Canyon."

Chris and Steph nodded.

"And third," Lia finished, "which in my opinion is the most likely culprit, we have Silver Lake. It's an artsy neighborhood, and Domingo lived there. Far enough away from the scenes of the other crimes to divert suspicion, but not terribly far from the canyon either."

Chris pointed out, "Far enough. I wouldn't want to drive from Silver Lake to goddamn Whittier with a body in the trunk, but then again, my mental health is a little better than this chick's."

"Noted," Lia countered. "I forgot to mention, Silver Lake is also closer to the various mansions where the art pieces were stolen. Before she turned to cutting up people along with paintings."

The others agreed that it was as good a prospect as they had.

"But," Chris wondered, "that's a ways from Bandini. How the hell do we get from one to the other if she doesn't show for the duel or whatever and we have to hunt her down to her home? I'm not sure it would be good for us to split up. Though I guess you plus Kera on the one hand, and me plus Steph on the other could work. One computer geek and one witch per team."

Steph liked the idea. "Right, right. Better than all four of us trying to rush all over town." She glanced at the gym area, where the sounds of Kera's furious battle with her heavy bag had not abated.

Chris looked too. "I'm a little worried about her. I think she's taking this personally. She was really messed up after that Barnes guy died. Blames herself, though I think I mostly convinced her that it wasn't her fault."

Stephanie got up. "I'll talk to her." She strolled over, getting close enough so she could address her friend without yelling but still at a safe distance in case Kera overshot one of her kicks. "Kera. How you doing?"

"Fine," she stated. Her eyes were narrowed but blazing, fixed on the bag as she pummeled it and dodged imaginary counter-attacks.

Steph had half a mind to join her since she was out of practice. She stretched for a minute or two, then gently stepped onto the mat and pushed the bag toward Kera after it swung away. "It okay if I practice a little, too? We might have to fight together, or we might need to split up. We were just talking about it. What do you think?"

Kera launched into a sidekick that practically sent the bag flying off its chain, though she had aimed it so it went to the side rather than at Stephanie. "I'll let you know shortly."

Steph sighed. "This ain't your fault, girl. It's not like when you were first out riding as Motorcycle Dude, you had any way of knowing an art thief would turn out to be a serial killer who for whatever dumbass reason would get obsessed with you. How the hell is anyone supposed to expect *that?*"

Kera stopped, breathing heavily and wiping the sweat from her brow. While she took a much-needed break, Stephanie drilled a few of the basic maneuvers she had learned from her friend.

"Yeah," Kera gasped. "It's not my fault up to this point. But if we don't stop her *tonight*, it will *become* my fault because I failed, and that's not going to happen."

The fire was coming back into her eyes. Noticing it, Steph warned, "Okay, but don't pass out before the fight even starts. Have a donut, how about?"

James Lovecraft had lived in upstate New York his whole life. He had traveled extensively, but his inner notion of what constituted "normal" weather and seasonal patterns was definitely a product of his home. September was well underway, and it was usually in September that a particular day arrived with a breeze, a feeling in the air that went beyond mere temperature, that announced summer was over.

That day was today, he was certain.

The wind was chilly and enigmatically threatening, and the sky was overcast with slate-hued clouds. The leaves' color had only begun to change around the edges here and there, but enough of them had started to die that when the first breeze of the season rolled in, it knocked a handful loose, scattering them, red and crumpled, amid the still-green grass.

It was beautiful, though it warned that winter would be along soon. James was surprised by his calm as he stared out the second-floor window.

Beside him, Zacharia McConnell fingered the coyote-fur shawl she wore. She had found the creature—dead, of course, since she would never have killed a living thing to make herself a garment.

"They're here," she stated. Her voice wasn't much stronger than a whisper, though they all heard it in the hush that had fallen over the mansion.

James nodded. "I noticed. They have good cloakers. Not *quite* good enough, but if we were one notch, maybe two, down the totem pole, they might have snuck right up to the front door before we noticed them."

Ezeudo was standing about five paces behind them. "How many of them are there? Can you tell? I cannot see anything."

Amanda Moore, standing at the next window and stroking the fur of her black cat, leaned forward to squint at what lay ahead, then rolled her head back as though listening for something behind her. Given that her specialty was animal engagement, she had the keenest senses of them all.

"Eighty at a minimum. A hundred at most, unless they have another auxiliary force waiting farther out."

Ezeudo made a choking, spluttering sound. "Eighty? One *hundred?* They outnumber us *nine-to-one!*"

James adjusted his glasses, keeping his eyes on the fields and hills and thickets beyond the window. "Your arithmetic is sound, assuming you went with the high end of Amanda's estimates rather than the mean number. Well done."

Mother LeBlanc sighed. "James, please be quiet. Now would be a good time for you to finally have *one* drink. It might actually do you good."

He walked over to an oak cabinet. "Your idea, not mine. This bottle has been here for a while as an emergency backup, but it's only half-empty. Wait, I mean half-*full*. Does anyone else want a sip?"

They ended up passing it around. It was old whiskey of middling quality, and everyone save Hugh, who was a teetotaler, and Lauren, who claimed dark liquors made her sick, had a drink.

By the time they were finished, the Orthodoxy's army had begun its advance across the grounds.

James watched. He was not shocked to observe that rather than send everyone forth at once in a coordinated, collaborative effort, their enemies began by unleashing a wave of uncloaked witches—younger recruits, most likely—to not only act as shock troops but as minesweepers. The Grandmistress had probably promised rewards to those who survived the experience.

The cloaking spell that hid the first of the attackers came to an abrupt end. Men and women (the balance favoring the latter) streamed across the grass at a trot or a jog, their bodies tense with excitement as they moved and their eyes shining with anticipation. There were twenty of them out front, and James guessed there were another ten advancing from the back of the property.

Most of them didn't get far. The vines enveloping the tree line to the west sprang into the air like grasping tentacles, seizing three witches in their coils. Screams of pain and alarm rose through the air.

At the same time, there came the rushing of disturbed wind and crystalizing water as Ms. Green's "turrets" fired a volley of icicles the size of daggers toward the intruders. One careless young man who was front and center went down shrieking with four of the projectiles embedded in his torso. A girl took another of the shards in her leg, then stumbled, horrified, into the clutches of a vine that was hidden in the grass.

"Oh, God." Ezeudo groaned. "I do not wish to see this. Are they just throwing away the lives of their youngest people?"

James shrugged. "Hopefully, yes. Wait, the others are moving in. Still cloaked. Oh, *crap.*"

With the first line of defenses having been breached and the traps sprung, the more senior and talented of the troops moved in to neutralize the council's defensive spells. The man who'd been impaled by icicles and one of the women who had been effectively broken in half between two vines that hung from two adjacent trees were clearly dead.

James doubted the Orthodoxy cared much about those two, but they *were* making an effort to save the others. Their leadership was willing to expose its lowly members to immense danger but was still smart enough to conserve its numbers when feasible. The better to overwhelm their targets.

To crush the council utterly, to erase it from existence.

As the senior members locked their powers against the traps, defenses, and counterattacks protecting the estate and began sweeping them aside with disturbing ease and speed, James turned to Lady Mitchell and asked, "Hey, didn't you have something else up your sleeve that could be activated on command? And Amanda, where's the cavalry?"

Mitchell was already going into a minor trance and raising her hands in the appropriate thaumaturgic gestures. Meanwhile, Moore's cat began acting strangely. It circled around her legs, looking up at her with impatience and anticipation as though it were awaiting orders. Amanda's gaze was on the woods surrounding the estate's grounds.

Ezeudo, who had taken to pacing between the rows of the thaumaturgists in his agitation, asked, "What are they doing?"

James replied in a soft voice, "You'll see. Wait a moment."

Mary Mitchell finished her incantation. "No, you will *not* see. Not yet, in any event. But our friends seem to have missed a little something. So far." A hard smirk formed on the corners of her mouth.

Ezeudo came up to the window between James and LeBlanc and watched as Amanda Moore's spell of calling reached its apex and its effects manifested below, to startling effect.

The woods rippled as forms darted out. Deer, coyotes, raccoons, snakes, and birds all emerged in a maddened wave, making beelines toward the advancing witches, most of whom froze. They had not been expecting a flanking attack.

It didn't take them long to react. Light flashed and noise rose as a dozen attack spells, mostly brute elemental force, were cast to repel the creatures.

Zacharia McConnell covered her face. "Oh, no. I cannot stand to see this. Why must they die in *our* fight?"

In a sharp tone, Amanda shot back, "I'm not happy about it either, but these are circumstances of dire necessity. The beasts and birds of the woods pledged to answer my call for help if the day came, and so they have. Their deaths may help us survive. If we are lucky."

James watched. Two more of the Orthodoxy's lower-echelon troops died screaming, one as he was trampled by a whole family of deer and gored by the buck's antlers. Another, a woman, found her legs entwined by snakes as birds attacked her face and throat, leaving her limp and lifeless when they fluttered off.

Mostly, the animals died by the dozen. The witches burned, blasted, froze, and electrocuted them, or crushed them beneath piles of earth or with pressurized gravity spells, scattering the earth with their blood, fur, scales, and feathers.

With a certain grim satisfaction, James nodded as two witches tried to escape a pack of coyotes and blundered into his immobilization spell, freezing in place as the magic trapped them, helpless.

But otherwise, the Orthodoxy's army proceeded across the lawn. Ultimately, the defenses the council had laid would do little more than dent their numbers. When the two groups met face to face, the Orthodoxy would be stronger by far, even after their minimal losses.

LeBlanc seemed to sense his thoughts. "It's your house, James," she pointed out. "Home field advantage."

"Yeah," he muttered. "And we're going to need every advantage we can get."

CHAPTER NINETEEN

The bathroom door opened and out stepped Chris, shrugging his shoulders and adjusting the lapel and sleeves. "Okay." He exhaled, standing up straight and looking around Kera's warehouse. "How do I look? Anyone? I liked what I saw in the mirror, but it's always good to get a second opinion."

Kera peered through narrowed eyelids at her boyfriend, half-amused and half-concerned that he had finally blown out his cerebral cortex from working too hard and might need to be institutionalized with due haste.

"You look, um, fine," she stated. "The weather's still a bit warm for that though, don't you think?"

Lia blinked, not saying anything, and Stephanie burst out laughing.

"No, no," Steph opined, waving her hand in Chris's direction. "He looks fabulous, at least according to what he seems to have in mind. The problem is, whatever he has in mind makes no damn sense."

Chris's face drooped in disappointment, and his body language suggested he was crestfallen. "What do you mean, 'doesn't make sense?' We're private detectives now! It makes *perfect* sense for me to wear a trench coat. Like, isn't that part of the official uniform of our profession?"

He extended his arms to the sides, allowing the full sleeves to hang off his arms, then spun to show the coat off from the back so its lower reaches twirled in the air.

"Um," Lia said, "you might be confusing present-day reality with old movies or something. I'm fairly certain most private investigators these days dress like ordinary businessmen. You might be better off dressing the way you do at your day job at the office, truth be told."

Chris sighed. "Well, that's no fun. But, um, the nights are getting chillier lately, so I'm going to wear the damn thing tonight and see how it goes. If it becomes a liability, I'll pawn it off to Goodwill or something. But none of you," he pointed his finger at the three women, "are going to kill and ravage my dreams just yet. Oh, no. I'm *wearing* this thing when we hit the streets later, and there's nothing you can do to stop me."

He walked forward, pretending to ignore them, and sat down at the computer desk next to Lia to help her with their last round of data analysis.

Kera laid a hand on his arm. "It doesn't look bad on you exactly, but even by LA standards, it looks...uncommon, I guess? Might attract extra attention. But you're going to be in the van... er, Jeep anyway, and I'll have the whole vehicle cloaked with a nice inattention charm, so it ought to be a moot point."

She paused. "Which means, if you were planning to show the coat off, then, well, sorry."

Chris tapped a few keys on the keyboard, bringing up a spreadsheet. Without looking at her, he remarked, "Well, having it on will make me *feel* better, and that's the important thing."

Stephanie added, "Oh, like how some kids need to have a security blanket with them at all times?"

"Hey!" Chris snapped. "I'll pretend I didn't hear that."

Lia, letting her breath out in a ragged expulsion to indicate that she was done with the subject, intervened. "Let's focus on work, please. Thanks. We still aren't entirely sure which location to stake out as a secondary target if the Alchemist doesn't show at the rendezvous point, but I think we can narrow it down. And in the meantime, let's go over our rough outline of the plan as a whole."

Kera nodded. "Yeah, you're right. We're running out of time and need to make our move soon. I don't like going into battle without even being positive of *where* the battle is going to take place, but we can't let this maniac kill another innocent person, so we're going to do the best we can with what we have *now*. And I couldn't ask for a better team, honestly. We've been through a lot together in a matter of weeks. We can do this."

It seemed it grew warmer in the broad space of her converted apartment. They drew closer, feeling mutual gratitude for each other's company.

Lia took a moment to add a new bit of commentary. "Before we get started, I just got an email from Johnny. He's willing to stake out one of the Alchemist's potential home bases, at which point he can either inform us so we can intercept her or possibly call the police and let them deal with it. The cops probably don't have enough to arrest her so far, but it would at least interfere with whatever she might have planned while she wrangles with lawyers, bail, and so forth."

"Right," Steph agreed. "Seems like that's the worst of the 'good' options, though, so I'm guessing our focus is still on catching her ourselves."

Kera's nostrils flared, and her hands clenched into fists. "Absolutely. If we take her—alive, if at all possible—then we have enough material for the authorities to put their case together and throw the book at her. She won't escape justice or have an opportunity to kill anyone, or even destroy any artworks, ever again."

"Good," Chris said. "It seems like the two crimes are connected—in her mind, anyway. Like, she murders a person if she doesn't get what she wants from a painting or something like that."

Kera again felt the inner cringing disgust, recalling her moments inside the Alchemist's head. Chris was probably right. She refused to let the memories distract her, however, because tonight was when they would put a stop to it once and for all.

They ran through the steps to come, making sure everyone was aware of their individual part to play and allowing for last-minute changes and adaptations as information about the Alchemist's location filtered in.

First, they would divide into four teams, one consisting of Lia and Chris, and three others consisting of Johnny, Kera, and Stephanie alone. "Normally," Kera clarified, "I wouldn't like splitting us up, but we basically have to, given the circumstances. And it's just one person we're after. We have to assume she's dangerous, but on the other hand, there's no reason to believe she has a bunch of armed men with her or anything like that."

I hope I'm right, she added in her head. *I don't like the thought of Lia and Chris having to confront this psychopath by themselves. Or Steph even, though at least she has magic on her side. But we've been through worse, arguably. All of us.*

Next, Lia would call the burner phone and give the location, then contact the reporters Doug Lopez and Mia Angel, who had previously specialized in covering Motorcycle Man and had leaped back into the proverbial fray after the most recent murder. She had managed to find their contact information, and it would be simple enough to drop a message to them. Having them there to witness what went down would kill the legend of MM once and for all.

Lia could not help admitting that it rankled her. "I just spent entire weeks trying to wipe this fictitious persona out of existence," she grumbled, "and now I'm going to stir everything back up again by deliberately involving those two. I understand *why* we're doing it, but...it's frustrating."

Kera turned to her. "Don't worry. We're only reviving him because this is our chance to finish him off."

"True," Chris added. "Did you have to put it *that* way, though?"

She ignored the comment. He was worried about her, but they were running out of time. Later, when it was all over, she could spend more than enough quality time with him to make up for it.

Each team, as Kera and Lia explained, would go to their respective location and wait. Since the goal was to intercept the Alchemist *before* she could reach the rendezvous point if at all possible, they decided to send Johnny to Bandini, which was the last resort. Everyone else would be at the places they had identified as the killer's possible lairs.

And the whole time, they would be in communication with one another, ready to shift course if new developments demanded it. Chris had acquired some headset microphones that would allow for two-way radio discussion. Kera knew they might have to shut the things off once the action started, but until then, she ought to be able to speak out loud without fear of bringing a small army down on her. It was different from when they had staked out El Peluquero's forces.

"Everyone clear?" Kera asked.

They all nodded. Past experience had taught them that, as the military was fond of saying, no plan ever survived contact with the enemy, but they had accounted for enough possibilities to narrow down the range of left-field bullshit that might happen.

Chris had parked inside the warehouse, and he got up and walked over to his Jeep. He and Lia had decided between them that it was once again the better candidate for a surveillance vehicle, given its larger size. It was also more conspicuous, but a quick spell from Kera or Steph could make it far less noticeable. Neither of the witches knew a way to magically create extra elbow room within a car into which people, gear, and tech equipment would be crammed.

"So," Chris pointed out, "with all this audio-visual stuff, we'll drive past the first location in the Arts District and scope it out. Short detour on our way to Silver Lake. Might help narrow down our prospects."

Lia stood up, closed her laptop, and slipped it into the satchel she had brought, then flipped her long black hair over her shoulder.

"All right," she concluded. "I believe we're ready to begin. As soon as I'm out in the Jeep, I'll call in the tip to those journalists Doug and Mia, which will get the ball rolling. We'll have to move fast and keep a sharp eye on things, but we will have time."

Kera nodded. "Agreed. Make sure you coordinate with Johnny as well, so he's in place before the time at which the Alchemist will have to leave for her supposed rendezvous with me."

"Yes," Lia agreed. "I'll remind him now to make sure."

Steph came up to Kera and gave her a quick hug. "Stay in touch. Don't be shy with the microphone in case anyone needs to come help anyone else. 'Course, we have all had to deal with shit by ourselves at the last minute before, haven't we?"

"Yes." Kera hugged her back. "Be careful, but we can't let her get away. She will kill again if not stopped. Keep that in mind, all of you." She paused and looked at her crew. "It's go time."

The lull in the chaos and carnage came, Anezka saw, just at the moment when they finally breached the council's defenses. It was a good sign—most encouraging.

Anezka, safe behind multiple layers of shields, general defensive charms, and trigger-delayed counterattack spells, stood motionless and looked around. She scanned the area with both her eyes and her mind. Things were going well so far, but it would be wise to reassess the situation before they plunged ahead with the next step.

The assault force she had taken to the Lovecraft estate had lost seven people thus far. No one too important; all of them were either recent recruits of questionable value or, in the case of two, unaffiliated freelance warlocks she had hired for a reasonable price. Two others, also low-ranking, had been wounded badly enough that they would need to remain outside rather than participating in attacking the mansion.

That still left seventy-six, including her, to move against the mere dozen council members. And perhaps a handful of servants, but they were unlikely to be of any real consequence.

The battle was practically a foregone conclusion, and Anezka gave a slow nod.

As ice spells rained down on the writhing mass of strangler vines to her right, a witch ran up. "Grandmistress!" the young woman reported in her awkward, mediocre Russian. Her name was Gianna, from Italy, if Anezka recalled correctly. "We have neutralized all of their defenses except the vines, and those will soon be dead."

Anezka glanced at the plants, which were withering and crumbling beneath the onslaught of an artificial winter storm. "Yes. Good. Return to your post. We are moving on to the second phase."

Gianna jogged back to rejoin her unit.

Anezka sent out a psychic message buried within layers of code and psionic noise to prevent the council from intercepting it and addressed the entire force at once, including those assailing the house from the rear whom she could not see.

Phase One has succeeded. Proceed to enter the mansion as previously rehearsed. All persons within the house are to be treated as enemy combatants and are not permitted to escape. Promotions shall be awarded to those who capture a member of the council alive, but no punishments will be issued to those who kill them on the spot. Also, please recall that you are not to damage valuable books or magical relics unless absolutely necessary.

A vague murmur of collective assent greeted her by way of response as the team members prepared to obey her orders.

She had, with her top subordinates and other senior members, discussed the possibility of simply destroying the house while the council huddled within. However, that would give them too many opportunities to band together on a collective defense spell and would risk the loss of the thaumaturgic paraphernalia they possessed. Anezka preferred to claim their possessions on behalf of the Orthodoxy.

Thus, they had decided instead to infiltrate, kill, and capture —to divide the council members from one another and deal with them individually.

The brunt of the team would breach the mansion from the front via a deliberately direct and unsubtle massed assault. Anezka herself led a group of twenty toward the front doors, while two other groups of thirteen prepared to shatter and leap through the windows to either side of the entrance. Meanwhile, the rear guard would attack the second-floor veranda as well as the back door at ground level.

The council would have no avenue of escape. The pincer would close around them, forcing them to fight a battle they had no hope of winning. Then the cowardly and submissive members of the various lesser covens would pledge allegiance to the Orthodoxy, allowing Anezka total dominion over North America.

She would be the most powerful witch in the world and among the most powerful in known history.

Anezka sent one more psionic message: *Now.*

The witches closed in. She, surrounded by her elite troops, stormed toward the front entrance as the vanguard blew the doors off their hinges with a powerful concussive spell, leaving the entryway wide open.

At the same moment, the groups to her left and right blasted out the windows and made ready to jump through them, drifting on the power of magic and avoiding the broken glass and other debris.

But something was wrong. At least a dozen of the people with her had frozen in place, slumped to the ground, or begun to convulse in agony.

"What?" she exclaimed, her head snapping from side to side as she surveyed the scene. "Stop! Find out what's wrong with them."

Anezka went to the person closest to her to examine the problem. A youngish man, a Latvian, with his arms wrapped around his midsection as he went into spasms of pain. There were tiny red dots all over his body. A fast mental scan revealed the council's treachery.

The strangler vines had been instructed to grow burrs and spines, which dug into the skin and then began burrowing their way deeper into the victims' flesh, doing gradual damage and perhaps poisoning the bloodstream. The effect was delayed, or they would have noticed it sooner.

Cursing, Anezka put her open hand over the man and used magic to draw the miniature blades back out. Further blood spots formed on his skin, and the spines formed a dark cloud in the air above him. Anezka cast them aside, then reached down, grabbed his jacket, and hauled him to his feet.

"Stand up! Pain is nothing. Victory is everything. You are not dead yet, and I will get a full day's battle out of you so long as you live."

The young man was choking and trembling. He would be able to function, though the pain of his wounds and the mild sickness induced by the venom of the plants would make it difficult.

While Anezka and three other senior witches and warlocks tended to the others who were incapacitated, someone on the second floor within the house tried to strike them with a flurry of lightning bolts. A single careless witch was caught amidst the storm and burned to a crisp, but otherwise, the attacks dissipated against their shields.

Anezka gritted her teeth. In addition to the secondary effect of the vines, which had afflicted four others of her troops, still more of them were suffering from an especially devious hex buried beneath the layers of the other spells the council had laid.

Specifically, they had been trapped by overpowering waves of remorse and horror at what they had done in the past or what they were about to do. The flashbacks and flash-forwards were so intense that they could not see what was happening in the present.

Anezka had two of her chief subordinates deal with removing the curses as she turned to re-strengthening the shields around the force in case the council took another potshot at them.

She frowned, watching the process of curing her people of their delusions. It had never occurred to her that their enemies would try to use weaponized *guilt* against them. But it probably should have; Westerners were obsessed with the idea that violence was inherently immoral. She would have to remember that dirty trick for later use.

A moment later, it was over. Two more minor minions of hers had died from the vine-burrs, but everyone else had recovered from both those and the guilt spell. Still, the momentum of their attack had been interrupted. The council would have extra time to prepare.

Anezka repeated her earlier order: *Now!*

Everyone charged, breaking into the mansion all at once. The vanguard of her main team spread out as they entered the foyer, with Anezka close behind. To the left and right, the other teams came through the windows like swarms of bats, and she could hear the rear team breaching the house's back door and windows as well.

Only one person was waiting for them—an attractive young-looking black woman in a bizarre, multicolored dress.

Anezka smiled. "Mother LeBlanc. Your reputation precedes

you. It is unfortunate, however, that your comrades are not here to support you."

LeBlanc looked absurdly unfrightened as the Orthodoxy's soldiers closed around her. She shrugged, and her face was placid and bemused.

"They can take care of themselves," she commented. "As for you people, you might as well get on with it, don't you think?"

She raised her hands, and Anezka did likewise.

CHAPTER TWENTY

Mother LeBlanc knew she might die in what was to come. The possibility was there, and she was prepared to face it. She had lived for a long time and accomplished much of which she was proud. Should her spirit move on to the next world, she would leave behind her present existence without regret.

But she did not consider her death to be *likely*. It was far from a foregone conclusion.

As the Orthodoxy's assault team, many times larger than the paltry number of her own friends, raised their hands to attack, she mimicked the gesture, and both attacked and defended at once.

A protective shield formed—not *around* her but in front of her, both vertically and horizontally. She conjured an entire wall's worth of barrier, cutting herself off from the mass of her foes. At the same time, a thin layer of arcane shield matter appeared on the floor, thickening as it rose beneath the attackers' feet.

Then LeBlanc pushed it all forward and up.

Most of the witches were hoisted into the air and shoved backward simultaneously. They realized what was happening after a second, and some of them started trying to cancel the spell or cut through the shield, but they were not fast enough. Many of them screamed or cursed as the shield slammed them hard into the front wall of James's house, with about half a dozen being trapped in the upper corner where the wall met the ceiling.

Others were thrown through the blown-out doors or broken windows to roll through the grass outside. One unfortunate woman stumbled into the mass of dead strangler vines and was pricked by dozens of the burrowing spines, which had retained their ability to do harm even after the parent plants were destroyed.

Of the members of the Orthodoxy who had breached the foyer, only Grandmistress Anezka and two other senior coven leaders remained, a man and a woman. The power of their individual shields was great enough that LeBlanc's mass shield had slipped around them like water over ice.

The three lost no time in counterattacking. Anezka had maintained a tenuous mental link with them both, and they were able to coordinate their response in the space of a single heartbeat.

While her cohorts struck at LeBlanc with bolts of lightning, fire, and ice, Anezka attacked the Creole woman's mind and power. It was a rare and difficult form of magical offense. When used against weaker casters, it either killed them outright or had no effect because such peoples' talent for witchcraft was too small to notice or was embedded within their personality and life force.

Against an old, experienced, and highly skilled thaumaturge like LeBlanc, the target she presented made it far easier, though it also came with more risks.

Anezka's mind pushed forward in a state of total, laser-like focus. She completely ignored the cacophony around her as her subordinates were flung away by the moving shield. She envisioned and perceived the source of LeBlanc's power as a huge, throbbing heart made of multihued fire like a rainbow sun, and her psychic attack upon it was like a tremendous blade or needle of ice and steel, penetrating it, separating it into pieces, and draining its vital strength with cold, hard malevolence.

LeBlanc's eyes widened, and she faltered back a step. With her left hand, she shielded herself from the barrage of flame and plasma Anezka's female cohort had unleashed, while with her right, she canceled the storm of electrified ice shards hurled by the male assistant so they melted into harmless, sparking patches of steam.

But Anezka's attempt to psionically impale her had shocked her. It was a spell she had not seen or even heard of in decades, a magical attack so advanced and deadly that she had almost forgotten its existence.

It did not kill her, not yet. She stopped it as its point pierced the surface of her magical heart, bringing her pain and fear but not death. The rainbow sun flared up, growing about it an anti-gravitational field that pushed the freezing needle away and softened it with blazing heat.

As LeBlanc's power swelled, the multicolored star gave off residual blasts of pure magic like solar flares. Anezka's companions stumbled backward, their magic momentarily dimmed by contrast.

Anezka did not falter, though. The attack had failed, but it only returned them to a stalemate. Her eyes and LeBlanc's were locked together, yet they did not see each other with mere vision. The most terrible fighting was going on in their minds and in the astral plane, where their essences were now linked in strife.

With both the Creole and the Grandmistress temporarily immobilized, locked in a state of neutrality as they saw the equality of might between them, the results of the next few seconds would be decided by outside factors. Anezka's confidence grew again. She possessed the crudest and most basic of all strategic advantages—raw numbers.

Her servants had mostly recovered from the moving-shield attack, and they closed in for the kill.

Upstairs, the rest of the council had been watching all that was going on. Since LeBlanc was the most powerful of their number, it had been agreed upon, albeit reluctantly, that she would face the attackers alone at first to test the full measure of their abilities. Now they had a far better idea of what they were up against.

"We're fucked," James Lovecraft concluded. "That gothy Ukrainian lady in charge of them is just as powerful as LeBlanc is, and after her, you have a bunch of people who are about on par with the rest of us. Then there are the rest of them. We should have hired Canadian mercenaries to help us or something. At least they would have provided a distraction."

Josiah Kane snapped, "It is not over 'til it's over, James. The number of the Grandmistress's followers who equal the eleven of us is perhaps half a dozen at most. That balances things out somewhat. Oh, and we have Ezeudo. Furthermore, they have divided their force, and their overall cohesion and discipline is not as great as ours."

Ezeudo glanced frantically around, hoping that more of the council would agree with Josiah than James. Most of them kept silent but moved into position for the next phase of the battle.

"Right." James grunted, straightened, and seemed to find his courage. "Let's save her, then. Zacharia?"

Zacharia McConnell had been the one who'd crafted the guilt spell, which had worked surprisingly well on some of the Orthodoxy's troops earlier. The residue of its effects had remained within their psyches and was open to further exploitation.

She raised her hands. "You who would harm us without cause, *dwell now upon this*," she proclaimed.

In those witches on the ground who had been frozen with shame and regret, a new emotion but one closely related to their prior ordeal arose with full force and overwhelmed their minds.

Fear of punishment. Horror at the consequences that might befall them for their wrongdoing.

Ten of the lower-ranking witches who were preparing to finish off Mother LeBlanc jerked or froze and stared into space as their conscious thoughts were blanked out by the emotional upheaval.

Mother LeBlanc, seeing her window of opportunity, pulled a hand in front of her as though drawing a curtain and vanished from sight.

Anezka snapped out of her fixation on the mental battle with LeBlanc. "You idiots!" she chastised them. "They are preying upon your weaknesses. It is all a trick. You must have no regrets. There will be *no* punishment for doing as I have instructed you to do. Kill them! Hunt them down and kill them all."

While LeBlanc slipped away, the council members watched as Anezka's army advanced into the house. They simultaneously kept their eyes on the screen attached to the foyer's security cameras and observed the movements of their energies with their minds.

"Hah!" Samantha Martinez chuckled. "They're splitting up. Perhaps we should, as well? To pick off some of the weaker ones?"

Hugh Buchanan insisted, "Not yet. First, let us perform the agreed-upon counterattack. It will work better if they are not bunched together beside their leader."

"Agreed," said Mary Mitchell. "Everyone, gather close and unleash the spell on my count."

They all joined hands as Mitchell counted down from three. "...two, one. Now!"

The Orthodoxy had been prepared for many things. Most of them were shielded against projectile or melee attacks. Some carried small charms designed to neutralize direct conjurations on their person, though these too were oriented toward physical damage. They had been instructed to expect a wide variety of magical effects to be hurled at any of them.

But they had not been prepared to resist the strongest, bluntest, yet most cohesive confusion spell cast by any group of witches anywhere in the last fifty years.

The combined strength of the eleven surviving council members (since LeBlanc lent her abilities despite still being physically on the stairs moving toward them), with Ezeudo contributing a little of his strength to boot, descended upon the invaders in a massive cloud of single-minded, brute-force disorientation. The spell was so intense that it broke through counterspells specifically designed to combat confusion enchantments, sending the weaker of the Orthodoxy's people into incoherent hysteria. Even the stronger members were stunned and befuddled, for a moment if not for long.

"Excellent," Rufus Mayer commented. "Now the rest. Good luck, everyone."

James turned to Ezeudo and clasped his arm. "Stay here no matter what. Don't feel guilty for 'not helping,' because in point of fact, you *are* helping."

The tall Nigerian managed a grim smile. "I know. Thank you, and be well."

The council separated into three groups. Two would head toward the front entrance to confront the main force, one on each of the staircases that wrapped around the sides of the mansion toward the foyer. The third would descend the back staircase that led to the kitchen and engage the Orthodoxy's smaller auxiliary team assailing the rear entrance.

They would still fight as a collective unit. Ezeudo had agreed to act as a conduit, a relay point through which their mutual consciousness could pass. It would keep him out of the worst of the fighting while making use of his considerable magical talent to maximize the potential of them all.

Ezeudo stood, feeling the link to his co-combatants remain

strong as they dispersed in three directions to take the fight to the enemy.

The group headed to the rear consisted of Zacharia McConnell, Amanda Moore, Hugh Buchanan, and Rufus Mayer. The four of them worked well together.

And they did not have far to go. The second-floor veranda was visible and accessible from where Ezeudo stood. He tried not to pay close attention to the fighting that almost immediately broke out.

The Orthodoxy's rear attack force was under the command of a tall, slender, gaunt-faced warlock who was among the most powerful of their order, perhaps third or fourth in the organization under the Grandmistress, as the council members would have guessed. With him were two moderately high-ranking witches as well as another two dozen or so rank-and-file casters.

They might have already breached the council's sanctuary had it not been for the mass confusion spell. They had recovered more quickly than the defenders would have preferred.

The two lieutenants were first to vault onto the veranda, magically floating while a half-dozen lesser witches jumped behind or to the sides of them and the gaunt man led the charge on the ground-level back door.

Rufus raised his hands. "You cannot fly," he stated.

Two of the lesser witches transformed, screaming in terror, into turtles and plummeted back over the railing to splatter on the pavement below.

Amanda and Zacharia, who both had affinities for animals, winced but offered no objection, for they understood the stakes. While Hugh locked wills with the lieutenants, battling them to a standstill in an invisible struggle, the two women beside him attacked the remaining minor witches.

Zacharia appealed to the animals that lay within them: their common primate ancestors among the apes, as well as the seabound creatures and protozoans who'd predated them by millions of years prior to the evolution of humankind. The attacking sorceresses had barely recovered from the confusion charm, and their higher consciousness withered under the assault.

Amanda, with her talent for commanding the creatures of the wild, seized control of the animal mindsets. "Leave this place," she ordered them, "and never come back."

Despite a brief effort by the commander to stop them, four of the witches turned and fled toward the woods at the edge of the property, hooting, slobbering, and occasionally running on all fours.

The gaunt warlock looked up at them from the back porch area. "You have won nothing," he vowed. "They will return soon." He raised his hand, the fingers twisted in an occult gesture.

The wood and carpet on the floor and the feet and legs of Amanda, Zacharia, and Hugh turned uniformly to granite. Hugh cursed. "Rufus!" he barked. In the momentary lapse in his concentration, the two lieutenant witches he had been fending off advanced, preparing attack spells of their own.

Rufus had mastered transmutation long ago, and as his eyes turned to the petrified legs of his comrades, they turned painfully back to flesh and bone. He left the floor as it was and attempted to reverse the spell upon the warlock who had cast it. The man resisted but could not counterattack, and while he was absorbed, the other council members engaged the rest of the rear attackers.

Ezeudo half-watched the fight out of the corner of his eye. He had to have faith in his comrades, all of them. The other two groups had problems of their own.

The second team, which had tackled the right-side staircase leading toward the front foyer, was composed of Samantha Martinez, Crystal Green, Josiah Kane, and Mary Carter Mitchell. On the surface, they knew themselves to be the most mismatched of the groups, given the mutual hostility of Mary's plants and

Crystal's ice magic, but past differences had taught them how to work together.

The Orthodoxy troops below them were still badly affected by the confusion spell since more of its brunt had been directed toward the main force at the front of the house than the team assaulting the back. Some of them were rolling around on the floor, and others stumbled against the walls as they struggled to get hold of themselves.

Crystal frowned. "Down, all of you," she said, not to her friends but to their foes. At a wave of her hand, the lower half of the staircase was coated with a slick rime of ice. The half-delusional witches in front slipped and crashed into one another, taking others with them as they slid back to ground level.

Mitchell seized the opportunity to weave a dense net of organic tendrils, tying the mass of bodies together in a bundle that would take them several minutes to cut through, especially when they were still dazed.

Three of the attackers, among the more lucid of them, slipped beneath the staircase. One cast a heat spell that burned a hole through the middle of the steps, and the council members had to jump aside to avoid it.

As Crystal extinguished the flames with a cloud of frost, Samantha dropped a small, fragile bottle through the hole. It shattered on the floor between the three hostile witches and a gas arose that worked its way into their noses, then their brains, which were still vulnerable.

The three turned on one another. The one who'd cast the heat spell cast it again, this time burning her friend to a pile of ash, while the third tackled her and began stabbing her with a hidden dagger.

Josiah Kane shook his head. "Pity." Bracing himself against the wall, he tossed his cane gently into the air. It spun, picking up speed, and collided with the skull of the dagger-wielder, knocking her unconscious before spinning back toward another wave of the invaders and breaking the leg of one who tried to climb through a broken window.

The final team of council members on the left front staircase was the smallest but perhaps the most cohesive, consisting of James Lovecraft, Mother LeBlanc, and Lauren Jones.

"Mother," James mused, "how long has it been since we've fought together like this? Oh, wait, Las Vegas. Not long at all."

LeBlanc had spent more of her energy than she'd intended in the struggle with Anezka, but she remained the most fearsome caster on the council. "Indeed."

She and James raised their hands in unison, and a gale-force windstorm arose beneath them, originating from nowhere in the foyer itself and blasting into the remainder of Anezka's forces. A couple of the projectiles thrown by the attackers flew wide, blasting holes in the walls around them but missing the trio.

One nearly struck them, but Lauren easily deflected it. It was a spiky ball of crystal and metal, and it bounced through the floor, collapsing part of the ceiling of James's study. "Oh, dear," she remarked. "Sorry, James."

Most of the remaining witches were driven out of the house by the wind. Anezka and her two most powerful subordinates remained, though, exactly as they had when LeBlanc had used the moving shield. The Grandmistress's eyes flashed toward LeBlanc.

"James," LeBlanc whispered, "attack her magical core directly."

Lovecraft blinked. "Okay. Haven't seen anyone do *that* in a while, aside from, uh, a minute ago when she tried to do it to you."

James sent his mind out in a lance of pure aggressive intent. It was easy to summon the necessary wrath, given how badly these people had fucked his house and knowing what they intended to do to the rest of them.

Like Damian.

His will to kill Anezka's source of power took the form of a blade of blue lightning with sparks crackling around the edges.

He perceived her magical core as a sphere of solid glossy black, lit within by an eerie green glow. The blade shattered against the sphere, jostling it but doing it no serious harm.

Shit, he thought. *I guess it's impressive that I got through her outer defenses, but I'm a grade or two below her.*

Nonetheless, the attack seemed to surprise Anezka, who froze and focused on defending herself as her subordinates hurled gravity-compression spells at the three council members.

Lauren had a talent for negating spell effects. As a teacher, it was helpful to know how to quickly undo her students' mistakes. "No, no, no," she muttered, catching the blasts thrown at them by the Orthodoxy's lieutenants and snuffing them out one after another.

By now, the witches forced out of the half-destroyed front of the mansion by the gale were climbing back in, and those trapped within Mary Mitchell's plant net were cutting their way free.

Ezeudo, back in the center of the building on the second floor, dimly perceived everything that happened and allowed signals to flow through him from one group to another. A consensus was emerging.

The council could not win. They could chip away at their adversaries' numbers and make them pay dearly for victory, but there were simply too many of them for a dozen casters to overcome. Stray thoughts sent to the group between bouts of focus on combat indicated that a plan to regroup and escape was emerging.

James's inner voice spoke loud and clear. *Couldn't we have rented a place to make our not-actually-last stand, then? Oh, no, we had to do this here. I get to abandon not merely my home but my family's home for the last hundred years. Better that than all of us dying, but goddamn!*

Mitchell said, *We appreciate your sacrifice, James, but houses and possessions can be replaced. Please focus on fighting.*

Zacharia added, *Let's gather around Ezeudo. We must weaken them a little more, then we flee as one by whatever route is available.*

For his part, Ezeudo stood in place, trying to keep calm. Each message that was sent through him took a little of his energy. Only a little, but by acting as a receiving board, he saved the council members from having to expend their own precious strength on communications.

A moment later, the sounds of battle drew closer. Lights flashed. Wood and stone and plaster cracked. Flames and smoke rose, along with ice, water, wind, writhing plants, and shrieking animals.

Madness, Ezeudo thought, hoping his feelings would not be transmitted to the others. *This is crazy. This should never have happened. After today, what kind of future can we expect?*

Suddenly, LeBlanc, James, Mitchell, and Hugh were at his side, and the others were converging past them, hurling spells at the encroaching wave of invaders.

Hugh nodded toward the southeast corner of the room. "That way. Easiest route by which to leave."

"Agreed," said LeBlanc.

James turned to Ezeudo. "I heard what you said back there about the future. Well, notwithstanding me being homeless and poor by tomorrow, I'd say we can expect—"

A dozen witches leaped toward them, and in front of the group, the wall collapsed in burning pieces. The Orthodoxy's Grandmistress stood glaring at them and raising her black-nailed hands as fighting broke out again around her.

"Future?" Anezka cawed. "You people have no future. Your country is a ridiculous mess, and you are weak, divided, confused, and decadent. Even if some of you escape today, you will not live to fight again tomorrow. You are doomed. Your council will cease to exist and never again come into being."

Her words struck a chord, and James found himself moving toward her almost unconsciously. In the back of his mind, while chaos raged all around him, he kept thinking of how the entire clusterfuck of the last few months had begun.

With him and the book. With his desire, initially supported by his friends in the council, to secure a future for their order and their craft through the recruitment of apprentices.

A cruel smile stretched across Anezka's pale face. "You will be the last of your kind, hunted down and destroyed as you age into irrelevance. You will never again train *any* to replace you."

James realized what she was about to do.

Hoping desperately that she was distracted enough for her defenses to have weakened over the course of the battle, he tried to conjure a blade of electromagnetic force within the center of her body, cutting her in half. But the spell fizzled, the blade cracking in half as it encountered the astonishing power within her.

Ezeudo started to turn around, oblivious to her intent, as she hurled a trio of jagged lances made of molten metal toward him.

"No!" James exclaimed. There was no time for a counterspell or to strengthen his shield. It had been weakened by both time and abuse at this point, but it would have to be enough. Without thinking, he flung himself into the path of the deadly projectiles.

As they struck him in the chest and shoulders, Ezeudo saw and shouted, "James!" His eyes bulging in horror, he ran forward, heedless of the danger.

LeBlanc and Mary Mitchell, having overcome their opponents, began to converge on Anezka, distracting her with a mass of strangler vines as well as a whirlwind of negative emotions and confusion spells. The three witches struggled in tandem, and the two council members would have been strong enough to overcome Anezka if their attention was entirely focused.

But both of them saw what happened to James.

The molten javelins had driven him back, denting his magical shield inwards, with two of them dissipating into a shower of hot fragments that left superficial burns on his arms and legs and caught a pile of wooden debris on fire beside him. The third, however, pierced through the barrier, its point entering his lower chest before it cooled into a semi-solid piece of dark, smoking iron.

The man gasped, gurgled, and fell over.

"James! *James!*" Ezeudo cried, kneeling next to his mentor. "Hang on. Keep your eyes open. I can heal you, I think. I can..."

James's eyes were already shut. He was breathing, but barely. Ezeudo canceled the shield around him, cradling him as he pulled him behind a shattered wall. Then, gathering what will and thaumaturgic strength he still possessed, he called upon the powers of the universe to do that which he hoped was not yet impossible.

CHAPTER TWENTY-ONE

Doug Lopez sat, his mouth full of half-chewed enchilada and a cold, sweating glass of lemonade in his left hand. He stared at the screen of his phone, which was on the table in front of him, with his right hand hovering over his keys.

"You have *got* to be fucking kidding me," he muttered as his eyes went over the message again.

The waitress who had been seeing to their table drifted by as he spoke. "Is everything all right, sir?" she asked, her voice thick with concern.

Blinking, Doug looked up at her. "Whuh? Oh, yeah, nothing to do with you. Sorry about that. We're fine. Can we get a box and our check though, please? Might have to leave early."

"Sure." She hurried off.

Doug hurriedly carved a couple extra bites of food and sipped his lemonade until what little was left in the glass gurgled between the ice cubes. Once Mia got back from the bathroom, he probably wouldn't get another chance.

His partner returned half a minute later. "What's wrong?" she asked. She knew him well enough to tell when something had happened to agitate him.

He held up his phone. "I just got an anonymous tip. Someone sent it through a third-party program, encrypted. Motorcycle Man is on the move again. That killer who was looking for him and who murdered the biker the other night? They've arranged a duel which will supposedly be taking place in Bandini near the tracks. Call me crazy, but I am inclined to suspect you would be interested in being there to catch the fun as it happens."

As Doug talked, Mia had picked up her glass of Sprite and begun to sip from it. She stopped, her cheeks bulging as she tried not to choke or spit it all over the table. Struggling for a second, she forced it down.

"Now," she gasped. "We need to go *now*. There's barely enough time to get there. You've still got your camera in the back, right?"

He stood up. "I do indeed. I requested a box and our check already."

The waitress returned mere seconds later, with Mia hurriedly thanking her and paying their tab while Doug scooped their half-eaten meals into the box. Then they rushed out the door to the new van they'd purchased. It was nominally Doug's, but Mia was listed as a second driver on the insurance.

Doug leaped behind the wheel as Mia fished in the rear area for the camera, pulling it up front to examine it and check the batteries as she buckled herself in and the engine roared to life.

"Christ," Mia grumbled, "couldn't they have given us an extra half-hour? Or ten minutes, at least. We'll be lucky to make it in time to get a good place to hide and film. The brouhaha might have started by the time we arrive."

Doug grimaced as he pulled the van onto the street, then navigated through traffic and passed slower motorists whenever he could. "Better late than never. The boss is already pissy about that report we did yesterday morning, so cracking the scab back open on the MM case is going to get us in all sorts of trouble."

He reflected on how peaceful, regular, and ordinary their lives had been since Motorcycle Man and the rumors surrounding him had gone into remission. Peaceful…and boring. He could use a change of pace.

"Who cares?" Mia replied. "I don't. If he fires us, our work on this scoop will only make us that much more attractive as hires to some other outlet. It's *still* the story of the goddamn decade. And since we did more than anyone else to bring it to the public's attention to begin with, we should be the ones who close the case on it. Shit. To think, we might actually discover his identity this time!"

Doug narrowed his eyes as they hit a yellow light at exactly the wrong time to risk running it. He stamped his foot down on the brakes. "Well, if this crazed killer wins their little duel, someone will be able to identify the corpse, won't they?"

Mia sighed, seeming to realize the danger of the whole situation for the first time since she'd heard the news. "That is one way of putting it, yeah."

The Alchemist closed her eyes and took a long, deep breath. In, then out. She lowered her hands and zipped up the light jacket she would be wearing to cover the body armor she had donned.

It was a bulletproof vest, III-A armor—the sort that would stop all but the largest handgun rounds as well as shotgun blasts, though it was ineffective against rifles. Still, she didn't expect to encounter anyone with an AR-15. Motorcycle Man might have a pistol, or at worst, the LAPD might be present with their own handguns and shotguns. If they called in the SWAT team, it would take long enough for her to escape.

She had always gotten away before and was confident she could again.

"Oh, of course it's a trap," she told herself, opening her eyes again. "But what choice do I have? There was no way to speak to Motorcycle Man in private so we could set up something mutually beneficial. I had to wait for him to set the meeting place and time. He chose a location that he thinks will benefit him, but he is overconfident. He has no idea who I am."

She smiled, brushing her hair away from her face. Earlier today, she had dyed it brown. She liked vivid colors, but recent events had drawn too much attention to her, and the bright turquoise hair would make her easier to identify. With brown hair, she looked more like any other woman.

Looking into the mirror, her smile faded, turning upside-down. Perhaps it was a trick of the lighting or a distortion of her mental state, but she did seem to look older. Well into her forties, or closer to fifty, perhaps.

Which was still far younger than she was, but it bothered her. Recently she had been confident she could pass for thirty-five.

The Alchemist's hands began to shake.

"No," she snapped. "There is no use, no use whatsoever in becoming emotional over nonsense we have no control over, is there? Whatever minor problems we might have, we will resolve them very soon. Yes. Afterward, we can worry about things like...that." She gestured toward the mirror, then turned away from it.

Despite the danger, she would have Motorcycle Man by dawn —the confluence of his vitality, his courage, and the aura of legend and myth that surrounded him. All those things, fawned over and talked about by other people that he wasted on point-less acts of vigilantism, would soon belong to the Alchemist.

Who could *appreciate* such gifts.

And it angered her that MM had forced her to work so hard for something that was rightfully hers to begin with. All these years, all these *decades* of ceaseless work for no purpose other than to gradually create the finest piece of art in history. Not only would it be regarded as brilliant in and of itself, but people would be awed by the choice of medium.

A masterpiece montage, constructed from the residues of

other artists' failures. Thus, the Alchemist would have transformed lead into gold. She would be remembered for rescuing those who could not realize their own potential.

She just had to stay alive a little longer to do so.

Striding back out to her studio, her mind buzzed with thoughts and plans and barely-controlled emotions.

Never before had she killed three people in the space of one week. Performing that particular procedure on living humans was something she tried to avoid. She had done it before, of course, but the risks were great. It created problems, drew attention to her and her operations, and inspired pushback from the normal populace and the normal authorities representing them.

Sighing, she mumbled, "And in Los Angeles, no less. What are the chances? Oh, it's ironic, isn't it? But fitting, I suppose. Yes."

The first time she had ever absorbed creativity by absorbing life had been in the very same city. It had been her first time in LA, and she had been little more than a girl, scarcely an adult. The war had ended recently, she recalled. About two years prior.

"And that," she concluded, "would mean it was...hmm. Seventy-five years ago? Yes, that, or close to it. Such a long time. Well, it's good I have lasted this long. My work is almost finished. The final piece is about to be claimed."

For reasons she could not have explained to anyone else and that scarcely made sense even to her, her mind began to pulsate with anger. It had taken so long to get to this point. Motorcycle Man was the last thing standing in her way. She was growing tired; after all, she was getting old.

"Why can't it be easy? It's as though everything grows harder the more time passes. I'm closer than ever to the point where you would think reality would understand that I *deserve* total victory by now. But no. Instead, the world forces me to confront a person who seems nearly superhuman. Everything grows more difficult the closer I get to fulfilling my goals. It's not fair."

Pouting, she examined her central setup: the juxtaposition of paintings, sculptures, tapestries, etchings, and calligraphy, all reconstituted by her from the detritus of the original creators' shortcomings.

Only the central piece was missing. And when the mysterious biker's blood flowed and he screamed in pain, the collage would take on a life of its own, and the Alchemist's work would be done at last.

She slowly breathed in and out. Her armor was fairly inconspicuous beneath the jacket. She strapped her knife to her leg under her pants and also slipped a .38 Special snub-nosed revolver into her waistband.

She disliked guns but appreciated their usefulness in certain circumstances. Notably, they were good for convincing people to cooperate with her—people who usually failed to realize that a far worse fate awaited them, courtesy of the knife.

The Alchemist giggled despite herself. People could be so stupid.

She glanced again at her incomplete masterpiece.

What if I have to shoot Motorcycle Man and he dies before I can complete the proper procedure? I might not be able to get the full complement of his life essence if he's dead when I strap him to the table. They have to remain alive for as long as possible, or the magic simply isn't there.

She went cold at the thought. If...*if* that ended up being the case, she would have no choice but to continue with her current program, gradually accumulating persons whose life-forces could replace that of Motorcycle Man.

She hoped it wouldn't come to that. She might need to kill another four or five people if so. It would all be extremely messy, complicated, and dangerous.

Sighing, the Alchemist steeled herself for the evening's work. She might have to face cops, angry bystanders, and other troublesome obstacles in addition to the vigilante biker himself. Old as she was, she had long years of experience at evading capture. Sometimes, her luck seemed nearly supernatural.

It was time.

She walked to the front door of her apartment, which lay within a derelict wing of a condemned building. Using the money and connections she had stored up over the years, she had conveniently had the apartment building scrubbed from any records where someone might want to look into it, and if they did, there were other records in place that would placate them and exonerate her. No one would find her here. At least, not until she was ready for the world to view her completed masterwork. Then she'd open her studio to the public and receive the vast hordes of admirers who would come to ogle her art.

The Alchemist opened the apartment door and stepped into the dark, dirty hallway. She got her electricity from an underground generator that could not be heard from the street. The rest of the building was without electric power, and she had ways of ensuring that running water was taken care of as well.

Her mind was on what would take place when she arrived in Bandini. She paid little attention to her immediate surroundings.

So, when she opened the side door of the building that led to an empty lot adjacent to the street, it shocked her to see a person standing there—a slim figure in a black helmet and a black leather outfit.

"Surprise, motherfucker," Motorcycle Man said in a young woman's voice and punched her in the face.

CHAPTER TWENTY-TWO

Kera could hear footsteps approaching. The person within the dilapidated building was accustomed to moving silently, but not *that* silently. They were good, but if indeed they possessed magic, as Kera suspected, they did not know how to use it to muffle their footfalls, or at least had not bothered to do so.

She took a deep breath and waited. The door opened.

The woman on the other side had clearly not expected to encounter anyone. In the split second before she realized she had a visitor, Kera's eyes fixed on her, and her consciousness probed for the familiar sense of cold disgust the Alchemist's vibe of violent psychosis induced.

It was her, no question about it. Aside from her hair being brown instead of blue, she matched the description Stephanie had given. At the sight of her, Kera's gut roiled with loathing. She could *feel* the aura of sick, murderous impulses, the bizarre hunger to kill and harm and destroy, that emanated from her.

"Surprise, motherfucker," she said, and before she knew what she was doing, her fist lashed across the woman's face.

The Alchemist stumbled back, letting out an "Oof!" and spitting as her head was knocked to the side. Kera had not augmented the punch with magical strength, nor had she spent time building up *ki* or anything. It was simply a basic, thoughtless blow, a reaction to how she felt about the murderess in front of her.

As the woman fell against the wall on the other side of the hallway, Kera raised a hand to her earpiece and spoke into the mouthpiece. She had not bothered to disable it since coming here had been a hunch.

"I got her," she stated. "The bitch was living in an abandoned apartment building in the Arts District all this time. Practically in the same neighborhood as me, for fuck's sake. Well, the next one over, more or less."

Chris's voice replied, "Well, I'll be damned. I thought you seemed agitated when the camera went by that place after we drove by it ten minutes ago. We'll be back shortly. Be careful. You have everything under control, right? It's only—"

Kera cut him off. "Shit!"

For a second, it had looked as though the Alchemist was going to collapse after the first, and hopefully only, punch. But the strange woman recovered as her mind caught up with what had happened, and she whipped a revolver out of her pants, aiming it at the black-clad figure's chest.

Kera dove aside as the madwoman fired. The first shot missed, so the Alchemist aimed at the portion of the outer wall behind which Kera had flung herself and fired again. Kera had hit the ground, and a hole opened in the plaster and wood about two inches above her face.

She rolled back and away, springing to her feet and conjuring a personal protective shield around her. There were no footsteps; the Alchemist was waiting for her to give away her position so she could shoot her.

Fuck. Somehow it didn't occur to me that this knife-happy wacko would be packing heat. She fired two shots. Is that a five-round snubbie or a six? Either way, she has enough left to kill me if I'm not careful.

She was protected for the time being, though.

Kera crashed through the window. The shield broke the glass ahead of her and drove it to the sides, protecting her from the shards.

The Alchemist had been focused on the door, and it took her a split second to swing toward the window as Kera leaped through. She had time to squeeze off one more shot, which sparked and ricocheted off the magical shield.

Grunting and bellowing, Kera plowed into her, kneeing the older woman in the stomach and knocking her hands aside. The gun went off a fourth time, and the bullet caromed off one of the door's hinges to work its way down the hall in the other direction. Then the revolver flew through the air and was lost in the shadows.

As the Alchemist doubled over Kera's knee, she somehow transformed the motion into a surprisingly agile leap. She jumped over Kera's leg and rolled over the floor toward where her weapon had skidded.

Kera pivoted toward her, trying to kick her in the back of the legs but missing by half an inch.

The Alchemist came out of her tumble in the pool of shadows where the gun had vanished, and her hands made whispering sounds as they scrabbled over the filthy hardwood floor, looking for the firearm.

"No," Kera stated. "You will *not* get away, and you won't kill me, either. This is your chance to give up. I came to meet you like I said. I just happened to arrive a little early and not where I told you I would be. Turn yourself in, and we can go to the police. You'll live, at least. But you're not going to hurt anyone else. *Ever.*"

She could only see the woman's silhouette. The hall was pitch-black aside from the angular areas of deep blue shade that were faintly illuminated by the lights from the street.

In her ear, Chris's voice shouted, "Kera! Are you okay? I hear your voice, but also gunshots."

"Yeah," she said. "Can't talk. Hurry over."

The silhouette slowly stood, and Kera couldn't tell if the Alchemist had found her gun again or not. "*Kera*? You're a woman, after all? That's interesting. I was expecting a man, but it doesn't change anything. You're full of life and courage. Or piss and vinegar, as people say."

At that, she burst into a fit of faintly raspy giggling that made Kera want to squirm where she stood. The Alchemist's voice was that of an elderly woman trying to imitate a girl in her twenties, and it sounded bizarre but appropriate for someone as far removed from reality as the Alchemist seemed to be.

Then there was the issue of how the Alchemist had overheard the conversation inside Kera's helmet...

Kera took one step forward. "This is your last chance. I don't want to—"

The silhouette raised its arm, and Kera hurled herself aside as the gun went off again. Since she had little room to dodge, the bullet would have ripped through Kera's right arm if she hadn't been shielded. As it was, it bounced off the shield.

The Alchemist had discarded the weapon and was bolting down the hallway.

Kera sucked in air and ran after her. *I guess it was a five-shot after all. I wonder if she has another one stashed somewhere?*

Halfway down the hall, when Kera was about to throw a moderate-strength blast of kinetic force to knock the woman off her feet, the Alchemist slowed, moved toward the wall, and grabbed at something before moving on. As Kera continued toward her, she realized that it had been a rope.

The ceiling collapsed.

"Ffffuuuuck!" Kera exclaimed, scraping her boot heels on the floor to stop herself and then throwing herself straight back. Wood and metal groaned, then shrieked as bars fell to the ground, followed by boards and chunks of plaster and half-decayed concrete. The impact of the cave-in shook the floor and Kera collapsed to her knees, narrowly avoiding being crushed.

Then it was over. Briefly, she had feared the whole building might collapse, but it was only a weak portion of the ceiling that had been sabotaged by the apartments' sole inhabitant.

She might not be that tough, but she's wily, I see. And this is her home turf, so she probably has other traps in place. That's assuming she wants to hang around and keep trying to kill me. She might have scampered out the back door by now.

She heard no sounds of movement out toward the street, though. And when she focused on the Alchemist's weird, unpleasant aura, it was still somewhere within the building.

Okay, hide-and-seek it is, Kera lamented. *Ugh, in some ways, this is worse than taking on El Peluquero's whole army. At least they came out and fought instead of trying to lure me into God-knows-what. Then again, that Neron guy tried something similar with his beach house.*

But at least he had been halfway sane. This chick was all the way off the deep end.

She jumped over the pile of debris from the fallen ceiling and advanced at a trot, her eyes and attention everywhere at once.

The hall ended at a corner that wrapped around to the left. Nothing indicated that the Alchemist had escaped through a window, so Kera focused on the line of doors leading to various apartments in the building's center.

As she moved, she cast a couple of minor charms on herself: one to enhance her sight, hearing, and reflexes, and another to bolster her luck. They ought to be enough, but she still had no way of knowing what to expect. She could see the Alchemist being crazy enough to try to blow up the whole structure with a pound of C4 for the sake of killing them both.

Kera called, "I know who you are. You've been to LA before. 1947. Elizabeth Short. Remember her?"

Her ears picked up a faint sound that would have been

inaudible without the aid of the augmentation spell—someone letting out a soft, high-pitched moan. Kera couldn't tell which door her opponent might be hiding behind. She narrowed it down to two and stood halfway between both of them. "Why did you kill her? I thought you only murdered artists."

To her surprise, the Alchemist answered the question.

"She thought she would be an actress," the woman blurted. "Though she didn't try very hard. She just wasted her time and potential. She was my first one before I focused on people who create things rather than just pretend to be things. But she *could* have been a star, maybe. If she wasn't so useless and lazy. I put her talent, her potential, her vital essence to good use. It put me on the road I'm on today toward creating the world's finest work of art where only wastes and failures existed before."

Kera was puzzled. *What the hell does that mean?* But she was pretty sure the voice was coming from deep within the apartment that lay beyond the left-hand door.

There was a rush of motion, and Kera tensed. The expected door flew open, and a dark form appeared within it. Kera saw the faint residual light glint off something metallic at the end of a long object in the figure's hands, and she threw her head back as if walking under a clothesline.

Without the amplification of her speed and reflexes, she might not have made it. There was a *thunk*, followed by the swish of air as either a crossbow bolt or a harpoon zipped past, missing Kera's throat by mere inches.

Then the Alchemist vanished back into the room. Kera swung toward the opening, tore the door off its hinges to throw it aside, and plunged in.

The apartment beyond, Kera saw, had been linked to one on the other side of the inner block to create a double-sized suite. However, the layout of the rooms seemed strange to her, and the Alchemist had further subdivided the space into multiple sub-rooms through the use of hanging sheets and curtains suspended from the ceiling.

"So, you're an artist too? What makes you think you're better than the people whose careers you ruined by murdering them? Domingo was a genius. Now, thanks to you, he'll never paint anything again. You're doing the complete opposite of what you claim to support."

The woman shrieked, "Bullshit! You don't understand, even though I just explained it to you. You're obviously not very smart. He sold himself out. He was well on his way to wasting his potential by becoming a *commercial* artist. I have channeled his spirit into a *pure* artistic endeavor."

Kera had no idea what to make of that, but she did have another notion. The Alchemist's supposed masterpiece was probably located somewhere within the suite, and she was likely to be protective of it.

Extending her hands, Kera cast firefly on the nearest hanging curtain. It burst into flames, which rapidly spread to another curtain, then the fire moved deeper into the rooms.

There was a gasp, noticeable even amid the crackling blaze, and footsteps moved closer to where Kera stood. Then a cloud of white half-gas, half-liquid sprayed everywhere, some of it coating Kera's body as the Alchemist tried to put out the nascent inferno.

Goddammit! Kera exclaimed as the intense, painful cold spread through her, slowing her heightened reflexes and interrupting the flow of her thoughts. *How fucking embarrassing would it be if I got my ass killed because someone sprayed me with a fire extinguisher?*

Still, she could now see where her adversary was. The strange woman was coming straight toward her, aiming the extinguisher's nozzle toward the last of the blaze.

Now.

Kera launched herself at the Alchemist, extending her foot in a powerful sidekick. Her boot knocked the fire extinguisher aside and then crashed into the Alchemist's ribs, audibly cracking at least one and sending the woman flying back into the apartment's interior. She hit the ground and rolled, yelping with pain.

I got her. She's going down unless she has one more trick up her sleeve. Where the hell are Lia and Chris and Steph? I suck at telling how much time has passed when I'm in the zone and fighting someone.

Kera stomped forward, her eyes fixed on the half-crumpled madwoman. "Who else?" she demanded. "Who else did you kill, huh? Where are the bodies? Are they all in LA, or have you been pulling this shit all over the country and the world? Was it you, all those times priceless pieces were stolen and cut up for no reason?"

She kicked the Alchemist in the stomach, sending her rolling again away from her, and continued her advance.

The woman swiveled abruptly, and with startling speed, she produced a knife. Kera jumped back, and it took a second for her to realize that the blade had passed through her leather pant leg and gone an inch deep into her calf.

"Shit!" she growled, collapsing to one knee and trying to determine if she had time to heal herself before the Alchemist moved in for the kill.

But her enemy had paused, hesitant, not sure what to do either. And for the first time, Kera could see the woman's art studio behind her.

The Alchemist's face, contorted with pain and rage, was framed by a bizarre display consisting of eight or ten art pieces. Some of them looked familiar. One was a blatant rip-off of Domingo's blue Expressionist painting. It was pretty damn good, but it was stolen goods, an unauthorized reproduction.

As the Alchemist slowly stood up, holding the bizarre ceremonial knife out with one hand while clutching her broken ribs with the other, she rasped, "I can't remember them all. I wrote it down somewhere, but who they were doesn't matter. What's important is who they will now *become*. After you die. You're the last piece. The only thing I'm missing is a work of taxidermy. A preserved human corpse, the body of a hero, at the center of all this genius. Imagine it! The art world will still be talking about it a thousand years from now. Don't you want to be part of something that will live forever?"

Kera stared at her. For the first time, she pitied the woman. Her latent creativity, frustrated by bad choices and growing mental illness, had expressed itself in her deranged obsessions. If a few things had been different, the Alchemist might have been the equal of Domingo.

"What's your name?" Kera asked.

The Alchemist advanced, knife out. "Be quiet. That doesn't matter. Now I'm giving *you* the chance to surrender. If you let me work the whole procedure on you—the table is right over there, in the other room—the results will be better for everyone. But if I have to kill you first, there might be holes I have to fill in with, um, someone else. Don't make me do that."

Outside, two vehicles pulled up, and in Kera's ear, her boyfriend's voice said, "We're here, and we will call the police as soon as you give the word."

The Alchemist's face fell. "What? You were working with the cops this whole time? I thought you were independent! You're not what everyone said you were!"

Kera didn't understand what the hell the woman was talking about, but it was obvious the situation had changed. "Hey, now. There's no way out of this for you. If you give up, you'll get a fair trial, at least, and maybe someone will write a review of your art that you can read in your cell. Better than nothing, right? Give it up."

When the Alchemist hesitated, Kera's hands lashed out and swatted the knife out of her grasp.

Screaming in rage and terror, the Alchemist stumbled back into the central portion of her incomplete montage. Her eyes frantically darted around, and her sweaty, disheveled hair flopped over her face.

"Fine!" she announced. "I see that no one else is worthy of completing my work. I should have known. I'll finish it *myself!*"

She grabbed a palette knife from a nearby stand.

Kera stepped forward. "Wait. Don't do that. Hey!"

As her friends' footfalls entered the building, the Alchemist looked toward the heavens and slashed her own throat. As the blood spurted across the floor, she drove the blade into her own midsection, under the ribs and into the heart, and collapsed in the midst of her forged masterpieces. By the time Kera got to her side, she'd lost two-thirds of her blood, and her heart was going still.

Attempting to bring the woman back from the very brink of death would have required so much healing energy that Kera might as well have sacrificed her own life, and somehow, it didn't seem worth it. She shook her head sadly, stepping away from the spreading pool of blood.

Chris and Lia burst in. "Kera, are you okay?" Chris asked.

She turned toward them. "Yeah, I'm fine. The Alchemist is dead. She offed herself before I could capture her. I guess she wanted to die along with her art."

Her partners looked at the grisly tableau. "Jesus," Lia whispered. "She had an easier end than some of her victims, but still. It's sad; she wasn't too bad a painter—or sculptor, or weaver. Did she make all these herself?"

Kera nodded. "Yeah, she was vampirizing other artists and thought she was channeling their talent into something better. In a way, maybe she *was,* since I was detecting a faint magical aura on her. She had a half-recognized ability to suck the vitality out of things and people and transfer them to herself, which is why she only looked middle-aged even though she had to be ninety or a hundred by now. Anyway, I'm not a psychologist, so I can't really figure it out."

Chris muttered, "There's another subject that I maybe should have studied instead of just tech stuff."

Kera shrugged as she tied a strip of half-burned curtain around her injured calf. "Help me search the place. She said she had, like, a diary or something where she recorded the other killings."

Lia headed toward the bedroom and Chris toward the kitchen as Kera searched the studio.

A minute later, Stephanie asked, "Everyone okay? What happened?"

Kera remembered the gash in her leg and spent two-thirds of her remaining stamina on healing it. It wasn't enough to bring it back to full functionality, but it stopped the bleeding and the pain and mended most of the tissue.

"Yeah," she replied. "Do us a favor, stay posted out there and call the cops when we find some more evidence. Oh, and call Johnny and tell him his help is appreciated, but we figured everything out without him."

Steph sighed. "That's no fun, but yeah, fine."

CHAPTER TWENTY-THREE

Chris poked his fork at the vague, syrupy residue on his plate. "After what we saw in that place," he commented, "I'm amazed I have this much of an appetite."

"Aye," said Kera. "Well, we all had a long day's work. That will make most people hungry regardless of how much blood they happen to see. Usually."

Steph frowned. "I didn't see any blood, not that I'm complaining. Then again, I didn't have to do much this time, so I wasn't burning calories. Think I'm putting on weight again. You need to have me doing more magic," she insisted, pointing her fork at Kera, "so I don't puff up next time you drag us all to some restaurant at three in the damn morning."

Kera laughed. Pancakes with friends, regardless of the time of day, was helping take her mind off everything she had been through.

It had taken about an hour. With the whole team working, they had managed, first of all, to eliminate every trace of their presence. The cops would find no evidence that Kera, Chris, Stephanie, or Lia had been there.

What they would find, on the other hand, was all the evidence of what the Alchemist had done. And Doug and Mia, who would likely arrive on the scene before the police could, would report on it all.

In the back of a cupboard in her bathroom, the woman had a couple of old leather-bound books. One seemed to be a tome of dark magic that Kera was tempted to steal and study for academic purposes, but since it included hideous diagrams showing how to ritualistically murder a person to steal their soul, it seemed like a strong piece of evidence for the police to study in building a case against the now-dead madwoman.

The other book was a journal. In it, the Alchemist had stuffed newspaper clippings and written down names, dates, and random commentary. The first entry was for the Black Dahlia murder in 1947. The last was for Luis Domingo in 2022. She hadn't yet gotten around to making one for poor Randall Barnes. Maybe in the Alchemist's mind, he didn't count since she had only murdered him as a result of mistaken identity.

Between them, creepily enough, were other entries that didn't involve killings, only art thefts. The dead woman, whoever she had been, did not seem to perceive a difference between the destruction of people's creative works and the destruction of their lives.

Kera had faced one final decision before they had tipped off the police and departed.

"Motorcycle Man," Lia had asked. "What do you want to do about him? Not that it would be pleasant, but you could dress *her* in your leathers. The two of you are about the same size. That might lead everyone to close the case on you once and for all."

Kera had paused, staring at the Alchemist's pale corpse. She'd considered it, but not for long.

"No. I don't want people thinking MM was a serial killer. It's one thing if they believe he never existed, and it was only random people trying to do good for their fellow citizens. But I can't stand the thought of my actions being associated with someone like the Alchemist. And it's not just vanity on my part. Ruining the legend means ruining it for everyone who believed in the spirit of what Motorcycle Woman was all about."

None of her friends had challenged her.

After that, Lia had placed another anonymous tip, then they had skedaddled with all due haste. They were lucky that no one had seemingly heard or acted upon the gunshots the Alchemist had fired at the beginning of their confrontation.

It hadn't taken them long to locate a nice little twenty-four-hour diner that specialized in breakfast food. After all, it was technically morning.

Lia generally ate like a bird, but surprisingly, she had managed to destroy an entire platter's worth of pancakes with butter, syrup, and strawberries.

"Oof!" She grunted, staring at the plate with low, simmering resentment. "I forgot how much I love pancakes, *and* how much they *don't* love me in return. I'm going to have a ton of work to do tomorrow, and here I am up at this ridiculous hour, feeling like I accidentally swallowed two pounds of mud."

Their waiter strolled by. "Something wrong with the pancakes?" he asked, blinking. He looked sleepy.

Kera waved a hand. "No, they're great. She just doesn't eat flour products very often. She's more of a healthy food person."

"Oh," the young man replied. "Well, let me know if you want anything else. More coffee?"

Chris held up his cup. "Sure."

The waiter was back half a minute later to give him a refill, then he left the quartet to the remainder of their meal. Only one other table was occupied, a smaller one on the other side of the dining floor where a young couple was steadily conversing in Spanish.

Puzzled, Kera asked Lia, "What is this work you supposedly have to do tomorrow? We finished the case tonight, and I don't have anything else lined up."

With exquisite patience, Lia explained, "I have to get back to the grind of spreading rumors on the Internet. Since you didn't want to pin the murders on your alter ego, not that I blame you, we'll have to concoct some other way of getting rid of the buzz concerning MM. We could, for example, say the Alchemist was obsessed with the *idea* of our mysterious vigilante, but he never showed because he wasn't real. Hence her murder of Barnes, followed by her apparent suicide when she realized it was all nonsense."

Kera tapped her lips. "That could work. It's worth a try. Don't work too hard, though. I'll contribute some to the rumor cleanup, too."

Stephanie finished the last of her pancakes. "Anyway, this case was gross if we're honest with ourselves. I didn't see the worst of it up close, but I saw those damn crime scene photos and heard all the details and shit. Some of it was *worse* than what we were dealing with against that Barber guy. And here we thought we were trying to avoid stuff like this."

Nods went around the table.

Lia offered, "I don't mind helping out. I don't regret putting in the work it took to stop her rampage and saving whoever the hell was next on the menu. But next time, let's try to pursue something a touch more low-key, shall we? We don't even get to claim credit for this one as a business. It's essentially a charitable write-off."

Kera scowled into her mostly-drained coffee cup. "That *was* the idea, yeah. Low-key. It's not our fault that an art-theft case turned into something out of a slasher movie. Like Mr. and Mrs. Kim said, I seem to be a magnet for trouble. Which reminds me, if I managed to make it to a reasonable time of morning before I fall asleep, I need to call them and tell them I'm okay. It's a little early right now."

"Deal," said Steph.

Chris raised his mug, gesturing vaguely with it as he swallowed another mouthful of its contents. "Actually, there's something worth pointing out."

"*Ackshually*," Kera mocked, kicking him gently in the shin. "Gotta love comments that start with *ackshually*."

"Silence," he shot back with a pantomimed slap. "Pretend I didn't say that particular word and focus on the rest. Yes, we got mixed up in something completely different from what we thought we were taking on at the beginning, but in point of fact, we did exactly what we intended. The primary objective was achieved."

Lia ran a finger through her hair. "We caught our suspect, yes."

Chris elaborated, "Yeah, and not only that. I'm talking the whole part about you not officially being a superhero anymore but still wanting to do good in the world. Well, you succeeded. The police didn't have enough to go on to catch that woman themselves. She would have remained at large, continuing to murder artists or random schmucks until she either got sloppy and made a mistake or finally died of natural causes. There's no way to be sure how many innocent people's lives you saved. Well, all of us, but mainly you."

Kera exhaled slowly. "Not mainly me. It really *was* all of us. I wouldn't have found her without all the help you guys provided."

Stephanie protested, "Eh, I didn't do so much this time around."

Laughing, Kera pointed out, "You deserved a break anyway. You saved my life multiple times before, not to mention you still wait tables by day. Anyway, next time, we'll find more for you to do. And Lia, you hopefully won't have to do quite as much."

Lia's mouth rose in a small smile. "I was taught to earn my paycheck."

"Oh, right," Kera remarked. "I'll pay you in another day or two, by the way. And if we can drum up some proper cases, Chris and Steph can finally quit their day jobs."

No one complained.

Looking uncertain, Stephanie said, "I dunno about that. I'd rather work with you all, but then again, no one tries to kill me when I wait tables. Kind of nice when you think about it. Still, I'll probably put in my notice at the Mermaid once more business rolls your way."

Kera put a hand atop hers. "It's up to you. You're welcome to join us anytime on anything."

Chris added, "I'm only glad justice was served. Still, it would be nice to make my living doing stuff I regard as legitimately important as opposed to the nonsense they usually have me do at the office."

Kera paused, reflecting on the word he had used: justice. By and large, he was right.

The murderer had been stopped, and the police would be able to put together the necessary case from the available evidence. The public would hear about it, and notwithstanding possible gossip about a shadowy bike-riding avenger being involved, be satisfied that all the loose ends had been tied up and the menace had been put to bed.

There was still one problem, though.

"Elizabeth Short," Kera pointed out, her voice wistful as a glum cloud drifted over her spirits. "We caught her killer after all these years, but no one is ever going to know that part. Sure, Short was in the diary, but nobody's going to believe that a woman who's still alive today was responsible for a crime from seventy-five goddamn years ago."

Chris grimaced. "Yeah, that's true. Officially, Short's case will remain filed under 'unsolved mysteries.'"

Stephanie folded her hands in front of her and flexed them. "They'll say it was a copycat, I guess. Like, this lady was obsessed with the Black Dahlia murder, so she killed those other people the same way for that reason."

"Probably," agreed Lia. "But there's nothing we can do about that unless we're prepared to deliver a detailed presentation to the authorities on how magical vampirism works, complete with evidence."

The way she says it, Kera thought, you'd almost believe she was giving the notion serious consideration. Maybe someday. Maybe there will come a time when the rest of humanity is ready to learn that magic is real and that, well, people like me walk among them. People like me, Steph, and the Kims on the one hand. But also, unfortunately, people like the Orthodoxy, the Duo, and the Alchemist. I don't think the general public would be comforted by the knowledge.

Still, she was feeling better. The horror, nausea, and awful guilt that had been eating at her since her misadventure inside the Alchemist's depraved mind were beginning to fade, replaced by a calm understanding that whatever terrible things might exist in the world, she had thus far done her part to alleviate them.

And had mostly succeeded.

"So," Chris offered, "what are we all doing with our day off tomorrow? Well, today. I propose sleeping in 'til, like, two in the afternoon. That way, after only a few hours pass, we'll be able to say it isn't too early to start drinking."

Lia sighed. "I already told you, I need to work the gossip forums."

Kera stood, stretched, and surprised Lia by planting a kiss on her cheek. "No, you don't. Not yet. As your boss, I *order* you to take the day off on pain of termination."

Stephanie laughed. "Damn, she's a hard woman to work for, ain't she?"

Lia rubbed her eyes. "Yes, ma'am."

CHAPTER TWENTY-FOUR

Kera woke up to the ringing of the phone. She wondered who the hell it could be the instant her dreams faded. Chris and Steph had spent the night at her place, and Lia had promised to sleep in and take it easy.

Possibly Johnny. She kicked off her sheets and sat up, groping toward the nightstand for the device and almost knocking over her alarm clock. It was 10:07, somewhat early by her standards.

Her eyes weren't working properly yet, and she had to blink three times before she could read the tiny numbers and letters on the readout on her phone's screen.

"No." She groaned as the residual warmth of her bed was replaced by a cold paroxysm of dread. "No, *no, it can't be.*"

She had known this fate would come, though. For far too long, she had fled from it, cherishing her idyllic existence yet knowing deep in the darkest corner of her mind that any escape, any freedom or joy she found was temporary. Sometimes she had even yearned for this moment, and perhaps that had brought her here. She was condemned, fated, *doomed* to the moment in which she now was stranded.

Coughing, Kera swiped her finger across the green icon. "Hi, Mom," she muttered.

"Kera, hello, it's your mother," Mrs. MacDonagh said, even though the phone had identified her and Kera had already called her Mom. "It's been so long since the last time we called that I was starting to worry you'd forget who I was. I'm certainly having trouble remembering what your face looks like, dear. I had to raid the mantelpiece for your graduation photos to be certain. Did you get the cookies I sent? I checked the delivery status online, and they reported the exact date and time when they were scanned as delivered."

Squirming in place and clenching her hands and feet, Kera responded, "Which part of that am I supposed to answer first?"

"Oh, I don't know," her mother rambled, "it's nice to hear your voice regardless, though it sounds like you just got up despite it presumably being well after *ten* out there in California. If you're going to run a business, you'll need to adjust to most people's working hours, you know. The cookies, though. Start with answering that."

Kera stood up and began shuffling toward the coffee pot. Chris and Steph snoozed nearby, he in the armchair with a laptop open on his lap and she on the loveseat. In the future, Kera decided, they would have to decide on an arrangement whereby anytime her mother called, one of the two of them immediately had to make a full pot of extra-strong coffee.

"Yes," Kera said. "Thank you for the cookies. They were honestly delicious. Some local baker made them, so they weren't *exactly* like yours, but close enough. I'm sorry I didn't call you and thank you for them. Wait, didn't I send you an email?"

Mrs. MacDonagh tittered. "Oh, good, I'm glad you liked them. Also, I'm flattered that you remember the *exact* taste of my cookies well enough to contrast them with someone else's. It's amazing, the little things we still recall with so much detail after years have passed. I remember when I was your age, there was this particular brand of lipstick I used to wear that tasted like cherries mixed with acetone, more or less. To this day, I expect all lipstick to taste that way. Not that it was *pleasant*; it simply formed my mental framework for lipstick."

Kera poured water into the coffee maker. "I didn't know you used to eat lipstick, Mom. I suppose that explains a lot, though."

Her mom laughed. "Very clever, Kera, but you know what I mean. Of course, you know that I *have* to ask this, so brace yourself."

"Oh," Kera murmured, "I've *been* braced, don't you worry."

"How are you and that boy Chris doing? Are you going steady yet? It's not technically any of my business, but I just want to make sure that he's treating you well and supporting your decision to run your own business. Some men feel inadequate if their girlfriend or wife makes more money than they do, and it can lead to long-term problems. I'm sure your business is taking off, isn't it? I was half-expecting you to send us your quarterly report so we can evaluate how you're managing your finances so far."

Kera scooped coffee grounds into the filter with her free hand, adding about thirty percent more than she typically used on normal, peaceful, pleasant mornings.

"Once again," she reported, "give me a second to mentally review all the stuff you just said so I can pick out which part of it to reply to first. Umm, me and Chris. We've been officially dating for a month or so now, I think. Everything's good between us. He doesn't care how much money I make."

"Really?" Mrs. MacDonagh asked though it was more a declaration than a question. "That's good insofar as it means jealousy won't be a problem between the two of you going forward. Well, at least as far as material prosperity goes. He's not trying to marry you for your inheritance, is he? I certainly hope not. But if your business is doing well, it's not as though you need to be shy in telling me as much since I'd want you to succeed regardless of what Chris thinks of it. What does he do again?"

Kera turned the coffee maker on, set a cup on the kitchen counter, and splashed about a tablespoon's worth of milk into the bottom of the mug. She added a tablespoon of sugar for good measure.

"Chris is an IT guy for a basic-ass white-collar tech company here in LA. And I couldn't say whether or not he's trying to marry me for my money because the subject of marriage hasn't come up. Let me get back to you on that in three years or so, okay?"

As she spoke, Chris stirred in his chair. His eyes fluttered open and focused on Kera. Seeing that she was on the phone, he didn't interrupt, though his nostrils flared noticeably at the smell of brewing coffee.

Mrs. MacDonagh sighed. "I suppose I can understand your reluctance to face adult responsibilities, though you *have* been out of college for around half a year at this point. Which reminds me, if you're still asleep at ten in the morning, it's probably safe to assume your business is still in the early stages, isn't it?"

Kera gritted her teeth. "Yes, though we, um, have had our first customer. We celebrated last night and are taking today off. That's all. Plus, we have things set up so that people who sleep like normal human beings can do the nine-to-five shit while I handle stuff that needs to be done in the evening."

"Oh." Her mom paused. "Well, that's good to know. I'll be sure to tell your father the good news, though as you can imagine, he'll probably want to see the invoices just so we're both certain you're charging enough to remain solvent. It's your business, dear, but we *do* have a lot of experience and advice to share. And of course your aunts and uncles and grandparents want to hear all about your successes as well."

Kera stared longingly at the coffee pot. It was thus far only half-full, but she debated pulling it and pouring herself a cup early, despite the potential loss of a few drops to the hotplate. But in her opinion, coffee was best after it had sat in the pot for one full minute after the dripping ceased.

"Well, Mom," she explained, "it's good to know that everyone is looking over my shoulder and panting and rubbing their hands together with anticipation so they can pore over every single thing I do and evaluate my performance." She took a deep breath. "But since, like you yourself said, I'm an adult now, I'd say I have the right to tell you all exactly as much as I want to about how things are going. No more, no less. And by the way, the money hasn't cleared yet."

Chris, watching her and listening, gave her a thumbs-up.

"Dear," her mother replied, "are you making coffee? When did you develop the habit of being so grumpy in the mornings before you had your caffeine? I hope you didn't pick it up in high school, but I really can't remember. Anyway, I was only curious so that everyone in the extended family could feel good about how you're doing. They're naturally interested, given that this is your inheritance from their side."

Anger and guilt clashed within Kera's mind, neutralizing one another like fire and water and leaving her awash in a haze of mental steam. She hated being guilt-tripped, but her mother was technically correct and sounded legitimately hurt.

"Sorry," she said. "I'll send you a summary of how things are going via email once in a while, okay? It will be easier for me to sit down and type something up than it is for me to think of how to say it when you're putting me on the spot first thing in the morning."

"Kera," stated her mother, "it's after *ten*."

Kera grabbed the coffee pot and dumped the steaming dark liquid into her cup. It was about eighty percent done, but she could not wait any longer. Three drops fell on the hotplate and sizzled into oblivion.

Kera cleared her throat. "Yes. You have correctly informed me of the time." She gulped down coffee, ignoring the fact that it was borderline scalding since she swallowed it too fast for it to do much damage.

"Well, dear," her mom went on, "since you seem to be relaxing and don't have much of anything important to do, have you considered a brief vacation? Your father and I would love to see you again. It's been so long, and the trees will start changing color shortly. Of course, he and I would both enjoy the warmer weather in Southern California, I'm sure, though arranging a trip down there would be a bit of a hassle, given that we have an actual house to think of rather than just an, um, what is it you rented again? A converted hardware store or something?"

"Warehouse," Kera clarified. She needed a second to respond to the rest of what she'd heard. After another sip of coffee, she did her best. "I, um, have considered a vacation, I suppose. Not sure now would be the best time since I'm, you know, trying to build a business. But—"

Mrs. MacDonagh interrupted her to apologize. "Oh, no, no, I'm sorry for even suggesting that you and Chris should be the ones to come back here. It's fine; we'll come out there instead. I'm curious to see what you've done with this warehouse since, from what I recall from when you were a little girl—before your father started indulging your obsession with sports and weapons and so forth—you did possess some decorating skills. I'm sure you have enough of a woman's touch that the place is lovely and that people who visit are impressed once they get past the fact of it being, well, a *warehouse.*"

Kera frantically motioned for Chris to come closer. He squinted but climbed out of the chair and hastened to her side. She gripped his hand, squeezing it to calm herself and keep from hyperventilating, fainting, or grabbing the coffee pot and hurling it through the wall.

"Now that you mention it," she replied, her jaw muscles tightening, "I would *love* to see the leaves change color in Connecticut again. I would love to have Chris see the old house, and maybe the townhouse in New York, so how about this. As soon as he can get some time off from the office, which hopefully won't be long, we'll fly out and pay you guys a quality visit, okay? It's *totally unnecessary* for you to go to the trouble of coming all the way out here just to evaluate my interior decorating capabilities. I wouldn't want to put you through all that hassle."

Her mother sighed again. "Hmm, I see. Yes, that sounds good. But when? I wouldn't want you to take too long and miss out on the leaves."

Chris said loudly, "Two weeks."

"Oh, dear, is that him?" Mrs. MacDonagh asked. "Hello, Chris. Anyway, two weeks ought to work well. Please inform us of the details so we can plan accordingly. Oh, and keep an eye on the weather. I understand Los Angeles doesn't really *have* what most people consider 'weather,' but up here, we still have to deal with rain, frost, and of course, all that turbulence when you fly through the middle of the country..."

Kera indulged her mother for another three or four minutes, by which point she was two-thirds of the way through her second cup of coffee. Finally, the conversation wound down enough for her to end it.

She nodded, though her mom couldn't see it; it made her feel better. "Okay. Okay, yeah. Thanks, Mom. I have to go. I'll send you the progress report on my business later. Via email, though, right? And yes, you'll hear more from me about the trip. I promise. Thanks again for the cookies, and tell Dad I said hello. Okay. Thanks. Bye."

She hung up, then stumbled over to her bed, collapsing face-first onto the mattress.

Chris nodded. "You've had a long day since you got up twenty minutes ago. You should probably get some rest."

"Yeah." Kera groaned. "I agree."

"She's damn good at that, I must say," Chris marveled, staring vacantly into the ether and stroking his chin.

Kera turned her head and glared at him. "Good at what, exactly? Identifying weak points and sticking needles into them?"

Chris took a sip of his own mug of black coffee. "Well, that too. But I mean, at getting you to do what she wants because it becomes the most attractive option. You end up wanting what she wants because it beats the alternatives. She'd make a good salesperson, in fact."

His girlfriend rolled over on her back. "That's one way of thinking about it, I guess. Or an interrogator for the secret police in a totalitarian state. Speaking of which, she is *not* coming here. I'm sorry I volunteered you for the journey, but maybe we can concoct a way for something to come up at the last minute. I'll still have to go, though, or she'll never be appeased."

"Nah." Chris shrugged. "I meant the two weeks part. I'm quitting the office, assuming you still want to hire me. I'll put in my notice tomorrow."

Kera stared into his eyes. "Okay." Her voice was soft and warm. "That's sweet of you. The trip might actually be sort of romantic, at least until we *arrive*." She frowned again.

Chris said in a mocking tone, "Ackshually... Just kidding, sorry. But yeah, I'm looking forward to it. It's been too long since I was out of SoCal. This 'weather' thing, whatever it is, sounds interesting."

He came over and sat next to her, and they enjoyed one another's warmth for a moment of pleasant silence.

Stephanie was still gently snoring on the loveseat.

"Damn," Kera said. "If we're gone for a week or two, she and Lia will have to take over the whole operation. I don't like the thought of leaving everything in their laps. Then again, if my mother were to set foot in this building and *suggest* I move to some awful condo in Beverly or hire a really expensive team of decorators to swankify the place, I would be forced to commit suicide. Then you, Steph, and Lia would all be *really* upset. Right?"

Chris kissed her on the nose. "Exactly."

Zacharia was not doing well. What had at first appeared to be a minor injury had become something else, something just as nasty as the rest of the Orthodoxy's tactics. Once it became clear that Zacharia would not live through the night, they had stopped off the main road to allow her to die in the woods. Everyone knew she would prefer that over perishing in a hospital or even a nice cozy house.

They had escaped from James's family estate—what little remained of it—two days ago, with nearly all of them badly wounded. Only Mother LeBlanc, Josiah, and Amanda had escaped relatively unscathed. They had minor injuries that would heal with time or with the application of medicinal thaumaturgy that would not be strenuous enough to slow them down.

No one else had been as fortunate. Lauren, Samantha, Crystal, Mary, Hugh, Rufus, and Ezeudo had all been lucky to be able to make it as far as they had without collapsing. They might not have made it at all had the Orthodoxy not been keen to claim the house and its treasure trove of books and relics and therefore wasted time securing the location rather than pursuing them.

As for James and Zacharia, the general feeling was that they would soon be joining Damian.

It was a beautiful autumn day, warmer than usual for the time of year, with a crisp breeze and bright sun. The day was waning; the magic hour would approach soon. They were near the James Kennedy State Forest in south-central New York state. They had wanted to be in Pennsylvania by now, but with two members who could not even walk by themselves...

Zacharia coughed. Josiah and LeBlanc had laid her on a grassy patch between two white-flowered bushes, where the sun was still shining between the trees that shielded them all from sight.

"Ah." She sighed. "Thank you. I can feel the Great Spirit here. It's the sort of place where coyotes would happily live. Am I still wearing mine?"

LeBlanc nodded. "Yes, Zacharia. Do you want to keep it on, or shall we remove it?"

She considered it for a moment as blood dripped from her mouth and her chest heaved, then convulsed and gasped as her lung collapsed again. Ezeudo turned away, covering his face.

"Remove it," she said once the pain lessened. "Give it back to the forest, please."

Hugh took the pelt from around her shoulders and set it respectfully on the earth between two tall, strong trees.

Josiah clasped her hand. "We will miss you. You know that."

Zacharia was having difficulty focusing, and her breath was failing. The muscles in her chest were contracting to try to close around the empty space created by her flattened lung. "I do know. I wish you all luck. It's too bad—"

An especially severe convulsion seized her, and she did not relax again after her body stiffened. But she lay still, and her now-glassy eyes stared at the sky.

Mother LeBlanc put her hand over Zacharia's face and closed her eyelids.

Ezeudo's breath shook as he exhaled. He kept his eyes on the ground and the grass since he did not feel like looking anyone in the face. "Why could you not heal her?" he asked. "I am sure it's an ignorant question on my part. Something I am missing. But I *must* ask why you let her die."

Hugh, the oldest and calmest among them, with the possible exception of LeBlanc, was the one who spoke. "She was cursed as well as injured," he explained. "The wound was hexed against healing magic. If we'd tried to cast a spell to save her, it would have siphoned off *our* strength, weakening us while doing nothing for her."

Ezeudo wanted to throw up, but he forced himself not to. "I see."

Amanda Moore, whose black eyes seemed to burn with hatred, remarked, "I was under the impression that that particular curse had been *universally* forbidden as of three hundred years ago." She and Zacharia had been close friends. They both loved animals.

"Well," said LeBlanc, "it would appear that some people are willing to employ it anyway. But let us not focus on that. There will be a time for redressing balances. For now, let us say a few words for Zacharia."

They stood in silence for a minute, then everyone spoke a sentence or two in memory of their mutual friend.

To everyone's surprise, James sat up, coughing and groaning, in the middle of the ceremony. They had all assumed he would pass away too within the next several hours.

"I heard," he muttered. "And don't tell me to lie back down and shut up. Zacharia was my friend, too, so I'm going to say this. I never ever should have put out that *fucking* book. I am sorry for that. I tried to make right what went wrong. I guess I failed, but they also failed to kill me, and once I'm better, we are going to put an end to this. They won't get away with it."

His voice was soft and shallow since the half-molten spear had damaged his diaphragm. Had it been cool when it stabbed him, he might have died of blood loss, but the heat of it had cauterized his wound.

LeBlanc touched his head. "You are right, James. But now you *do* need to lie back down."

He coughed. "Okay." He lowered himself to the ground again and passed out.

Finally, it was Ezeudo's turn to speak.

"I did not know Zacharia well," he admitted, "but she seemed like a nice person, and I am sorry to have lost her. I regret all of this, and I regret doubting you. I was wrong to think that we could negotiate with those people, and I should have been firmer in my commitment to help you defeat them. Now, seeing what they have *done*—" his voice cracked, "there is no more doubt. I am with you until the end."

Mary Mitchell nodded. "Thank you, Ezeudo. James thanks you as well, I'm sure. I can see why he wanted you to join us. These days, we can use all the friends we can get."

CREATOR NOTES
APRIL 29, 2021

Thank you for reading this story and through to the back with these author notes!

If this is the first time you have read something by me, welcome! For those who already know me, please just jump past the 'about me' section below to the latest thoughts and musings on the next page...or two. I'm not sure where it will show up.

ABOUT ME

I wrote my first book *Death Becomes Her* (*The Kurtherian Gambit*) in September/October of 2015 and released it November 2, 2015. I wrote and released the next two books that same month and had three released by the end of November 2015.

So, just at five years ago.

Since then, I've written, collaborated, concepted, and/or created hundreds more in all sorts of genres.

My most successful genre is still my first, Paranormal Sci-Fi, followed quickly by Urban Fantasy. I have multiple pen names I produce under.

Some because I can be a bit crude in my humor at times or raw in my cynicism (Michael Todd). I have one I share with

Martha Carr (Judith Berens, and another (not disclosed) that we use as a marketing test pen name.

In general, I just love to tell stories, and with success comes the opportunity to mix two things I love in my life.

BUSINESS AND STORIES

I've wanted to be an entrepreneur since I was a teenager. I was a very *unsuccessful* entrepreneur (I tried many times) until my publishing company LMBPN signed one author in 2015.

Me.

I was the president of the company, and I was the first author published. Funny how it worked out that way.

It was late 2016 before we had additional authors join me for publishing. Now we have a few dozen authors, a few hundred audiobooks by LMBPN published, a few hundred more licensed by six audio companies, and about a thousand titles in our company.

It's been a busy five years.

LATEST THOUGHTS AND MUSINGS

I'm a huge fan of chili. Now, one can't usually say that without declaring if you are "beans or no beans."

I'm no beans.

I'm also "no big chunks of tomatoes, onions, or practically anything else." I'm a fan of adding either potatoes or rice and occasionally spaghetti, but at the core, it needs to be about meat and spices.

When I was growing up, the chili my mom made had toma-toes, and I have never been able to duplicate that taste by using either tomato sauce or tomato paste. She passed a couple of years ago, so I can't ask her (again…I've done it many times over the last forty years.)

So, the last couple of weekends, I've tried peeled and diced tomatoes.

It both worked and failed miserably.

It worked because I know that part of my mom's flavor was peeled tomatoes. It failed miserably because both times, I had big enough chunks of tomato that I was spooning them out of my bowls to get to the good stuff.

"Good stuff" is defined as everything but chunks of tomato and onions.

Now, I realize she only used whole peeled tomato from Hunt's. I had hesitated to add those to my pot because I thought it would be a pain to take out when it was finished cooking. Using diced, I only succeeded in making it worse.

SMH (shake my head.)

So, the next time I go to the store, I'll grab a couple of cans of Hunt's whole peeled.

I'm on the right track. I seem to remember it is a can of whole peeled tomatoes and 8 oz of tomato sauce or to taste.

Plus, I finally figured out it was probably 85/15 on the meat (fat content), and she spooned the grease off of the top. I've been buying 93/7 or even 95/5 to make my life easier by taking away the need to spoon off the fat.

Apparently, I also took away a necessary flavor ingredient.

Well, I'll let you get back to your next book. Just know that I'm on the right track to cooking what I remember as a favorite dish as a kid.

If you have a favorite dish someone in your family cooks? Maybe sit them down and record them telling you how they did it. One day, they won't be there to answer the questions for you.

Mom, I know you are out there. I'm going to figure out how you did it.

When I do, that bowl will be for you. Love you!

Ad Aeternitatem,

Michael Anderle

CONNECT WITH MICHAEL

Connect with Michael Anderle

Website: http://lmbpn.com

Email List: http://lmbpn.com/email/

Social Media:

https://www.facebook.com/LMBPNPublishing

https://twitter.com/MichaelAnderle

https://www.instagram.com/lmbpn_publishing/

https://www.bookbub.com/authors/michael-anderle